Melyndie
a75b99r84GE

BOOK ONE

By: Barbara Pelham

Contents

Dedication

To my daughters, without whom this book would never have been written. Thank you for your love and support throughout the years. I love you all dearly.

Year: 2375

The atmosphere within the room was suffocating, a palpable tension hanging in the air, as visible as the sterile white walls surrounding them. The Chancellor's voice echoed through the silence, a tremor of uncertainty creeping into his usually composed tone. "Can we not find an alternate solution?" he queried with a sense of desperation.

Kishida-Guan, lead scientist and one of only three individuals who'd attained the level of holy one, cleared his throat before responding, his voice resonating with an ominous gravity. "Chancellor," he began, his words heavy with regret and resignation. "I have run countless simulations and yet the outcome remains unaltered—"

"Your projections?" The Chancellor interrupted him abruptly, his tone dripping with worry.

A sigh escaped from Kishida-Guan as if he bore the weight of their entire world on his shoulders. "If we do not expedite the construction process—"

"I did not ask that you elaborate!" The Chancellor's voice sliced through the air like a blade. "I am fully cognizant of our urgency! How much time do we have?"

"My apologies, Chancellor," he acquiesced with a respectful nod. "Fifty years."

A deep silence enveloped the room, hanging in the air like an impending storm cloud waiting to release its torrential downpour, as the Chancellor processed this revelation. Kishida-Guan stood rigid; hands clasped tightly together in an attempt to stifle any sign of nervousness. He wished he could decipher what went on behind those steely eyes as easily as their advanced technology translated the Chancellor's thoughts into speech.

Eventually, after what felt like an infinite wait encapsulated in mere seconds, the Chancellor spoke again, his voice soft yet laden with implication. "Fifty years if construction is unsuccessful?" His voice echoed ominously around them. "And how long would it take for you, and your fellow scientists, to finalize this project?"

"Given that we are venturing into uncharted territories," Kishida-Guan replied cautiously, "an accurate estimate is difficult to provide. However, we anticipate it would take approximately twenty to twenty-five years."

"That long?" The Chancellor's voice reverberated with disbelief and disappointment.

"Indeed, this endeavor has never been undertaken in our time," the holy one reminded him gently. "While we do have rudimentary formulas from the before time as a starting point, none have successfully transformed theory into a working prototype, let alone a functional model. I feel I must emphasize, Chancellor, that the fifty years is only an estimate. After all, there is no way to provide a date with precision, any more than I can state, with certainty, the length of time in which this project is likely to be concluded."

"So, it could be fifty years or more…or less." The Chancellor fell into another contemplative silence. After an agonizingly long span of time, he spoke again, his tone grave and somber. "With things disintegrating so rapidly…perhaps it is time, Saik, for us to yield to the inevitable."

Kishida-Guan's eyes widened in shock—not only because the Chancellor addressed him by his first name; a name he'd not heard in more than a century, as no one beneath him dared address him thus as the holy of holies—but also because of the dejection in his tone. He'd known the leader of their realm for all of their lives, even before the Chancellor's metamorphosis, and never had he heard him speak with such defeatism. "Evander?" He queried briefly, using the Chancellor's given name in response to his being used—although it had taken him a moment to even recall it since he'd not used it in an eternity. Still, he felt that if the Chancellor could address him thus, he could return the favor.

The Chancellor snorted, "It sounds strange, doesn't it? Hearing names we haven't used since we were but younglings."

"I was taken aback by your sudden decision to address me thus, I must admit. Why did you? Given our elevated status, it seems a sparkless echo of what once was."

"If things are as dire as you have portrayed…I guess I wanted to briefly return to a time of innocence."

"Are you really ready to give up on all that we have worked so hard to achieve?"

"We have done much for humanity over the centuries. Perhaps it is time for us to let our society perish," he continued with an air of resignation. "Especially considering that the genetic template from which we fabricate—"

"I vehemently disagree, Chancellor," Kishida-Guan interjected passionately, dropping the informalities. "Our society represents perfection that took centuries of painstaking effort to achieve—"

"And yet," the Chancellor interrupted him again, his tone bitter, "centuries ago, there was pestilence and war, famine and genocide, but the human race staggered onward in its rebelliousness, daring adversity with a stubbornness that defied prudence. And through that resolute boldness, humankind survived. Our ancestors lived through the tail end of that era; was at the forefront of the change that brings us to where we are now. There is an antiquated saying that hindsight is twenty-twenty, and never before have I felt the truth of that as I do now. Where did we err in our beliefs that society would be enhanced through the eradication of individuality, the elimination of free will, and the obliteration of human emotions?"

"We did not remove all of that, we simply suppressed things so that humankind became more effectual," the holy one argued. "And our efforts have evolved into an enviable society that functions seamlessly in harmonious productivity."

"And within those efforts, we have forgotten what it means to be human," the Chancellor rejoined quietly.

The holy one opened his mouth to respond but found himself momentarily speechless; none had ever dared question their societal evolution before—certainly not one of the creators of that society. After a moment of contemplation, he responded defiantly, "I firmly believe that there was no error in our societal evolution—"

"Yet here we stand on the precipice of oblivion." The Chancellor cut him off again grimly.

Kishida-Guan faced the Chancellor; his voice filled with unwavering conviction. His eyes glinted with a deep-seated belief in their mission, and he gestured emphatically as he defended his stance. "I am adamant, Chancellor, that if we succeed in our endeavors, we can step back from this precipice of doom and herald a new era of perfection—a future that many like-minded individuals have toiled tirelessly to achieve—that will ensure the survival of humanity for centuries to come."

"Your faith in a brighter future is almost staggering." The Chancellor's voice echoed from the unseen speakers.

"I would argue it's less about faith and more about practicality. Our society may be facing adversities of an unprecedented scale, but I am convinced that these adversities are not insurmountable."

"Sounds like optimism to me," retorted the Chancellor, a disembodied voice resonating through the sterile room. A rare chuckle punctuated his words, sounding out of place in their somber surroundings. "Answer me this, if you can?"

"I will give it my best effort, Chancellor."

"Suppose your project reaches completion successfully. What exactly fuels your confidence that you will be able to pinpoint the exact moment in history that needs alteration? The moment when humanity took a wrong turn leading us to our current predicament? That your created one will be able to affect this change you seem certain needs making?"

"Us holy ones have been tirelessly revisiting this ever since we first noticed…no, not noticed…realized the existence of imperfections within our societal fabric."

"And have they reached any conclusive certainty—"

"No definitive answer yet, Chancellor. However, we are confident that by the time our project concludes, we will not only be ready and able to replenish our stores but to also know precisely what needs changing, eradicating, or simply modifying to prevent further issues. We won't know what it is that we need to accomplish, with precision, until we study the fabricated makeup of our citizens further to determine whether the error lies in them or if it lies in something which was set in motion centuries ago. This is a task that our scientists are running in unison with us holy ones' efforts."

"You place immense trust in, and responsibility onto, your fellow holy ones and scientists—an admirable trait considering they lack first-hand knowledge of history."

"They have access to historical texts—"

"Do you genuinely believe that words stored within a mainframe can provide sufficient data to identify an exact moment in history—"

"I cannot say for sure. However, our mainframe can analyze this information and generate potential scenarios giving us a starting point. The archivist works tirelessly, every day, to upload millions of physical works into the mainframe, which is analyzed regularly for that one piece of pertinent data…" He trailed off, knowing that there was no way to fully assuage the Chancellor's doubts over their project—at least not in this area. Instead, he decided to deflect. "May I ask something of you, Chancellor?"

There was a brief silence before the Chancellor responded, "Proceed."

"Are you certain that your desire to end humanity stems from practicality? Or is it possible that you've grown weary and simply wish to conclude your term as Chancellor?"

"Are you questioning my dedication to our world?"

"No, not at all. The effort required to maintain the delicate balance of this world demands unwavering dedication. My question pertains more to your personal feelings. Are you hesitant about finding a solution for our world's current predicament because you're tired...of living?" Kishida-Guan's hesitation did not go unnoticed by the Chancellor.

Ignoring the question, the Chancellor retorted with a query of his own, "Did it ever occur to you and your fellow holy ones to consult me directly?"

"Chancellor?"

"Did it slip your mind in your eagerness to commence this project that I might have insights to offer? After all, I am the oldest surviving member of this society and the closest one to have lived to that bygone era."

"I see," Kishida-Guan responded curtly, clearly displeased at having his question sidestepped. "Your inclusion was discussed at length among the holy ones and we concluded that, although your knowledge base, no matter how defective, might prove invaluable from your perspective, we ultimately decided, as a whole, that your participation was futile. After all, much of the work that we'll be doing will require hands-on laboratory work…" Kishida-Guan trailed off, knowing that his words were cruel.

After a few moments of silence, a robotic voice echoed through the room: "Received and understood." Indicating that the Chancellor had exited their conversation.

Kishida-Guan bowed respectfully towards the preserved body encased within its transparent polycarbonate pod before exiting the chamber.

"Did he sanction our endeavor?" 71PQv inquired, a mimicry of eagerness threading his voice as his fellow holy one stepped into the austere antechamber, where his two fellow holy ones stood waiting, bathed in the dim, cold light.

71PQv and 41GB were engineered a few decades after Kishida-Guan using new processes that became the norm in their society: genetically designed to be more productive with less emphasis on emotional needs. Even though they possessed emotions, they were taught from youngling years that emotions were a hindrance to productive levels and were not to be nurtured. Being in the company of Kishida-Guan, almost daily, they eventually started mimicking him as he was one of the last individuals in their community to possess fully developed emotions. They thought that by behaving like him, they could attain his level of esteem without tapping into that which would occasionally make him behave in unpredictable ways. Though they couldn't completely grasp the root of their ambition, they embraced it as a fundamental need to achieve their highest potential. As time went on and more individuals were fabricated, most adopted this same mimicry, while others chose to fully embrace the teaching from youngling years that emotions were useless to the human existence.

Kishida-Guan recognized this behavior in his fellow holy ones—as well as other members of society—and neither opted to encourage nor discourage it. To him, as long as society functioned as a tightly coordinated unit, his colleague's behaviors—and that of others—concerned him little. Until emotions—mimicked and genuine—began to interfere with his plans.

"He terminated our discourse before granting explicit approval. Yet, I am unwaveringly convinced that he would have consented if not for the affront I inadvertently delivered before his abrupt departure," Kishida-Guan replied, his voice echoing slightly in the emptiness of the corridor.

"So, you disclosed our intentions to him?" 71PQv asked, his tone measured and cautious.

"Not entirely. I merely emphasized the critical need to advance and accomplish our project—a notion to which he seemed receptive." Kishida-Guan was aware that he had overstated the Chancellor's acceptance; their conversation had ended prematurely without securing an official green light. Still, he couldn't afford to wallow in regret over misleading his colleagues at this crucial juncture.

"We must expedite our efforts then; time is a luxury we no longer possess," 41GB declared with an authoritative nod. "And along that vein, I have news to impart. The current archivist has located data which, I believe, is of great importance to our needs."

When his colleague didn't elaborate, Kishida-Guan let out a deep sigh, "Would you like to explain?" 41GB tilted her head slightly, unsure why the doctor's voice carried a note of annoyance. Before she could comment on this unusual emotion—one she noticed was becoming more prevalent in Kishida-Guan as their project advanced—he interrupted her. "Is this something you're uncomfortable discussing here, in this vacant space, void of other people?" he asked. His voice was laced with sarcasm, which she didn't quite grasp, as he waved his arms about.

She looked around and then refocused on the doctor, "I believe it is sufficiently secure, and the information isn't particularly sensitive. As I was mentioning, the archivist is confident that he's verified your inquiry regarding the Chancellor's lineage."

"He has definitively confirmed that Jeffrey Saltzer, who was the President of the New Confederated States of America in the past, was indeed an ancestor of our current Chancellor?" 71PQv asked with a hint of doubt.

"I'm confident that he is indeed confident," 41GB assured.

Kishida-Guan nodded. "And since we've already established that my direct ancestor, Dr. Riku Jang, was his chief scientist during that era, as well as his confidant and co-lead, we have a starting point in which to target our focus. This is good news, indeed."

"One day soon you must divulge how you unearthed these identities amidst eons passed and buried within countless records from the before time. The task seems insurmountable considering it would take someone many decades just to sift through even a fraction of those documents scattered across various realms," 41GB posited with a hint of awe.

"No great enigma lies therein," Kishida-Guan shrugged nonchalantly. "I simply inquired it of the Chancellor."

41GB gasped, "And he divulged willingly?"

"And he retained such memories?" 71PQv echoed with surprise, simultaneously.

"We may have purged our world of individual identifiers—that which was once referred to as names—but that doesn't imply the Chancellor's memory is devoid of such recollections. After all, he and I share this antiquated form of address, even now. When I inquired about his…and my…ancestry, he willing shared much about our forebears and why only we two remain from that timeline, which is why I still bear a name. The Chancellor, however, elected to forsake his name for his title," Kishida-Guan responded, his voice tinged with a rare scorn for their society's eldest member. "Thus, when I requested you task the archivist with locating information on these individuals, it was with confidence that he would be able to locate the data I was hoping for."

"Sometimes we overlook that your longevity is nearly equal to the Chancellor's and that both of you have outlived any conceivable lifespan," 71PQv noted, his tone laced with reverence.

"While this historical discourse holds interest, it bears no relevance to our pressing predicament or the measures required to mitigate it," 41GB interjected pragmatically.

"I disagree. While we are still miles away from completing the necessary steps to reach our goal, we now have a firmer grasp on where, in the before time, we need to target our return. So, we in essence, have fitted yet one more piece of the puzzle."

"Do you suppose he suspects your covert intentions?" 71PQv whispered apprehensively.

"Improbable," 41GB asserted.

"And what about our candidate? Have we fabricated one sufficient for the proposed tasks ahead?" 71PQv asked pointedly.

"Now that the Chancellor has been apprised of our objectives, I'll initiate the fabrication of the one who will execute our plans. This created entity will remain oblivious to those goals known solely amongst us here, until the time in which they are needed." Kishida-Guan stated.

"Will they be informed of their fate upon completion—" 71PQv began but was abruptly cut off.

"Do you deem that prudent?" Kishida-Guan retorted sharply.

His two colleagues shook their heads in unison.

"Why question then?"

"I must admit," 41GB started cautiously, shifting the topic. "While I understand the gravity of issues mandating change, I harbor apprehensions about this course of action. What if we fail?" she asked.

"Or worse still, what if our interference in the past inflicts greater harm than our present predicament?" 71PQv added, his voice echoing a similar concern.

"Worse than the potential extinction of the human race in the next half-century?" Kishida-Guan asked incredulously.

"Indeed, as it is highly probable that our intervention could precipitate humanity's downfall even sooner—" 41GB began.

"That is just apprehensive supposition," Kishida-Guan interrupted and then sighed loudly. "My dear colleagues, we have discussed this at length and agreed that we must act, which is why we brought this before the Chancellor. This is not the time to doubt, nor to turn from the path before us. We must set aside those doubts that flitter into our minds and see this through. Agreed?"

"Agreed," his companions murmured.

"Then we will send the order to the geneticists so that our GE archivist will be of age and suitably trained upon completion of our project."

"We have never tested the GE aspects before. Is it wise to do so now when so much is at stake?" 41GB asked.

"It is precisely because so much is at stake that we must modify this fabricated one. Our current populace is designed for a singular purpose—" Kishida-Guan began.

"And you feel that our current design is insufficient for our needs?" 71PQv interjected. "What if we act carelessly in modifying the base genetic template, use our limited supply of synthetic genes, only to have the fabricated product fail when it is needed most? Will this, in fact, resolve the current degradation issue which currently plagues the general populace?"

"Allow me to ask this question," Kishida-Guan went on, his patience with his colleagues wearing thin. "Would you really want to delegate such a crucial task to just any fabrication, or would you rather rely on my expertise to guarantee a perfect tool for our objectives?"

"We would, of course, prefer that our chosen one be flawless, but you are making assumptions based on a non-existent foundation," 71PQv countered.

"I'm making a prediction of failure, if you must know, should we rely on the current state of our fabrications. Preliminary lab results indicate that the reduction in their productivity is likely due to a breakdown in their genetic base. While this is not confirmed as yet, we do not want to risk—"

"Go ahead and send the GE instructions to the geneticists," 41GB caved immediately, nodding to 71PQv to ensure he also concurred. "I'm assuming, of course, that you have already determined which enhancements you feel would be best suited to our needs. Let us trust that we complete the project by the time our created one is of age and that they do not demonstrate adverse side effects, because I do not wish to test fate with a second attempt; especially as we will likely use a majority of our limited reserves on this first trial run. There can be no errors."

They continued the contemplative banter until they entered the research lab, where the comforting hum of machines filled the air. Side by side, they analyzed data and studied designs, trying to piece together the puzzle that held the key to their destiny.

Birth of the GE

The laboratory was bathed in an ethereal glow, a spectral blue light that danced and flickered over the polished, chrome-edged tables, casting long, distorted shadows. The air hummed with tension as the duo of geneticists huddled in quiet consultation, their voices no more than whispers that echoed eerily through the cavernous chamber. They were deep in discussion about their latest mandate from the revered holy ones.

"We are to fabricate thirty new beings using rapid embryonic synthesis," G9983 stated, his voice imbued with authority. "The order specifies accelerated zygotic development and full genomic sequencing within three cycles."

G13654 paused before responding, causing her colleague to lift his gaze from the directives and question her lack of response. "Did you not—"

"I heard," she interjected quietly. "The sheer volume is staggering. We've never been required to initiate this many zygote-to-organism pathways in such a short time. Is it possible this is meant to support a new infrastructural build, perhaps needing increased bio-mechanical labor?"

G9983 arched a brow, eyes narrowing in mild reproach. "Since when do we speculate on the intentions of the holy ones?"

"Is it subversive to entertain a moment of intellectual curiosity?" she countered, defensive but measured.

Dismissing her query with a curt huff, G9983 returned his focus to the directive paper in hand. "There's no mention of structural engineering, although the list does appear to be the standard fare." His brow furrowed momentarily before he regained his composure and proceeded. "The genetic expression profiles are as follows: agro-specialists, systems maintenance, a single sentry, and...one archivist."

G13654 drew in a sharp breath through her nostrils. "But A9021 has not shown any telomeric attrition beyond baseline. No sign of age-related mitochondrial decay. Nor is he due to transition to the next realm for years yet. So, why replace him?"

"I cannot answer your questions," G9983 snapped back impatiently. "Given the standard ontogenetic timeline, the new subject would require a minimum of fifteen years to reach productivity deployment readiness, so he isn't likely to be replaced anytime soon."

"Yes, of course. It was just a shock to hear that news is all. I do hope that this means he'll transition; not that he'll be terminated."

"Whatever is decided is what will be," G9983 replied tersely, causing G13654 to sigh heavily.

"Well then, if there is nothing else required of us today," she ventured cautiously after retrieving the necessary templates, "I will begin the oocyte activation protocols."

As G9983 remained silent, engrossed in their directive, a wave of concern washed over G13654. She'd noticed that her colleague was becoming more emotional and distracted as their years progressed. Even more so than even herself, causing her to question whether his cognitive efficiency was declining? Being of an earlier version of fabricated humans, their genetic makeup varied greatly from the newer fabrications; however, that also meant that they were prone to declination more aligned with natural-born humans, only on an extended time scale. If he were declining cognitively, should she report the anomaly to a neural assessment unit...or a nearby sentry? The thought of doing so caused a shiver of dread to race along her spine. Another thought struck her then: had he gone quiet because he was thinking along similar lines related to her? He had expressed concern over her propensity of late in questioning their directives. Was he considering reporting her?

Suddenly, G9983 blinked rapidly as if their conversation had never paused. "The archivist is to be a genetically enhanced specimen," he noted, eyes fixed on the augmented phenotype parameters. "It must be ages since we've had such a specific request. Do you recall—"

"There's never been one," G13654 interjected, eyes wide with both interest and intrigue. "Maybe it's a trial. An attempt to address population imbalances with enhanced gene expressions, particularly given the increasing number of terminations for failure to maintain requisite levels of productivity. Maybe they're trying to fill the widening gaps in societal needs with enhanced beings."

"One GE does not constitute a systemic reform," G9983 interrupted. "And your speculation and incessant questioning borders on deviant cognition. We are here to enact the will of the holy ones—"

"I'm not trying to guess their thought processes, nor am I questioning them," she responded, "I just find it all so puzzling. Don't you ever feel the need to ask questions? Not all questions are a direct assault on the Chancellor or the holy ones, you know."

"We cannot risk our concerns being overheard," he warned in a hushed whisper. "Any questions, directly or indirectly related to their directives, could be perceived as deviant behavior."

She shook her head and quickly changed the subject. "What genetic enhancements are required for this GE? Did they specify any particular balance in genetic makeup?"

After reviewing the specs, G9983 shook his head again. "The specifications include enhanced mnemonic retention, increased myostatin suppression for muscular development, extended telomerase activation, and systemic immuno-enhancement…and much more—"

"Immuno-enhancement?" she repeated in disbelief. "Pathogenic vectors have been eradicated for over a century. Do we even retain the alleles for resistance factors?"

G9983 shot her a sharp glance, "Search the archived SNP databases for alleles linked to broad-spectrum resistance. Use retroviral vectors if necessary."

"On it," she said, fingers already scrolling through epigenetic overlays and CRISPR-optimized constructs.

"You didn't mention suppressing the emotions. Was that not on the list of requisites?"

"It is a given," G9983 stated shortly after glancing over the list of requisites again. As senior geneticist, G9983 was in charge of the records. As a matter of course, he generally recited the needs and G13654 made a mental note before beginning work. This case, however, was far removed from the norm. He pressed a button on his tablet and transferred the data onto a larger shared screen. "There are so many enhancements that it may be best if you review them yourself."

"You know," G13654 continued conversationally, "we didn't even start suppressing emotions until—"

"Until the last cognitive uprising," G9983 asserted. "A mandate by the Chancellor following a wave of non-compliance and mass terminations. I suppose you count us among those fortunate few who were not suppressed? Personally, I would have preferred it." After a contemplative moment, G9983 continued. "Perhaps the holy ones left that directive unwritten because they determined it would be unwise to suppress the emotions in this new fabrication.

After all, if she is being manufactured for a specific purpose, would it not be counterproductive to have her emotional—"

"So, you've already determined it should be a *she*," G13654 grinned as she pulled the sequences designating the GE as female. "No take backs. You said 'she', so she it is."

"For some reason, I thought I read…" G9983 trailed off with a huff, but didn't argue the point, "Gender doesn't matter one whit. What matters is that we enhance her with the requisites as outlined in the holy ones' directives, and suppressed emotions was not listed."

"No arguments from me." As she worked, she asked, "How's your progress on the thirty? Have you adjusted for polygenic load balancing?"

"The allelic combinations are within range. I'm stabilizing regulatory regions to ensure they meet productive thresholds post-development."

She nodded. "This one will need significantly more post-natal monitoring. Her polygenic scores span cognitive and physiological domains."

What designation should we give the genetically enhanced? After all, she will need to stand apart so that the holy ones will know how to identify her—"

"They could do that simply with any number that we designate for her," G9983 argued. "Why must you make things so complicated?"

"I just think that since she will be special, her designation should be special," G13654 countered.

"Of course you would think that," G9983 huffed again. "Preset alphanumeric identifiers have sufficed for centuries, so why should anything be different—"

"I'll just add 'GE' to the end of her designator, for 'genetically enhanced'" G13654 interrupted, and proceeded to mark the vial with the designation a75b99r84GE, then announced, "I'm set to begin."

"I'll be ready in another minute or two, so stand by. We'll begin production on all simultaneously."

G9983 carefully placed each of his vials next to the one marked a75b99r84GE. They initiated the fabrication sequence together, activating the multi-chambered gestation system. Aseptic pressure filters engaged, and the room filled with the low hum of synchronized bio-synthesis.

"As the genesis cycle commences, I find myself entangled in a web of moral quandaries," G13654 confessed in a hushed undertone, her words barely louder than the gentle purr of surrounding machinery. "The morality of it all—"

"Morality?" G9983 halted mid-action, his brow furrowing in contemplation. "Our duty isn't to dissect morality. We are mere executors of the holy ones' mandates. It's as straightforward as that. What has gotten into you today?"

"I am uncertain," she admitted, her voice laced with unease. "This process, the deliberate creation of a potentially superior organism using untested recombinant pathways—it feels like we're crossing an invisible ethical threshold."

"You're jumping to conclusions," G9983 cut her off sharply. "The holy ones didn't specify that this GE will be exceptional beyond its designation as a GE."

"The enhancements make it exceptional," G13654 argued confused by her colleague's lack of a logical argument.

"Perhaps it is exactly as you suggested—a trial run. If so, it's potentially a step forward—a way to evolve past the entropy affecting our production outputs." He paused, his gaze distant and thoughtful. "Genetics is about evolution, not stagnation. We've been mired in complacency for far too long in our quest for perfection, relying on temporary solutions rather than pushing boundaries."

"Evolution is non-linear." She murmured. "Even beneficial mutations can destabilize entire systems. So, we have to ask ourselves what price we are willing to pay?" she pressed on stubbornly. "The incumbent archivist—"

"Is inconsequential now," he interjected sternly before she could finish her sentence. "We don't lament over fallen leaves making way for new growth." His eyes bore into hers with an intensity that made her flinch slightly. "You need to recalibrate your cognitive processes or I'll have no choice but to report your subversive queries to the sentries."

"I understand," she conceded with a sigh of resignation. "I'm ready to continue."

With practiced synchronicity, they instigated the creation stage by flipping a switch together. The chamber came alive, bathing their masked faces in a spectral blue glow. They fell silent as the GE vial's bioluminescent swirl intensified. Inside, engineered stem cells were rapidly differentiating under the guidance of synthetic transcription factors. Mitochondrial pairing was underway, and neural crest cells flickered with potential.

"We were talking earlier about the current archivist possibly transitioning to the next realm," G13654 initiated a new line of conversation, her voice slightly steadier than before as they watched new life form before them. "Do you ever contemplate what that move will entail? Moving from that of laborer to cognitive exploration?"

G9983's gaze remained fixed on the increasingly radiant vial. "I strive not to let my thoughts stray too far into uncharted territories," he responded after a moment. "But yes, at times I do indulge in such musings. Picture this—instead of being confined within these metallic walls," he gestured expansively towards their high-tech lab humming with machinery and awash with blinking lights, "we could be delving into unknown realms of cognition, perhaps even manipulating realities or conceiving new ones."

G13654 nodded slowly, her visor reflecting the ethereal light emanating from the chamber. "It sounds liberating yet somewhat daunting." She paused briefly before continuing, "You and I have been entrenched in our production phase for countless years, so long, in fact, that…well, have you never observed how the alphanumeric designators grow progressively longer with each fresh fabrication? I mean, look at our genetically enhanced. Even if I hadn't tacked on the GE, her designator is still nine digits in length, and would be longer if terminated designations weren't recycled."

"We should be honored to be where we are, for as long as we've been. We are renowned for our proficiency; it is an honor that the holy ones place such immense trust in us." He paused for effect before adding ominously, "Be grateful that they haven't deemed it necessary to replace us...yet."

"Do you ever ponder over whether we'll be fabricating our own successors one day? Do you think that when that day arrives, the holy ones will permit us to ascend to higher wisdom? That's the norm, but we are far older than many who transition…" G13654 trailed off, unwilling to admit that they may eventually face termination due to their advanced years, rather than be allowed to ascend.

"I have no concern that when the time arrives, we will move to the realm of the wise ones. Are you, perhaps, apprehensive about the fate of the current archivist? You did seem to automatically jump to the conclusion that he would be terminated," G9983 replied.

"I am indeed, and I know I did," she admitted candidly. "He seems too young to already have a replacement being fabricated; far too young to already be considered for ascension, so my thought is that he must have been targeted for low productive levels."

"Although the current archivist is a few generations removed from us, he too has many traits that the newer fabrications lack," he reassured her. "This has either served him well, or bode ill for him. We simply do not know nor should we attempt to guess. As for us, I am certain that we are irreplaceable as we are highly efficient, so even if the archivist, though younger in years, may be selected for ascension that doesn't mean we are being overlooked. We are simply invaluable where we are."

With that, they returned their attention to a75b99r84GE. The liquid inside the vial was swirling more vigorously now, tiny luminescent particles beginning to coalesce in the center like a constellation of stars forming a new galaxy.

"It has begun," G9983 murmured, his voice filled with awe and reverence.

G13654's pulse quickened imperceptibly, her enhanced physiology responding to the gravity of what they were witnessing—the birth of a being like no other. She allowed herself a moment of silent reflection, pondering the paradox of their existence. Here they were, creators, yet still bound by invisible chains of obedience and function.

Awe filled G13654's chest despite the reservations that had overwhelmed her this day. She considered their legacy—creators constrained by ancient mandates. "Each new sequence moves us further from the ancestral genome. What happens when divergence renders us obsolete?"

G9983 considered this in silence, his eyes never leaving the glowing vial. "Evolution cannot be tethered entirely to past blueprints," he finally responded, his voice carrying a rare undertone of conviction. "Perhaps it is time we embraced these deviations as not mere errors but as potential enhancements."

"But enhancements suggest improvement, an ascent towards something greater," G13654 countered quietly. "Are we prepared to handle entities that might surpass our own capabilities? What then becomes of us?"

"That," G9983 replied, turning to meet her gaze directly, "is a bridge we will cross when we reach it. For now, our duty is to forge ahead with the tasks assigned to us."

The chamber emitted a soft chime, signaling the completion of the genesis cycle for a75b99r84GE and the others. The vial slowed its swirling and settled into a steady glow. They both approached the chamber, their movements synchronized in practiced harmony. G13654 carefully extracted the vial, holding it up against the light. Inside, the luminescent particles had now settled into a distinct pattern, resembling a delicate, swirling galaxy with a bright nucleus at its center—a visual metaphor for the new life they had just engineered.

"As always, the forming product is mesmerizing," she remarked, the awe evident in her tone despite her earlier reservations. "Yet each time I can't help but wonder about the destiny we have charted for them."

G9983 nodded, his expression unreadable behind his visor. "It is not our place to question the paths laid out by the holy ones. We engineer; we do not steer destiny."

"But isn't it possible," she persisted softly, "that in our role as creators, we are inadvertently shaping their destinies more than we realize? Our choices in their design, though limited, could be dictating their futures in ways we can't even begin to comprehend."

This seemed to strike a chord with G9983, who paused thoughtfully before responding. "Perhaps you are right. But then, every creator must eventually release their creations into the universe and let them find their own way. It's the natural order of things. But you speak as if we have greater sway over their purpose when we do no more than combine what amounts to an ingredients list provided to us by the holy ones."

"Is that what we're doing now? With this GE? Are we not making decisions beyond the parameters given? Have we not done this before?" G13654 continued, stubbornly.

"It is as you said—we make choices, though limited. Now, can we focus on our work? All of this debate is getting tiresome."

"Yes, of course." The murmured softly, "Every new beginning comes with its own set of uncertainties. I wish it were possible to see what lies ahead for them. Especially for this GE."

G9983 glanced back at the vial with a mixture of pride and trepidation. "In many ways," he replied slowly, "it is perhaps a mercy that we cannot see the future. It allows us to focus on our present tasks without the burden of potential consequences that are beyond our control. We have done what we were tasked to do," G9983 stated, his tone final, reverberating slightly within the now quiet bay. "Now, it is up to her to navigate the complexities of existence."

"Yes," G13654 agreed quietly, her thoughts drifting towards the broader implications of their work. "And though I know you find our conversations tiresome at times, I do enjoy our philosophical debates. I do believe that it is important that we continue questioning and reflecting on our role in this ever-evolving narrative."

"Without being caught out, of course."

"What do you think our world would have become if we hadn't begun suppressing emotions?" G13654 queried softly. "What if we stepped away from the holy ones' dictates, as we did with the GE, and created all with emotions?

"Was not the before time a chaotic disaster because of emotions?" G9983 asked. "Were the uprisings just a century past not answer enough, which is why the Chancellor mandated things be changed?"

"That is what we were told, yes," G13654 responded, a twinge of doubt in her tone.

"Whether it is what we were told, or whether it is fact, is irrelevant. What matters is the now, and right now, those few of us who were created with emotions intact are being systematically terminated because we do not know when to keep those emotions in check." G9983 snapped softly.

"That isn't why and you know it. It's because they are slowly replacing the older models with the emotionless newer ones. But that makes no sense either, since we cannot influence those who have no emotions—" G13654 began, but G9983 interrupted with an argument that she did not anticipate.

"You speak in absolutes when the data does not exist to support your hypothesis? Have we ever tried to gauge our impact on individuals whose emotions are almost absent, akin to a well where the water isn't fully drained but is still inaccessible due to its depth? These creations are not without emotions, they are merely suppressed, which means that any one of them can choose to—"

"Without an example, someone to lead them—"

"I think that this particular debate needs to cease. I, for one, do not wish to risk my ascension to the next realm should someone overhear our discussions and misinterpret them for rebellion."

G13654 nodded with a heavy sigh.

They left the integration bay side by side, their steps echoing softly in the vast corridor. Each was lost in thought, pondering their own place within the intricate tapestry of creation and destiny. They had engineered life but remained bound by their own limitations and directives—a paradox not lost on either of them as they contemplated their next steps in a world that balanced precariously between progress and tradition, innovation and control, rigid structure and unforeseen potential. The silence between them was laden with unspoken questions about autonomy, purpose, and the true nature of progress.

As they reached the end of the corridor, G13654 paused, turning to face G9983. Her voice was more hesitant than before, a reflection of the internal conflict she felt. "Do you think what we do is right?"

G9983 stared at her for a long moment, his usual composure seeming to waver under the weight of her inquiry. Finally, he spoke, his tone more subdued than usual. "Right or wrong may be irrelevant. But I believe what we do matters. And that is enough."

She nodded, but her thoughts lingered on the GE. A life born from code and curiosity, caught between obedience and unknown potential.

a75b99r84GE woke up promptly at her designated time, stretching and yawning loudly. She glanced over at her classmates, all the same age as her, and couldn't help but envy their ability to jump out of bed without any hesitation. She had tried once to remain snuggled, but their instructor scolded her in his cold, unfeeling tone. It wasn't that she wasn't as alert or ready to start her day; wasn't that she was lazy or defiant. Staying nuzzled beneath her blankets just felt good.

At only six years old, a75b99r84GE knew she was different from her classmates, far older in her mental acuity, even though she was still too immature to comprehend why. She questioned and nurtured a curiosity that the others seemed to allow to lie dormant. When she was even younger, she'd raced about, laughing; attempting to engage her classmates in play, but it was soon made clear that her behaviors were not acceptable and that she needed to learn to contain herself for the greater good; to focus her attentions on her training, studies, and preparation on future productivity. There was no room in their society for frivolity, she'd been warned, repeatedly, by her instructors. Learning to suppress her inclinations hadn't been enjoyable for her, but to prevent standing out, she'd quickly learned to blend in. On occasion, her desires would get the better of her and she'd find herself engaged in unacceptable behaviors again. Sometimes indulging, when no one noticed; most times, fighting against her innate urges.

What she didn't realize was that her enhancements had given her an advantage over her fellow classmates both mentally and physically. a75b99r84GE had been enhanced with greater neural plasticity, advanced myelination, a more active hippocampus, myostatin inhibition, superior proprioception…and many other mental and physical enhancements which made her academic progress smoother and her physical development advanced. This was also, without her knowledge, why she wasn't terminated immediately as a flawed fabrication after her initial irregular behaviors were noticed. Kishida-Guan had instructed her teachers to pay special attention to her and her progression, to ensure she had every advantage in her academics.

Just as a75b99r84GE was unaware of her own uniqueness, so was Kishida-Guan oblivious to the emotions swirling within her young mind complicating his directives for the instructors, who initially struggled to reign her in so that she wouldn't prove a distraction or poor influence on the other students. So, when, at the age of five, she appeared to suddenly start self-regulating, the instructors displayed a rare emotion themselves: relief. Though it ended up being short lived.

As she climbed from her bed to stand next to her classmates, her thoughts drifted to the lessons of the day, which were displayed on a readout every morning. Today, they were scheduled to learn about their realm's history, a subject that always intrigued her more than it did the others, perhaps because she'd been fabricated to become the next archivist.

Her classmates seemed content with absorbing the information provided, never questioning its depth or source. But a75b99r84GE found herself often wondering about the spaces between the lines of their textbooks; what wasn't written.

Today, however, there was a stronger restlessness pulling at her. She felt a strong urge to explore beyond the usual boundaries set by their curriculum. So, when they lined up for their morning routine, and she noticed that the interior door to the archives was slightly ajar—a rare oversight in their otherwise closely monitored environment—it proved too much to ignore.

Her heart raced as she contemplated what might lie beyond. The archives were off-limits to students—or anyone other than the archivist and holy ones—without purpose or permission, a rule that had been drilled into them since their integration into the educational system.

It ignited the recurrence of a subtle defiance within her that she'd never considered acting on before. But today, her curiosity was simply too compelling, pulling and tugging at her until, before she could change her mind, she found herself slipping away from the line and inching towards the door, splitting her gaze between the distracted instructors and the doorway, careful to remain unnoticed.

She gently nudged the door ajar, slipping through the narrow opening with caution, eager to uncover the secrets of the archives and discover why the contents were restricted to only a select group. After all, she reasoned tacitly, if she were to be the next archivist, surely its contents weren't off limits to her. It was a justification that she didn't care to fight against.

Inside, the archives were a maze of digital and physical records, stretching far along dimly lit corridors. Her fingers hovered over the interfaces, each one promising a wealth of knowledge. With a tentative touch, she inadvertently activated one of the panels causing it to power on. Holograms flickered to life around her, displaying events and figures from epochs past. Why would such intriguing information be forbidden? After all, knowing one's history often ensured a better future. She knitted her brow, wondering where that thought originated and why she'd be fascinated in a history she knew nothing about. Again, her young mind, though advanced, simply supplied that she was to be the next archivist and therefore was likely fabricated with a burgeoning curiosity over all that entailed.

She was so engrossed in a hologram about a world unfamiliar to her when she was startled by the sound of footsteps echoing from down one of the hallways. Panicked, she quickly turned off the panel and hid behind one of the larger data modules. Her heart thumped loudly as she held her breath, longing to remain unseen. The footsteps grew louder and then paused, as if the person had stopped to listen or look around.

She peered around the corner. It was her primary instructor, his sharp eyes scanning the room. a75b99r84GE jerked back when he turned, drawing nearer to her hiding spot. She knew that getting caught would mean severe reprimand, possibly even reintegration training. But as fear clutched at her throat, a deeper part of her stirred—a part that was driven by the same curiosity that had brought her here. A curiosity that begged whether she would be able to talk her way out of trouble were she to be discovered. Her mind raced with the possibilities on how she could explain her presence there. Could she, perhaps, suggest that she was fabricated for that position and was merely taking initiative to explore her future role within their society?

Before she could reason out a cohesive excuse, she heard the sound of the instructor's footfalls moving away. She released the breath she hadn't realized she'd been holding and let out a quiet sigh of relief. She waited a few more moments before cautiously emerging from behind the data module. Rising on tiptoes, she dashed back the way she'd come and quickly made her way to the hallway outside of their living quarters, where her classmates stood, not the slightest confusion etched on their features, devoid of expression, over the delay in their day. She shook her head and slipped in line behind the last student.

Her instructor emerged a moment later and approached, "Where were you?" He demanded.

a75b99r84GE drew a mask of innocence over her face before glancing up at the elderly man, who did nothing to hide the irritation he was feeling. It was a rare occurrence for anyone to show emotion, that it startled her when they did. "I forgot something in my locker and then I needed to run to the bathroom…"

"Next time you need to depart the line, speak up!" he barked. Before she could acknowledge the reprimand, he turned and marched back to the head of the line where the other instructor had returned from her search. She glanced at a75b99r84GE briefly, then took command of the class, while the primary instructor marched off to perform his other duties.

In the months that followed, her ordinary routines took on a dual nature. Externally, she performed her tasks with the mechanical precision expected of her, but internally, she wrestled with the burgeoning need to understand more about the world beyond their controlled existence. The more she thought about what she'd seen in the holograms, the more she realized how isolated they were from whatever reality lay outside their meticulously crafted community.

The next opportunity to explore these curiosities came unexpectedly near the end of their academic term. During the morning session, their instructor announced that they would begin the final phase of their academic journey, which would require them to access specifically-provided archived materials as a part of their job-specific training. a75b99r84GE couldn't help feeling excited, but as she'd done for most of her life, she hid this excitement behind a mask of indifference.

Deep within her soul, however, she'd chafed at the opportunity to access the forbidden archives again in a legitimized way. She glanced around at her classmates wondering if they were just as excited as she was. Though she tried to suppress her emotional response, she couldn't hide it altogether as her eyes were alight with delight. Yet, her classmates remained completely unresponsive. They sat stiffly in their seats, their faces as expressionless as she tried to make hers. For them, it was merely another routine day in academia, spent in mute compliance.

A realization dawned on her, that their days always passed in this manner. Their existence was choreographed with such precision that spontaneity of speech and action seemed not just rare but nearly nonexistent. Even their teacher spoke succinctly, and only when necessary for instruction or direction.

She couldn't quite put her finger on why this unsettled her so much. There was a nagging sense that something was absent from her life. This lack of understanding tugged at her young heart, turning her enthusiasm about delving into the archives into a confusing swirl of inexplicable sadness. She pushed down on her turbulent emotions, which threatened to erupt from her chest like a storm ready to break, until the mask she wore to conceal them felt less like a facade and more like a natural expression. With this newfound composure, she redirected her focus to the words her teacher was imparting. Even though her equilibrium was restored, a profound sadness lingered within her, not for her own sake, but for her classmates who appeared indifferent to...everything.

"Today, we begin your final academic journey before moving to your individual areas in which you will begin the download process specific to your fields of study. Over the course of this next year, this phase of your academic journey will test your ability to learn, process, and retain information as well as an increased emphasis on physical training to strengthen your bodies, which will, in turn, strengthen your minds. Those who fail in this process will face termination," their instructor droned on, "which would mean less individuals entering the workforce. Therefore, I urge you to do your best. Not only to prevent ending your progress at the early age of six and a half, but to prevent putting undue stress on society who is depending upon you all to take your places in a couple of years, after your individual work data download sessions have concluded.

"As you have been selected for the field of archival studies, a75b99r84GE, I will introduce you to the current archivist so you can become familiar with him. The reminder of you will break off into your individually assigned cubicles to begin your studies. As of this week, you will undergo individual testing regularly to ensure that the information provided for your review is being comprehended and retained. Because you are in your academic phase, limited failure will be permitted, emphasis on the word limited. Repeated failures will be seen as either intentional disregard or as functional degradation. Neither of which will be permitted into society. Now, after our morning repast, we shall make our way to the archives. Let us now proceed with the day."

All the children responded their readiness in unison by standing and moving to line up outside of their classroom.

"Let me inform the archivist that we will be ready for him to meet with us in three-quarters of an hour." The instructor stepped away for a few minutes, leaving the students clustered in the corridor. a75b99r84GE seized this moment to attempt communication, eager to share both her excitement and her reservations with some of her classmates. This endeavor was one she had tried discreetly over the past couple of years, always hoping for a response, but her efforts had yet to yield any successful interactions. Nevertheless, in her mind, they were now six and a half years old and rapidly approaching their productive phase. Surely, she thought, this milestone was ample reason for someone other than herself to express their own thoughts and emotions.

She turned to the closest student, "Hi, I'm a75b99r84GE." He turned and looked at her with an expressionless face.

"I am aware," he replied shortly, though a mild flickering in his eyes seemed to counter this proclamation.

"You must be c479956cf, right?" she said, testing her memory of a fellow student's identifier. They seldom had a reason to remember such details, so she was surprised at how easily she recalled it, especially since instructors were the only ones who addressed students by their designators. No one had ever emphasized the need to remember a classmate's identifier. His eyes widened slightly, showing his surprise that she remembered such a trivial detail.

"That's accurate," came the flat response from c479956cf, his young voice devoid of any emotional inflection, which spoke of the years of training they all had that emotions were volatile and useless and therefore the minute levels each were fabricated with needed to be quashed. This meant that the tiny spark of surprise that had initially registered in his large, innocent eyes was quickly extinguished.

"Pleasure to meet you," a75b99r84GE responded with genuine warmth, trying to ignore his indifferent demeanor. Her eyes sparkled with the enthusiasm she wished to express about their upcoming academic chapter. Unfortunately, his reaction subdued her enthusiasm.

"Why?" c479956cf asked, his question seeming more like an automated response than genuine curiosity.

Surprised by the lackluster response, a75b99r84GE hesitated before replying. "There's not...a particular reason," she replied trying to hide the disappointment in her tone. Due to her genetic enhancements, she was more mature than all of her classmates, which confused and challenged her, and in recent months she found herself, inexplicably, wanting to assess their emotional intelligence and social engagement. The lack of opportunity and response by her peers, however, intensified her ever-increasing frustrations. Nevertheless, she stayed optimistic; each encounter was a chance for learning and an effort to forge a connection.

c479956cf took her continued silence as the end to their conversation and turned his back on her. Just then the instructor returned and motioned for them to follow her to the cafeteria. Each student collected a plate, sat down in their designated spot, and ate in silence. Precisely three-quarters of an hour later, the students lined up and returned to stand before the door to the archives. After a moment to ensure that the archivist was prepared for their arrival, the instructor stood aside and bade the students enter.

"Students, this is the current archivist. His designator is A9021. This designator, you'll commit to memory. Especially you, a75b99r84GE, as you have been selected to take over this position in the next year and a half.

So surprised by the fact that they were now being instructed to memorize designators, something she was just thinking about earlier as being of little importance, that a75b99r84GE interrupted the teacher's instructions.

"Excuse me…" she paused, not even knowing how to address the person who had been training them all for the past two and a half years. She decided to simply ask her question, "Are we expected to learn designators for everyone now, or specifically just significant figures such as the archivist? Will we now address you as other than 'teacher'?"

The instructor's gaze narrowed marginally, his expression betraying a flicker of shock and annoyance at the brazen interruption, but he quickly masked it and responded with a neutral tone. "Significant roles only. Since you will be working alongside A9021 for a period of years, you will need to know his designator. Each student will be provided the designator of their mentor also, when entering production phase, which will need to be recalled as needed. Other than those instances, and because our society does not encourage socializing…"

"Why not?" a75b99r84GE interjected again, much to the teacher's mortification, which he expressed more openly at this second interruption. Unnoticed by her, and the others, a sentry had moved away from his guard position and had begun transmitting the interaction to an unseen individual.

The instructor compressed his lips, repressing his anger at this disruption in their day, in their routine. Had this student not been singled out by the holy one as one to treat differently than the others, he would have signaled for a sentry to remove her from their presence immediately. As it was, he feared that her ever-increasing divergence from societal expectations would become a serious issue. Still, it was not his call to do other than instruct, so he drew in a deep breath and replied, "Socializing promotes emotional connections, which in turn can affect productivity and focus. It is paramount that each of you performs at optimal efficiency. Emotional distractions can ruin the very fabric of our system," he explained in a patronizing tone that stated she was already aware of this information, as this perspective was deeply ingrained in their society's philosophy. Emotions were seen not as human necessities but as impediments to the functionality and output of its members. "Now, I highly suggest that you curb your sudden proclivity to interject your unnecessary and unwelcomed curiosities so that we may proceed with our academics."

a75b99r84GE digested this information, feeling the cold weight of the words settle around her as though they were physically constraining her. It was a reiterating clarification she had not wanted to hear and it reminded her, again, that those traits which made her unique were not welcomed. She was not meant to stand out, rather to blend in.

"Now I will turn all of you—"

"a75b99r84GE, you will accompany me," the sentry interrupted, moving toward the group.

All eyes turned to the classmate that the sentry was addressing, expressions ranging from zero interest to a mild curiosity, with the exception of the instructor who appeared to have a cross between smug and relief etched on his features. The instructor quickly stepped forward, "Students, go with A9021. He will go escort you to your cubicles and explain what you will be doing." As her classmates dispersed, a75b99r84GE followed the sentry out of the archives.

"Where are we going?" she queried, but the sentry did not respond. Instead, she led a75b99r84GE out of the main building and, after a short walk across the courtyard, they entered a building in which she'd never gone before. Within a few minutes, they were standing outside a large door. The sentry entered her identifying information onto a panel, then stepped back and waited in silence.

When the door hissed open, the sentry signaled that a75b99r84GE step inside, all without speaking another word to her.

When a75b99r84GE complied, the sentry turned and walked a few feet away, taking up a post nearby and leaving a75b99r84GE alone inside a medium-sized sparsely-furnished space. She noticed a chair swivel slightly at the opposite end of the room and started moving toward it. Before she could announce her presence, the chair swung about and before her sat an individual whom she recognized to be a holy one.

The image they had been shown years before seemed unimaginable, but to stand before him now…she had never seen anything so old still drawing breath.

The figure before her wasn't just aged—he was ancient, like time had folded itself around him and forgotten to let go. His skin was thin and papery, stretched delicately over a frame that looked more sculpture than man. Every breath he took seemed to echo in the sterile silence, a slow, deliberate inhale—as though the air itself had to be coaxed into his body, summoned like an old memory returning from exile. His eyes weren't clouded with age, but sharpened by it. They shimmered like memory crystals, catching light and knowledge in ways no child's eyes ever could. When he blinked, she could sense the centuries which had passed behind those lids.

The holy one's voice—when it came—was less sound and more presence. A resonance that she felt in her bones before she heard it with her ears, like an echo from a planet she'd never visited. She knew him to be more than two centuries old, which to her, made him seem inhuman—or at least he wasn't human in the way others were. He was a myth that had decided to keep breathing—and he was angry.

"Your conduct today crossed the line and has caused discomfort among your peers," he reprimanded.

"They didn't seem uncomfortable; they barely show any signs of life, let alone emotion," she countered, fearlessly.

"That's because they aren't flawed," Kishida-Guan accused. "They know that emotions are not a part of a cohesively functional society founded on a core of productivity. There's no place for the type of disparate behaviors the likes of which you displayed here today."

"Then why am I still here?" she fired back, sounding more like a petulant child than an enhanced advanced. She stood defiant, recalling the chilling instances when their populace was forced to assemble for public executions. Those who failed to keep their scant emotions entirely under wraps as per decree or whose productivity had gradually dwindled over time were eliminated; an event becoming all too common.

The fire in Kishida-Guan's gaze diminished and he sighed heavily, "You are still here because the holy ones fabricated you for a specific purpose. Until that purpose is revealed and implemented, you need to learn to control yourself. Do you understand?"

a75b99r84GE nodded slowly. The gravity of his tone in that short explanation revealed more than his words, which revealed nothing; yet, she somehow comprehended the enormity of what was being asked of her: to live within the boundaries of a role she didn't yet understand and, until it was revealed, to stifle any hint of individuality or emotion that constantly threatened to surface. She remained silent, feeling each second stretch taut like a wire, relaxed only when Kishida-Guan spoke again.

"You are not like the others, a75b99r84GE. This will prove both beneficial and difficult as you continue through your life. I cannot comprehend, myself, why you struggle with emotions since your primary fabrication protocols are no different than that of your classmates. Though we all have emotions, they are greatly suppressed in the newer generations and, as you are aware, all are taught at the beginning of their academics, as younglings, that they are useless and to be ignored and repressed. Yet, with your level of intelligence and enhancements, you appear unable, or unwilling, to control them as easily and this is baffling to me." He paused for a moment before continuing, speaking more to himself than to her, as if making a mental note. "Perhaps I need to address this with the Chancellor. Consider not just suppressing emotions in future fabrications, rather eliminating them altogether." He glanced at her then, his gaze hawk-like, "For now, you must learn to quell that which separates you from the rest of society. It would be prudent to observe and adapt rather than to attempt to resist the norms."

"How am I to do this?" she asked quietly, genuinely seeking guidance in a world that seemed bent on erasing her personal identity.

Kishida-Guan leaned back in his chair, his eyes narrowing thoughtfully. "Observation. Note how those around you interact within our prescribed structures. Emulate them. Not just in behavior but also in mindset, until it becomes second nature."

"Blend in. Not stand out," a75b99r84GE murmured sadly.

"Precisely. You must learn to wear the mask that everyone has on naturally, even if yours feels heavier by virtue of your awareness of it. To do anything other risks more than just your existence, it risks the purpose for which you were fabricated. Now, you must return to your classmates," he continued before she could question him on what her true purpose for existing was. "It is my understanding that you are to graduate within the next two years and will take your place among society. It is my sincere hope that we do not meet again under these circumstances—or have the need at all before time." With that he stood, effectively concluding their meeting. He waved his hand over a section of his console and the doors to his office hissed open. The same sentry who'd escorted her there, was standing in wait.

a75b99r84GE walked out of the room on the heels of the sentry, her mind swirling in confusion and a newfound fear of the future. She knew that blending in was not something she excelled at, nor did she fully understand why she should have to suppress what felt natural to her. Nevertheless, it had been commanded by the holy one and that command resounded in her mind as a grim prophecy.

The walk back across the courtyard felt longer than before. Everything around her seemed so different now, somehow unnatural. She tried to digest the reality of her existence and the seemingly impossible life before her, but struggled to do so. The towering walls of the buildings cast long shadows over her path, as if reflecting the weight of her thoughts.

When she reached the archives, A9021 was still moving about explaining expectations to her classmates, signaling that she hadn't been gone nearly as long as it felt. No one but A9021 acknowledged her return. The uniformity of their behavior struck her now more than ever—a stark contrast to the storm of emotions raging inside her.

After a minute, A9021 walked toward her and extended a skeletal hand in greeting. His grip was cold and bony, but firm. "Welcome to the archives," A9021 said, his voice as dry as the pages of the books around him. "I understand you're to replace me in the next few years. I hope you find clarity and purpose here, just as I did."

"May I ask you something?" she ventured.

"Since you were delayed in starting work with your classmates, don't you think your time would be better spent than assuaging your curiosity?"

"True, but this is to be my future vocation. I would think that querying you, the current archivist, would prove beneficial."

"I will entertain a single question, and then settle you into a cubicle to begin your studies."

"Do you ever wonder about what lies beyond these archives? Beyond our lessons and routines?"

"That is two questions."

"More a question and a clarification."

A9021 paused, turning his gaze upon her. For a moment, she thought she saw a flicker of curiosity in his eyes, or perhaps it was just a reflection of the holograms. He seemed to weigh her question carefully before answering. "The world beyond the archives is vast and filled with complexities that our structured environment shields us from. It is also of no concern to us," A9021 began, his voice carrying an uncharacteristic hint of wistfulness. "It is our duty, as archivists, to preserve the knowledge that has been stored within these walls for centuries, not to seek that which is outside of them. In short, it is for us to do, not to question."

"I have heard that repeatedly over the last couple of years," a75b99r84GE stated in mild frustration, but she kept those frustrations internally, though inside her thoughts churned with rebellious ideas. If they were only to preserve, never explore, how would they ever grow in knowledge? She opened her mouth to question him further, but his gaze stopped her. Instead, she thanked him and then turned toward the cubicle he pointed to. Before she stepped away, however, he had a final thought to impart, which he did in a mere whisper—for her hearing alone.

"One more thing, little one," he said. "While I caution you against unnecessary exploration, it's clear you have an innate desire to understand deeper truths. I implore you to bury that urge, deep within you; lock it away and never let it loose. Our Chancellor and holy ones do not look kindly upon heterogeneity."

"What is—"

"You are different than your classmates," he asserted, interrupting her. "You have within you, for some inexplicable reason, a nonconformity that could see you terminated if you do not learn to conceal it, and conceal it well."

a75b99r84GE felt the weight of A9021's words settle like a cold stone in her stomach, even though the holy one had assured her that her fate was not to die, rather to serve some mysterious purpose later. Still, she nodded slowly her acknowledgment, her eyes tracing the intricate patterns of the floor tiles as she processed his warning.

It was a warning that she was beginning to realize that all citizens faced: step away from the norm at the risk of death. It did not seem to lend itself to a contented life. While the fear of termination was real and omnipresent, so was her thirst for knowledge, an unquenchable flame that no threat could fully extinguish. Though, through an unfamiliar need for self-preservation, she would do as instructed and attempt to hide it. "Thank you, A9021," she managed to say, her voice steady despite the turmoil within. "I will consider your advice carefully."

As she walked to her designated cubicle, her mind raced with conflicting emotions. The safety of conformity battled against the dangerous allure of curiosity. She logged into the system and began her research, her fingers mechanically navigating through digital archives while her thoughts wandered to forbidden territories.

She Wasn't Prepared

One year later

"The following students are to step forward." The instructor's voice was devoid of any emotion. "a3167lu30, c479956cf…"

It was graduation day, which meant that only those students who'd excelled in their physical and mental requirements would be moving on to the download phase of their academic journey. She glanced about at her classmates, a few of whom had received warnings for the forewarned 'limited failures' wondering if they'd adjusted their physical and/or mental efforts sufficiently to graduate with their classmates…or if they'd be terminated. In reality, she knew that any one of them could be called forward to graduate or face termination because no matter how one thought they performed personally, it was ultimately their instructors who determined success, which is why she stood now with a feeling of uncertainty gripping her nerves which fought against the confidence she held that she'd indeed excelled and would graduate. It didn't help her nerves when her gaze scanned about the area and she spotted two sentries standing against a nearby wall…waiting. One holding a rod and the other carrying a bucket. She jerked her eyes away, drawing in deep, calming breaths.

Her thoughts echoed back to the year before when the holy one had assured her that she was meant for some future purpose, which immediately worked to dispel any doubts she harbored over being terminated. She straightened her shoulders and waited for her identifier to be called.

"a75b99r84GE," the instructor beckoned. Her heart raced as she stood up even taller and lifted her chin in pride. She could feel the weight of the moment resting on her small seven-and-a-half-year-old shoulders.

"Out of the thirty students fabricated over seven years ago, only these ten have a proven performance with zero entropy. The remainder of you—all twenty—have failed to meet the expectations required for graduation insofar as you each have demonstrated levels of performance indicative of premature degradation and therefore are unsuited for life as a productive. Thus, you will not move on to the download phase of your education, rather you are each hereby instructed to present yourselves to the sentries for termination."

Those few words uttered by their instructor hit a75b99r84GE like a barrage of swords, piercing through her with their harsh reality causing her shoulders to slump and her pride to deflate. She felt tears form in her eyes. She stood there, wide-eyed, alone in her sorrow and distress for those twenty individuals with whom she'd spent her youngling years. And because they didn't meet the high restrictive level of expectation, they would meet their end at the tender age of just seven-and-a-half. It was almost too much for her to bear witness to, so she turned her back, seeking an escape from the overwhelming tide of emotions.

In the shadowy recesses of the cavernous room, the two geneticists, G9983 and G13654, stood in somber silence as they watched the emotional response of the genetically enhanced. Their eyes fell shut in unison, as if tethered by an unseen thread of shared apprehension. A fleeting glance passed between them, an exchange of unease that hung heavy in the sterile air. The disturbing reality was now undeniable—over half of their meticulously engineered students had faltered on their predestined educational journey.

"The degradation within our fabrications is manifesting prematurely," G9983's voice trembled as it barely reached his partner, his words sinking into her ears like an ominous warning that chilled her to the core.

"Yes, it's deeply troubling," G13654 agreed with a tense nod.

"We have to notify Kishida-Guan about this alarming trend immediately," G9983 urged, his tone heavy with the pressing gravity of their situation.

"I am certain that he is already aware," came G13654's soft agreement, tilting her head toward a sentry who appeared to be broadcasting the event to someone unseen.

"You think he's watching?" G9983 murmured as he watched the ten graduates shuffle out under the harsh fluorescent lights and the first underperformer halt before the impassive sentries; emotionless, as the rod of termination was lifted.

"Considering he had us create something unique as a potential test subject for future fabrications? I'd say it is likely he, and the other holy ones, would be as interested in that progress as we are," G13654 broke the gloomy silence with a note of hope.

"That's presumption on our part; although, the genetically enhanced did perform admirably." Her voice held a glint of pride that cut through the pervading gloom. "When we next meet with Kishida-Guan, perhaps we should propose focusing solely on fabricating genetically enhanced moving forward; show him that we stand in solidarity with his efforts."

"That might indeed be our salvation from this crisis," agreed G9983 with a hint of relief threading through his response, his gaze lingering on the remaining younglings as they awaited their fate.

"Surely, you do not believe that he would hold us personally responsible for the ever-increasing degradation of the citizenry!" G13654 exclaimed in a voice barely above a whisper but screaming with worry.

"We cannot presume he will not, so I suggest that we compile all the data we can in defense of our work, and also as it relates to a75b99r84GE. It may be our saving grace. Let us discuss this on the way back to the laboratory."

Meanwhile, a75b99r84GE followed the line of graduates, her mind swirling with a mixture of relief and sorrow. Relief that she was among the chosen few allowed to continue, but sorrow for her classmates who were not as fortunate. As they made their way to the new facility where their vocational download would commence, she couldn't shake off A9021's warnings from a year ago. Despite the joy of success, his words about her innate nonconformity haunted her. Was she only spared because Kishida-Guan commanded it be so? If that were true, was she just as flawed as those who were kept behind to be terminated? Would her aberrancy make it difficult for her to process and retain the data she'd be receiving this coming year? She wracked her brain trying to determine whether she'd ever felt the effects of degradation. Was her high opinion of her abilities factual or purely subjective on her part.

She entered the new facility with a determined stride, trying to portray an aura of compliance and confidence with the predetermined path laid out for her…for them all. The facility was impressive and overwhelming, filled with an advanced technology, which was only just visible above the doors of the tiny rooms which encircled the entire interior wall. In the center sat a main console at which sat a single technician. Seeing it all lifted a75b99r84GE's spirits and sparked renewed curiosity and anticipation. Her heart buzzed with a hidden excitement about the vast knowledge she was set to receive.

"Here, the final phase of your education begins," the instructor stated. "This is t859672k." The technician stood and made her way over. "She is the technician who will be overseeing your individual downloads in the coming year. Depending on the level of information required, along with your retention and recall levels, you can expect to be in this phase anywhere from three- to twelve months. It was a privilege to have worked with you all and I wish you a long and productive life. I will now turn over this next phase of your journey to her.

Back in their laboratory, the two geneticists concluded their conversation in agreement to send a communications request to the realm of the holy ones. This was a rare occurrence since messages were generally relayed through the office of sentries and then, if deigned necessary, a holy one would communicate directly with them. If deemed unnecessary, a message was relayed back through the office of sentries. Today, however, G9983 decided that the information related to today's graduates needed to be relayed immediately and directly. He only hoped the holy ones agreed and didn't determine his actions to be aberrant.

"I don't think Kishida-Guan is one to answer citizen's calls directly. Even from his geneticists," G13654 speculated when the screen before them remained dark.

"Perhaps not, but we may be able to reach a more junior holy one. That is, we may be able to connect with 71PQv or 41GB," G9983 replied.

When the screen remained black, the geneticists looked at each other in doubt. "Perhaps," G13654 sighed, "we should just relay a message through the sentries that we wish an audience with Kishida-Guan."

G9983 nodded, but just as he reached over to disconnect, the screen before them lit up and the visage of an elderly man appeared. Immediately, both geneticists bowed in respect.

"G9983, G13654, your direct communication is noted," the holy one's voice resonated with a tone of solemn authority with a hint of accusation that had them glancing side-eyed at other in worry. Before they could explain the breach in protocol, Kishida-

Guan continued, "however, I am surprised that you would think that there is something within our realm to which I would be uninformed."

The geneticist blinked in surprise and their faces reddened with humiliated embarrassment. They were about to begin apologizing profusely, when Kishida-Guan continued, "I assume that the reason for the direct communication was not simply to inform me that we lost two-thirds of our latest crop of citizenry, but rather to notify me that you believe our current genetic material to be degrading. Moreover, is it possible you believe you have a proposition to put forth to alter the inferior genetics with which we are currently faced?"

G9983 nodded rapidly, but seemed unable to speak, so G13654 spoke up, "We cannot begin to fathom why so many of the fabrications are degrading so rapidly, especially as they are created using the same genetic materials that we have used for centuries; why some thrive—" she began.

"Do you plan to give me a history of which I am already keenly aware?" Kishida-Guan interrupted sharply.

"My apologies," G13654 replied quickly, timidly. "We propose that we consider instilling all future fabricated citizenry with the same genetic enhancements as a75b99r84GE—"

"Out of the question." The abruptness of Kishida-Guan's response left G13654 momentarily speechless. She exchanged a glance with G9983, both of their expressions mirroring the shock and confusion they felt. Kishida-Guan's image on the screen paused for a moment, as if calculating his next words carefully. "I understand your concerns and while the apparent success of fabricated citizen, a75b99r84GE, does suggest a solution to our current crises, enhancing all future fabrications to that genetic standard is not feasible. For one, the resources required are substantial and our society must think sustainably. Had you taken the time to inventory the genetic material currently available, before contacting me, you would have seen that it is woefully insufficient as a remedy. Also, it does not address the underlying issue with the base genome. The genetic enhancements of a75b99r84GE may very well be serendipitous. Only one-third of this latest batch of fabrications proved viable. Who's to say that, if we did have sufficient base materials, we'd see a greater number of successes within a group solely comprised of genetically enhanced?"

"Then why create a genetically enhanced at all?" G13654 queried, realizing too late the insubordinate tone in which it was asked.

The holy one's eyes narrowed slightly, "The purpose for the creation of a genetically enhanced is not for your knowledge."

"With all due respect, sir," G9983 jumped in, finally finding his voice, "but surely the current rate of degradation among our citizenry threatens our society's structural foundation more than resource allocation does."

"Again, your point is noted," he turned his glaring gaze from G13654 to her colleague, his tone softening, "however, consider this: what if the enhancements do not take uniformly—as I just stated? What if the inclusion of genetically enhanced material leads to unforeseen consequences, even greater failures? Take, for instance, a75b99r84GE's present state of emotional unrest. I am still uncertain why the enhancements requested have made it difficult for her to control her suppressed emotions to such a degree…" Kishida-Guan trailed off, eyeing his geneticist with a suspicion that had them squirming, but they remained silent, unwilling to confess the part in tampering with her genetic base code. After a moment, he continued, "If all of our citizens suddenly began behaving emotionally, it would set back our society's advancements. Reverting our arc of progress centuries; perhaps even to that of the before time. Still, if it will put your mind at ease," he continued, his tone suggesting that he could care less about easing their concerns, "the Chancellor, myself, and my fellow holy ones, have been—and continue to be—deliberating on the proper course of action to reverse the issues facing future fabricated citizens. Now, as you are the ones who initiated this discourse, was there anything further, before I close this conversation?"

"Do you wish for us to begin fabrications for the twenty that were lost in today's graduation?" G13654 asked meekly, hoping that her earlier infraction would be swiftly overlooked.

"The sooner we can move to replace those lost, the smoother our society will continue to function, so yes, begin immediate fabrication of those replacements needed as directed more seven years ago. I do not need to ask that your records of that directive are in pristine order."

Before either could respond in the affirmative to his statement, the screen went black. G9983 and G13654 remained still for a moment, the weight of their failed proposal heavy in the air between them. They turned to each other; the unspoken consensus clear. After a moment, G13654 spoke up, her voice barely above a whisper, "Do we dare?"

G9983 shook his head and replied, "I need some time to think about it," glancing around nervously. "Let's just make the replacement batch for now. We can talk about what to do next afterwards. If Kishida-Guan is correct, we are lacking the genetic material for this to be a long-term solution." G13654 gave him a strange look, as if he lacked a backbone—which he didn't deny. However, there was no need to reveal that to her. "Also, I confess that I'm hesitating because our society has always put complete trust in the Chancellor and the holy ones—for centuries now—and we have thrived because of it. But now when one problem arises, suddenly we doubt their abilities?"

G13654 listened, her expression unreadable. "I agree that we've thrived, or possibly merely survived?" she countered softly, her gaze intense. "But should they not also put their trust in us? We are, after all, the geneticists. Should not our expertise be taken into account?" She paused, sighing heavily. "I am curious how the holy ones are more knowledgeable about our stores than even we are. After all, we work with them—"

"We work with the primary materials, not that which was used to create the genetically enhanced," G9983 argued feebly. "Did you bother to take an inventory when we gathered what was needed for a75b99r84GE, or did you simply collect what was needed by rote, as we do with every new batch?"

"Very well. I concede your point, and I agree that we should go ahead and fabricate a new batch right now, but afterward, let's consider taking a serious look at the degradation rates, the anomalies that have been appearing more frequently." She sighed, her shoulders slumping slightly as if the weight of their secret debate was physically pressing down on her. "I'm just saying, maybe…maybe it's time for a change. For us to take a risk."

G9983 weighed his words carefully as they stood in the bustling laboratory, surrounded by the constant hum of machines and data processing. The soft glow of monitors cast shadows on their faces as they contemplated straying from protocol. "Maybe we can start small," G9983 suggested. "Make incremental changes instead of a complete overhaul so that the modified fabrications don't resemble a75b99r84GE too closely at first." He moved closer to G13654 and pulled up a tablet filled with genetic sequences and notes, swiping through them with his fingers until he located the file from the fabrications that we terminated today, still murmuring about their plans while he worked. "We could adjust the epigenetic markers in just a few fabrications without altering the core genetic structure..."

G13654's eyes widened with interest. "That could potentially yield significant results without causing the fabrications to stand out." She paused, considering the implications. "It's worth trying. We can test new variations without risking a full genetic overhaul."

G9983 nodded feeling buoyed by the potential, his voice radiating with sudden excitement. "And if it works, we can inform Kishida-Guan then. If successful, we might even be given the opportunity to fabricate our replacements so that we can ascend soon. Maybe we won't even need to go through the realm of wise ones first."

"We could be elevated directly to holy ones," G13654 finished with a grin.

Watching from his office, Kishida-Guan listened with growing concern. That hint of defiance when they'd conversed with him concerned him greatly. Thus, instead of disconnecting the communications, he'd simply darkened his screen to see if his concern was warranted.

He knew they were among the few remaining from a time when emotions were not suppressed at all in fabrications. And now he understood more than ever why suppressing emotions was necessary for the greater good of society. Acts of rebellion done covertly could not be tolerated. And if they began to mess around with the genetics of future fabrications, it could impede upon his plans.

He summoned a sentry, "From now on, you are to act as sentry on duty within the genetics laboratory. Record all activity; however, should you notice anything of immediate concern, notify me immediately. I think it's time that we prepare for their termination. Present them with the following orders to add two replacement geneticists to the next batch of fabrications."

The sentry, a tall and imposing figure, nodded solemnly, then left to take its post. Kishida-Guan leaned back in his chair, his fingers steepled. He knew that the geneticists within this realm were valuable assets who were pioneers of sorts, since they were there at the beginning when the new protocols for fabrications were put into place. But their current behavior suggested a burgeoning defiance and dissatisfaction with the status quo which could prove disastrous if left unchecked. Hopefully, giving them a sense of hope that they would soon be ascending would put an end to their rebellion. If not, and he had to terminate sooner than their replacements came of age...it was an unthinkable possibility that would halt citizenry production for more than a decade. He clenched his jaw in fury. He was already contending with degradation on a large scale and a potentially aberrant GE who he needed to forward his plans. He didn't need another wrench thrown into the works.

"I've worked too hard to see this project completed and I will not have them derail my purposes by becoming meddlesome."

His fingers glided across the console, composing a message to his counterpart in Realm 3275. In the centuries since the realms were created, he'd never had a reason to reach out to the holy ones in another realm. It had new questions whirling about in his mind, as the Chancellor was the only one who knew of events on realms other than theirs. He could send this message out only to discover that Realm 3275 never advanced beyond the intelligence of apes. He sighed heavily. He needed to know, for the sake of their own realm's future; especially if he needed to call on their geneticists for interim backup. He paused in composition of the message, deciding to consult with the Chancellor on the matter first.

Rapid Degradations

a75b99r84GE lie on the chilled, stainless-steel table, her mind struggling to focus. The final words from her instructor felt like a warning. In essence: remember what is being fed into your brain, or face termination. Her training wasn't that complex, so retention shouldn't be an issue for her. She felt fortunate that her daily memory exercises were hours fewer than her classmates, for they faced jobs more mentally and physically taxing than herself. She also reminded herself repeatedly that no matter how poorly she performed, she wouldn't likely face a sentry's rod. It was a constant battle within her—the certitude versus the uncertainty.

For her, graduation was only a month out, and she was confident that she would move from a student to that of a productive—but only if her mind stopped wandering, which it did at every turn. And she fought back at every turn.

Still, her curiosities were eating away at her. Primarily about who she was and why she was so vastly different from her classmates. Second to that, but equally distracting was her curiosity. She'd had a peek into a world enormously dissimilar to her own. It was a mere glance, but it was enough for her mind to want more. She'd been genetically tasklined to become the archivist, and now was exceptionally grateful for that. Not because of what the job entailed, but because of what it could reveal.

The archivist position was not just about maintaining records and ensuring the accuracy of data. It was a role laced with potential access to files, obscure protocols, and forgotten histories that were placed far beyond the reach of most within her society. For a75b99r84GE, it represented a beacon of knowledge, an ocean of undiscovered truths waiting to be navigated.

As she lay on the cold steel table, her instructor's voice continued to echo in her head, blending with the monotone hum of machinery. "Focus is key," the instructor repeated like a mantra designed to condition hers, and her classmates', minds for compliance and functional efficiency. But her mind rebelled, drawn irresistibly towards the forbidden allure of hidden knowledge. She needed to be careful, very careful—A9021's warnings still clung to her like a second skin.

In the final few weeks, a75b99r84GE forced her mind to focus on what was being taught to her during training, and the extra effort paid off. She showcased an impeccable retention rate and demonstrated her abilities well beyond what was expected. Her technician in charge of her avocation downloads noted her performance with clinical approval but remained oblivious to the underlying drive that fueled her excellence—her rapidly approaching position as junior archivist.

When her personal graduation day finally arrived, at the age of eight, it was with a silent breath of relief and a carefully masked enthusiasm that a75b99r84GE received the announcement of her progression to that of a productive. She had played the game by its rules—mostly—and emerged victorious. However, this victory was just the beginning.

As she stood at the front of the room in front her classmates, who were still months away from completing their requisites, she felt prideful, but it waned quickly when the teacher made a post-graduate announcement.

She fought to return her expression to one of neutrality as she saw two sentries move from their position at the side of the room. With no ceremony and in a tone completely devoid of affect, the instructor announced, "a75b99r84GE has successfully completed her requisites, and the following three are on track to do so successfully within the next few months: a3167lu30, c479956cf, and p4e69832h. a75b99r84GE, please present yourself to U5912, who is waiting by the door to the courtyard. He will escort you to your new living quarters. The other three, await my return in the corridor; and, a75b99r84GE, may you have a long productive life." With that, the instructor turned back to the remaining six students, and without any fanfare, announced their fate. "As you six have shown a rapid decent towards degradation, you are to present yourselves for termination."

As a75b99r84GE made her way to the door to meet up with U5912, who was the supervisor of the housing authority, the first of the remaining eight years olds lined up to emotionlessly meet their fate, like lambs to the slaughter.

Without any acknowledgement, U5912, an octogenarian with a slender figure, turned and began walking across the courtyard. Instinctually, a75b99r84GE followed along behind her.

Entering the housing unit, they climbed up several flights of stairs before turning down a narrow corridor. The older woman consulted her tablet for a moment before turning to finally speak. "Acknowledge your designation."

"a75b99r84GE"

"Acknowledged; data entered. Now, this is your new residence. Commit to memory the building and room number: building three, room eighty-seven. Committed to memory?"

a75b99r84GE could only nod in the face of the woman's towering and intimidating manner.

"Now," she continued, "place your palm on the center of the door panel and hold it there until instructed otherwise." Lights and sounds indicated that her palm print was being scanned and registered into the system. "You will place this palm, only, like so, each time you wish to enter your premises. When you exit, your room door will automatically lock behind you. When you place your palm on the panel, the door will open automatically. Now that you are entered into the system as the resident of this unit, you may enter your quarters."

a75b99r84GE pressed her palm against the panel again. The door immediately swung open and the lights flickered on. She stepped inside with curiosity at the small space, which measured no more than five-hundred square feet.

"As you can see, the lights activated upon entrance, and will turn off after sixty seconds when it reads that you are no longer inside, or have moved to your sleeping area. You've probably noticed that there is only room here for one individual. Now that you are no longer a student youngling, you will not be required to share living space as you have done for the past six years. Follow me." It only took U5912 three steps to make it across the floor space. "This is where you will bathe and sleep," she stated, stepping aside so that a75b99r84GE could step inside. If she thought the outer room was tiny, this room was even tinier, at no larger than fifty square feet. To the left side was a sink and a toilet and on the right side, beneath an angled clerestory window, which offered a pleasant vantage of the sky, was a bed currently too long for her five-foot height. She could only imagine that it was meant to accommodate her from now through adulthood.

"Please step over to the wardrobe," U5912 stated, ticking something off on her tablet, before tapping to retrieve some information, which she read off as a75b99r84GE eyed the single jumpsuit hanging inside and the cloth footwear on the bottom. "Now, obviously, since you've only just transitioned from a youngling and have many years of growth ahead of you, the jumpsuit and indoor booties inside will be switched out each annum until you reach your full height. I have made a notation in your file to return each year to ensure proper measurements are taken. Once you've reached your adult size, you will be provided three jumpsuits and an additional pair of indoor booties which you will need to tend to until your ascension to the next phase of your life…if you are not terminated before then," she muttered beneath her breath. "The outdoor booties you are currently wearing should be left by the door. They are for outdoor wear only; however, as this is just a tour of your residence, I have made an exception.

"Now, on the wall next to the sink, you see that there is one wash cloth and one towel. These will be for your personal use. At the end of each month, you will deposit them into this receptacle…" she paused, moving to wave her hand across the wall next to where the towels hung. A panel, invisible to her sight, slid open, revealing a small chute. "Once they are deposited, a fresh set will be left outside of your door for you to retrieve at the end of your productive day. Follow me back to the other room.

"Here is where you will take your morning and evening meals. These are your meal rations," she stated, pointing to a tall basket standing next to the stove. "As you are no longer a youngling, you are responsible for preparing your own food. You will also be responsible to ensure that this basket is rolled out at the end of each month, so that your supply can be replenished. While missing the linen drop may not cause you any distress, I assure you that you do not want to miss your ration refill, so do not ever fail to place your basket by your door on your way to work on the last day of each month. Make a mental note, and don't forget it. Now, step closer so that I may instruct you on the preparation of your food. Again, make a mental note so you do not forget." She stepped over to the bucket, which had already been filled with sufficient water for this demonstration. She then reached into the basket and pulled out a sizable pouch. "Take a cup of water and pour it into the pot which is on the heater…just so. The heater will turn on automatically when it senses a difference in weight. Once the water begins to boil and you remove the pot, the heater will disengage. While the water boils, you will tear open your pouch, pour it into your bowl, and then pour the boiling water into the bowl. Allow the water to absorb into the food stuff until it solidifies. Your meal will then be ready to consume. Your cup, which you will use to drink from, is hanging just there, next to the water dispenser. You will retrieve a single cup from the bucket of water. You may drink one cup in the morning and one cup in the evening. Once your meal is completed, ensure that you clean and replace all items. Of greatest importance is the following: water is scarce; so, you do not wish to miss your ration. In order to ensure that you receive your morning ration and your evening ration, you must place your bucket beneath the spigot at precisely six in the morning and again at six in the evening—"

"Why can't I just simply leave the bucket on the floor?" a75b99r84GE asked, confused over why such a task required a convoluted solution.

"Because that it how it is done," U5912 responded, her expression showing one of genuine shock.

a75b99r84GE wondered whether that shock stemmed from the question or the fact that she'd dared to ask a question…or both. In a moment of mischievousness, she determined to see how the housing authority would react were she to press the issue. "That isn't really an answer. After all, if I were simply to place my bucket beneath the spigot before going to bed for my breakfast ration, and then again before I left for work in order to ensure I receive my evening ration…well, I would never be at risk of missing out, right?"

a75b99r84GE had to force herself not to grin at the look of aghast on the woman's face; convinced that if she were a robot and not just robotic-like, she would have, for certain, blown a fuse. Feeling a moment of pity for her, a75b99r84GE supplied what she decided was a plausible answer: "Perhaps it is simply meant to force a level of responsibility on people; to ensure that all live their lives by a strict routine." After all, she thought in a moment of surprising clarity, it's far more difficult for a society to mount a rebellion if they can be forced to focus on mundane tasks instead of thinking for themselves. It helps maintain control also, if that same society has negligible emotional output.

"Quite right," U9512 sputtered, then quickly shifted back to her own routine, "Now, on Sunday evenings, you will be allowed an extra allotment of water for your ablutions. Do not waste it. That is the end of our demonstration. Make a mental note, so you do not forget. As your evening meal is ready for consumption, I will depart and leave you to it. Report to the archives at zero-six-thirty hours tomorrow morning. Your alarm in your room has been pre-programmed to wake you each day at zero-five-fifty hours to give you time to eat, dress, and walk across the courtyard to the archival building. As in your time as a student youngling, you must remember to be timely in all that you do."

Without further word, she turned toward the door, "Oh, to leave your room, simply wave your hand over the side panel…here…and the door will open." Without another word, she stepped out and marched away. a75b99r84GE chuckled at the abrupt departure, "Likely still chafing over being challenged," she mused allowed. As the door closed, and she found herself alone, the moment of humor faded. With a heavy sigh, a75b99r84GE turned and sat down on the stool in front of her table, picked up her fork, and dug it into the all-too familiar foam-textured mound. Tear formed in her eyes as she looked about her room, suddenly feeling very much alone.

First Day as a Productive

On her first day at the archives, a75b99r84GE was re-introduced to A9021—the chief archivist—a gaunt figure with sharp eyes that seemed to miss nothing.

"It has been a while, A9021. I'm pleased to be joining you here," a75b99r84GE greeted her mentor, but the elder man looked at her as if he was seeing her for the first time. His face was devoid of expression, as glanced down into her youthful brown eyes. Gone was the meek, kind man she'd met nearly a year prior, and in his place stood one that appeared carved from marble, for all the warmth he exuded.

"Your role is important; however, it can also be repetitive and tedious at times," he started, forgoing any form of official welcome. Without pause, he continued, turning to move toward the centralized database. "You will manage, catalog, preserve and scan into the database items of historical significance. Precision, speed, and discretion are your utmost responsibilities. We are here to expedite and preserve, not to waste time frittering the days away with unwelcomed curiosities," A9021 instructed with a stern tone.

"So, we're not allowed to read materials we're scanning? I mean, surely, we need to read through the data to ensure it's categorized correctly," a75b99r84GE countered as politely as she could manage—though she already knew the answer.

"Did you not finalize your download session with an exceptional retention rate?" He queried sharply, eyes narrowing suspiciously.

"Indeed," she replied with a sigh, already aware of what he was about to say.

"Then you should have known that our database is quite remarkable. The computer reads through the information that we scan in—far quicker than we ever could—and sorts it accordingly."

Without further conversation, he turned and walked away, down one of the corridors of the massive building. It didn't take much mental effort for a75b99r84GE to reason that she should be following behind him, and sprinted to catch up. He was in the process of pointing out the various sections she must familiarize herself with. "Among this section is where you will spend most of your time," he said as they walked along amidst row upon row of pre-data age writings. The air was thick with the smell of old paper, which stood in contrast to the brilliance of the electronic equipment nearer to the front of the room.

a75b99r84GE followed closely, absorbing every detail. "You will start by digitizing these," A9021 continued, gesturing towards a stack of manuscripts; the appearance of which bespoke of centuries long past. "They're from before the Reformation. Fragile and invaluable. Handle them as if they were the last remnants of our past—because they are. As your time here progresses, we will go over other areas of expectations. You may begin your work."

"May I pose a query?" a75b99r84GE questioned before A9021 could depart, which he seemed overly eager to do.

"Only if doing so does not result in a prolonged discussion. We must not forgo productivity in favor of our own vain curiosities."

a75b99r84GE pursed her lips to refrain from retorting against the unnecessary reprimand and went ahead with her question, "It's my understanding that our realm is more than two centuries old now. With so much time behind us, why hasn't all of this information already been processed? I realize, by looking at just this small sampling, that there are mounds upon mounds of historical documents, but certainly there's been sufficient time to have digitized it all."

"In this two centuries since the birth of our realms, there have been a grand total of six archivist, including yourself. Do you truly believe that a singular individual could have processed so much, when working alone? As you will be, once I depart—"

"How long do you think it will be before I take over and…I expect…for you to ascend to the realm of the wise ones?" a75b99r84GE asked suddenly, delaying his departure yet again. "That is why your demeanor has shifted so dramatically since last we met, isn't it? You don't want to do anything that might be perceived as aberrant; anything that could put you at risk of being terminated when you're so close to ascending?"

The façade that A9021 had erected fell away, startling a75b99r84GE with his sudden vulnerability. "That's it, isn't it? But why would that concern you? Surely your work has been exemplary nor, I would assume, have you been experiencing a reduction in productive output?"

He shook his head, closing his eyes for a moment, uncertain whether he should be communicating his concerns to a child less than ten years of age; even if that child did seem to possess a maturity far greater in years.

"If you need more years in which to prepare for ascension, I can accommodate you and extend my mentorship—"

"You will do no such thing, little one," he reprimanded, sharply, then immediately amended his tone, "I am sorry. I do not need you risking your own productive future because of the fears of an old man."

"I do not think that slowing my progress just a little bit would be cause for concern, since I am assured that I am…" she stopped speaking, uncertain whether it would be wise to reveal that which the holy one had shared with her. After all, knowing that she was fabricated for a future purpose and was unlikely to ever face termination might not be received by someone whose fate always hung in the balance. The pendulum continually swung for the citizenry in her realm, while it remained unmoving for her. Somehow that didn't seem fair; and it certainly wouldn't be fair for her to reveal it.

"I am concerned," A9021 finally spoke, his voice slightly quavering, "because no one has mentioned the possibility of ascension in the eight-and-a-half years since you were fabricated to be my replacement. I spoke to several people and they were advised of their fate the moment a replacement was in the works."

"And since they are all to be terminated, you fear that will be your fate also?" a75b99r84GE queried with an accuracy that had A9021's gaze widening in surprise. "Perhaps," she continued, when it didn't appear as if he was going to respond, "the reason you weren't notified is because you are to ascend, not be terminated. Those facing termination—who are notified of their fate well in advance, of course—surely need time to process that fate. Perhaps it is meant as motivation, albeit a rather skewed one, to squeeze the last bit of productivity from them before their end, as many are terminated due to a breakdown in productive levels. After self-reflection, you're convinced that your productivity has not slowed?"

"It has not, no," A9021 acknowledge, straightening his shoulders in a rare display of pride.

"There you have it then," a75b99r84GE exclaimed. "The holy ones are simply waiting to inform you of your date of ascension until after I have finished my internship. Once I am fully trained, you will likely move on to the realm of the wise ones."

"Thank you, little one," he whispered, his tone filled with gratitude. "I do not know if you are correct in your assessment, but I take heart in the fact that you offer a fair argument in favor of ascension. Now, we really should get to work. Ever since you were marched away to have words with the holy one last year, I have heard murmurs that individuals with emotions are being monitored more closely. There are growing concerns that we may be influencing the newer generations in ways that is not beneficial to society."

"I wasn't aware of this," a75b99r84GE murmured thoughtfully. Surely, Kishida-Guan did not believe that she, and those like her, could possibly create havoc simply because they felt deeper than those fabricated with their emotions suppressed. She certainly would know that it was not an easy task to pull near-dead emotions from what amounted to a walking corpse, as she well knew, since she'd attempted many times, in her youngling years, to get her classmates to laugh and play, only to have to them look at her with bland expressions or the occasional confusion. "Where did you hear these murmurings?"

"I don't…"

"Who am I going to tell?" she encouraged, when it didn't appear as if he was going to reveal his secret. He gave her an uncertain smile, but then must have decided that she could be trusted.

"The geneticists, G9983 and G13654, stopped by yesterday. Long ago, before things became the way they are now, we would have been considered friends—"

"What's a friend?"

"Now is not the time for that lesson, little one," he interrupted her question. Despite enjoying this small bit of freedom to discuss the topic at hand, he was still fearful of being caught out. "Anyway, they told me that they'd fabricated you with genetic enhancements on the authority of the holy one, Kishida-Guan; that they wanted me to be aware of this because…well…I might be confused over how smart you are for one so young, and I must admit, your intellectual maturity is startling. They also shared…" he paused again, a slight tremor in his tone as his gaze shot up and down the corridor. So fearful had he become, so rapidly, that he literally started quaking in front of her eyes.

"Please do not fret yourself, A9021. Perhaps we can carry on this conversation at another time…when you are feeling less apprehensive," she offered. "After all, I really should begin work now."

"Thank you, little one. When you are done with your day, meet me up front and we will close up together." Before she could reply again, he spun about and nearly ran up the corridor, vanishing from sight around a corner. Her brow knitted, wondering what it was that he was going to reveal to her. Should she dare to seek out the geneticists who fabricated her? Would she be able to do so without placing them in jeopardy? She decided it would be best to wait until after she spoke to A9021 again. After all, the information could be quite innocuous and certainly nothing for her to get fretful over.

She picked up the scanning rod and moved to the stack of books. She carefully opened the first page and ran the rod over the top. A beep sounded and her brow knitted. Surely, she hadn't done anything incorrectly. She glanced down at the rod and a message appeared "document already scanned". "Well, that's a good feature to have," she murmured and closed that book, then reached for another. She'd only just reached a rhythm when a soft bell rang out, echoing into the distance. It took her a moment to realize that it was the end-of-day notification. She switched off the rod and placed it in its case, then laid it atop the book she was currently working on.

She stood up, stretching her arms high above her head, then twisted at the waist for a minute, to stretch the kinks from her body. She yawned widely, then turned and walked languidly up the corridor back to the front of the building.

A9021 was already standing at the door waiting on her. "We must go. Need to reach our quarters before the water ration arrives, so pick up your pace please. Thank you."

a75b99r84GE grinned lopsided and sprinted the remaining distance. She decided not to reveal to him that she didn't need to rush at all, because she'd defiantly placed her bucket beneath the spigot after her morning breakfast. She could take a circuitous route to her building and still not have to worry about missing out. She could have said all of that, but decided that this was one secret she should keep to herself. After all, she couldn't have everyone suddenly acting contrary. That would seriously raise the holy ones' concerns. Instead, she simply said, "Have a lovely evening A9021. I'll see you in the morning."

"You too, little one." With that, A9021, turned and strode across the cobblestoned courtyard toward building one. a75b99r84GE paused a moment longer to take in the setting sun, then headed off toward her own apartment building. As she walked past others returning to their homes after their productive day, she couldn't help but wonder just how many of them struggled to keep their own emotionless mask from slipping for fear of being terminated. Were there many more fabrications out there like her whose emotions felt more like a volcano, constantly on the verge of erupting; or were they all like her classmates: empty vessels created for the sole purpose of furthering humanity's existence.

She trudged up the stairs to her living quarters and pressed her palm against the scanner. The door swung open, the lights flickered on, and a75b99r84GE froze in dread. Her ration of dinner water was puddled onto the floor beneath the spigot. She quickly scanned the room and spotted her bucket sitting in its placement next to the stove. Her brow knitted in confusion. She knew that she had placed it beneath the spigot; had no doubt whatsoever about her actions of that morning, so then how had it moved? It certainly hadn't sprouted feet and walked itself back to its spot. A chill raced along her spine, wondering if her living quarters were being monitored. And, if so, had someone entered her apartment during the day, after observing her actions, which were contrary to given instructions, and repositioned her bucket? If that were the case…she carefully moved into the room, her eyes scanning for any other discrepancies.

Nothing else seemed out of place, but the movement of the bucket was enough to unsettle her. In this place of stringent—and often ridiculous rules, in her opinion—deviations like this were not taken lightly. She went into the bathroom and collected her towel, but then stopped and returned it to the rack, determining that the water would eventually evaporate without assistance from her and she needed that towel for at least two more weeks.

She returned to sit on the stool, eyeing the bucket with caution. Should she test her theory about an intruder by placing the bucket beneath the spigot again, for her morning ration? Her stomach chose that moment to grumble loudly. "Your actions have already deprived you of your dinner," she chastised herself. "You certainly don't need to miss out on eating your breakfast also."

Later that evening, as she lay in bed, her mind raced with possibilities about who could've move the bucket and why. Had the housing authority, U9512, returned to check on her after she'd dared questioned the rigidity of their schedule? It wouldn't surprise her, since U9512 made it clear that the query was a sign of defiance. Perhaps Kishida-Guan had sent someone to check up on her quarters since she was only one day removed from being a youngling, and was now a productive.

The morning light eventually filtered through her window, signaling the start of a new day and a fresh chance to uncover the truths hidden in the shadows of her life. As she got ready for work, she bolstered herself with the belief that knowledge was power and resolved that the archives would be the best place to pursue it. While tidying her living space after breakfast, she felt a strong urge to put the bucket under the spigot, battling with the cautious voice in her head warning her against unusual actions. Did she really want her every move being monitored, especially during her time at the archives? If she attracted too much unwanted attention, she'd lose the opportunity to use her position to seek answers to the many questions troubling her. With determined defiance, she set the bucket beside the heating unit, then surveyed her quarters to ensure everything was in order. Once satisfied that her room would pass another surreptitious scrutiny, she waved her hand over the door panel and exited her room.

Mysteries Before Us

a75b99r84GE's piercing gaze meticulously dissected the archival documents spread before her, her visage alight with curious wonder. The enigmatic pages that lay in front of her were an enticing puzzle, their purpose shrouded in layers of mystery that beckoned to her inquisitive nature. "Of what do these pages speak?" she finally ventured, directing her query towards the A9021, who worked nearby.

"I thought we went over this yesterday. You are to scan, not read," A9021 sighed heavily.

"What's the purpose for ascending?" she asked, abruptly shifting the topic.

A9021 blinked rapidly for a few seconds trying to decipher what she was getting at with the odd question, "I'm not certain I understand your query."

"Once you have ensured that I am sufficiently proficient and you move on to the realm of the wise ones…what will you be doing there?"

"Oh…well…while I am not entirely certain of all that transpires daily in the life of a wise one, I do know that the transition is meant as a reward for those who live full lives, showing no degradation in the quality or quantity of productivity. Once it is determined that they have performed their duties admirably, they are given the opportunity to rest their bodies in favor of enhancing their minds. Once they attain a level of mental superiority, they may then be selected to become a holy one." The tone in which the explanation was delivered bespoke of the longing in his soul to reach this level of existence.

a75b99r784GE appeared to ponder the explanation before asking, "Who makes that decision?"

It was A9021's turn to pause and ponder, "I…well…I don't know, to be frank. I suppose it must be the other holy ones. Perhaps, as overseer of all of the realms, it could be the Chancellor, but I'm certain that he is far too busy to spend his days deciding the fate of his citizens."

"As the archivist, one would think that you would ascend far sooner than your fellow citizens—"

"What would make you leap to that conclusion?" A9021 interrupted, again feeling the fingers of dread creep along his spine as to why he had still not been selected.

"Well, it stands to reason that if the realm of the wise ones is where productives move from a life of labor to one of cognitive pursuits, and you work daily in a field where you have the knowledge of the centuries at your fingertips…and, if no one is permitted to read these documents…well, from what source do the wise ones glean the knowledge required in their pursuit of cognitive advancement?"

"These documents are of the before time; before the creation of our realms. They contain information millennia old of humanity's existence before the realms were created and humanity evolved into the lives that we live now. It holds little value to the citizens of the realms, aside from the holy ones and the Chancellor, of course. Whatever data that wise ones need from which to pursue a life of knowledge is likely parsed from information provided them by the Chancellor and the holy ones—"

"Have you ever met a wise one?"

"How would I meet one when they ascend to a different realm?"

"I've met a holy one," a75b99r84GE murmured. "Other than appearing far more ancient than anyone with whom I've encountered before, he didn't seem any wiser than you or I. Just more…emotional."

"I think that this conversation is over, little one. You are treading into dangerous waters with your curiosities and I'll not be a part of it. I have work to complete at my desk. I'll leave you to your duties here. And, may I remind you that your role is not to question, simply to execute," came the curt reply, a sharp reprimand designed to quell her curiosity. It worked momentarily, and also stopped her train of thought…but only for a short moment.

"Don't you ever grow weary of the dreary repetition, of never truly delving into that which we view daily?" she persisted doggedly.

"You have been here all of two days, so how could you already—"

"Not me, you."

"Again, I'll remind you, we are not permitted to know, only do," challenged A9021, with an air of condescension. "What has happened to you today? The little one I met yesterday was a curious sort, but today you are bordering on defiant insubordination." His voice was tinged with frustration and worry, almost fearful of the potential consequences her continued questioning might bring upon them both.

a75b99r84GE sensed the stress in his tone and paused, reflecting on the implication of her actions. Her curiosity was a burning flame, but it seemed to singe those around her who were caught within its glow. "I understand," she said softly, a layer of regret smoothing the edges of her words. "But my mind races with thoughts and questions about all that surrounds us—questions I fear will remain unanswered unless I ask."

A9021 looked at her with a mixed expression of exasperation and sympathy. "That much is evident," he admitted quietly. "And truth be told, there are nights when I lay awake wondering about the very same things. But we have our roles, our duties. We must trust in the system laid out before us; it's the only way to ensure the safety and prosperity of our realms."

"But isn't questioning a part of learning? Isn't it how we grow?" she pressed gently, trying not to push him too far yet unable to stop herself.

A9021 sighed deeply, his eyes shifting away momentarily before returning to meet hers. "Perhaps in another time or another place, that would be true. But here, questions can be dangerous. They can unsettle the order of things. And besides, some questions might lead to truths that are best left undiscovered."

a75b99r84GE nodded slowly, absorbing his words with a solemn intensity. She decided to change the subject, softening her demeanor, "I know that I am not what you expected," she said softly. "But I appreciate your patience with me as I navigate my new position as a productive."

A9021 gave her a small smile, "I don't know why you were fabricated so far removed from other citizens within this realm, and I certainly don't know why it was determined that you would be paired with me for the duration of your training, but I will endeavor to remain patient if you promise to try to reign in your curiosity…if only a little. Now, let's see if we can't get at least one book scanned into the database today. It's only your second day and your questions outpace your work level. If you continue along this vein, I shudder to think how long you'll be at this job before being permitted to ascend," he finished, his tone joking.

a75b99r84GE grinned and returned her focus to the book she held, discreetly reading the text while gradually passing the scanning rod over each page. Although A9021 might prefer not to challenge the holy ones' rule of doing rather than learning, she was resolute in her desire to gather all the information available to her, simply because she could.

"Good morning, A9021. I trust you slept—wait, what is that?" She paused, staring at the relic—a flat, glossy square—lying on A9021's desk. It sat there as though waiting to be discovered, patient and impossible to ignore. The image confined within its surface shimmered faintly, tugging at something deep and primal within her.

She stared at it silently, uncertain whether to inch forward or retreat. The air around it felt charged. Not threatening, exactly—but unstable, like something sacred had been disturbed. Old tech, perhaps, or some kind of visual record. She had seen stylized renderings of ancient cities and diagrams of extinct machines within the texts she'd spent the last two days scanning into the database— but nothing like this.

It looked alive.

A creature stood frozen in the image: it stood on four limbs, not two like them. Its body was covered in what looked similar to the hair upon her head, though denser, more chaotic—wild. Eyes dark, glinted with unknowable thought. Its ears were pointed, alert, and its stance—steady, watchful—suggested strength. Jagged teeth peeked from its slightly open mouth, yet there was no malice in the expression, only...expectation. As though it was waiting for someone.

She couldn't name the shape, but knew it wasn't human. It wasn't machine. It wasn't *them*.

She staggered back; breath caught in her throat. Her pulse— normally a steady rhythm—sped into something erratic and uncertain.

"Is this...real?" she whispered, as though the word itself might summon it to life.

For the first time in the archives, the past didn't feel distant. It loomed. Wild. Beautiful. Dangerous.

And free.

A9021 interjected into her musings, his voice trying for neutrality. "I am uncertain, as I have not taken the time to find a reference to it among the pages of the archival records," he confessed, the tint in his skin revealing his embarrassment over viewing the image.

There was something in the way he sat, shoulders tight, eyes darting—not fear, not exactly. But the strain of having stepped beyond a line he didn't know existed until he crossed it.

"I just stumbled upon it…after deciding upon a course of rebellious action." He continued speaking, his words tumbling out like a frenzied storm, as if his mind were a live wire sparking wildly, teetering on the brink of a catastrophic implosion. "To waste such valuable productive time in doing such a search would be impractical, and definitely unwise. So, I am content to merely look at it, though it will remain forever a mysterious being. Although its designation is unknown, can you not perceive its captivating beauty and inherent power?" His fingers traced the photo's edges with reverence, but also hesitation—like touching it might reveal too much.

"Are you doing okay today?" a75b99r84GE inquired with a voice tinged with genuine worry; her eyes attempting to search his lowered face for any sign of distress.

"I am…not sure, but I think I've made a dreadful mistake," he murmured, his gaze still pinned on the picture.

A heaviness settled between them.

"Where did you get this?" she asked, a feeling of unease creeping into her mind. She hadn't really thought it possible to affect others with her idiosyncrasies, but something inside accused her of being responsible for A9021's current state; a state that appeared to be bordering on a manic episode.

"I couldn't sleep," he admitted, his voice shaky as he glanced up at a75b99r84GE, who took a step back in shock. It was clear he hadn't rested, and the tears pooling in his eyes were a testament to a deep sorrow which tugged at her heartstrings.

"Your questions shamed me, forcing me to confront just how willingly ignorant I've been. Then I thought it would be a loss if I ascended without ever seeing the wonders hidden in this vast expanse..." His voice faltered, eyes wandering over the immense archives. "But now, knowing I've disrupted productive protocol, I'm terrified I might not ascend at all. Was it worth it, letting my curiosity lead me astray? Or have I cost myself everything by seeking what I shouldn't?" His voice cracked on that last word, and for a moment he looked more lost than guilty. Like a child realizing the world was far bigger—and far less safe—than they'd been taught.

"May I?" she requested, reaching for the intriguing item.

A9021 acquiesced and allowed her to immerse herself in the photograph's allure. As a75b99r84GE drank in the picture's beauty, he watched her reaction apprehensively. Would she view the vault's contents with his equally inquisitive eyes or blindly follow the Chancellor and holy ones' edicts, as she should?

When he saw her features light up with curiosity, something in him both soared and sank. He sighed heavily: "Oh, little one, I fear your tenure here will be tragically brief."

"You mustn't assume that our inquisitiveness will be discovered." Her fingers trembled slightly as she held the photograph, transfixed by the image of the peaceful creature. A part of her wanted to believe it was harmless—to believe *they* were harmless. But another part knew better. "There is much to be learned, not just stored," she whispered, trying her best to provide him a sense of peace.

A9021 nodded, his expression a blend of resignation and deep-seated dread. "The interests that drive us can also set ablaze the fears of those in power, potentially sealing your fate before its time."

a75b99r84GE looked up from the photograph, her eyes alight with a mix of fear and determination. "If I was fabricated to be more than a mere custodian of forgotten knowledge, how can I exist simply as vessel for data without understanding its significance?"

"It is a paradox that keeps us bound in an endless cycle of obedience and ignorance," he replied, his voice tinged with bitterness. "You must be cautious. The path you seem inclined to follow is fraught with danger."

"What is that called? Do you know?" She asked, deciding it best to change the subject as she placed the photograph back on the table.

"This square thing, or the image contained in it? I already said…"

"The square thing. I know you said you didn't know what the thing on it is. Where exactly did you retrieve it from? Did you cut it from one of the pages—"

"Good heavens, little one! Do you sincerely believe I would desecrate—"

"No, no, of course not! I just don't recall having seen squares of this sort before…that were not a part of one of the books that we scan."

"I went further into the recess of the archival records," he admitted.

"Have you never been back that far before?" a75b99r84GE asked, her tone incredulous.

A9021 shook his head, "There are simply so many books and other written materials that preoccupy my time…so much information of which I know nothing about…" His voice trailed off again as his eyes seemed to glaze over with self-loathing, his mind tangled in the enormity of what he didn't know.

"And yes, in one of those untouched corners, I found boxes filled with these types of files. The writing on the box, though faded with time, appeared to spell the word 'pictures'…although I am uncertain whether I am pronouncing that word correctly." He repeated the word slowly, tasting the novelty of it.

a75b99r84GE nodded thoughtfully, "Pictures," she repeated, storing the new term into her memory. "Apparently, this is a visual record of time immemorial, capturing an unknown entity for eternity."

"Apparently, people in the before time had devices by which to capture these vibrant images from their lives—impressions of a reality so potent that even now they evoke emotion."

The concept intrigued a75b99r84GE to no end. It stirred a yearning she hadn't known she was capable of. The idea that objects from the past could still stir feeling was almost revolutionary. "This is why citizens aren't allowed to explore the archives," she murmured, a sudden clarity settling over her. "It's the fear of awakening dormant emotions—feelings that could disrupt the order. The Chancellor and the holy ones believe that curiosities are dangers, not doors to understanding."

A9021 nodded, the dim light of the archiver catching his troubled expression. "Curiosity breeds contemplation, and contemplation breeds defiance. The Chancellor and the holy ones fear what might happen if individuals begin to question."

"Blend in, don't stand out," a75b99r84GE murmured softly.

"What did you say?" A9021 asked.

a75b99r84GE shook her head, "Something the holy one, Kishida-Guan, commented to me. That I was to work hard to emulate those around me; to wear the same mask of emotionless compliance even if the weight of that mask wore heavy on me. But if the knowledge within this building threatens all that the Chancellor and the holy ones strive to maintain, why not destroy it all; why keep it preserved?"

A9021's eyes widened slightly, a spark of rebellion flickering within as he contemplated her question. "Perhaps even they cannot bring themselves to obliterate the past entirely. They keep it, hidden away, perhaps as a reminder of the power they hold in deciding what is known and what remains hidden."

She nodded slowly, understanding dawning, "So, by allowing limited access, they dangle the illusion of transparency while ensuring control remains firmly in their grasp." She paused, looking around at the vast archives surrounding them. "Or maybe, in their arrogance, they truly believe this information, this knowledge, should be for their eyes only."

"Plausible hypotheses," A9021 agreed, a mixture of awe and fear in his voice. "And now, we are here, standing amidst truth and knowledge that is not meant for us. What good does this do us, knowing that we too must keep its contents a secret from those around us?"

a75b99r84GE glanced down at the picture again, her fingers brushing over it as though it could be enticed to reveal its secrets. "We continue to explore; to learn all we can."

"We could start by trying to identify more about the creature within this picture," A9021 suggested. His voice was less shaky now, almost excited as the opportunity for discovery unfolded before him—an opportunity he had long denied himself. "But we mustn't do anything that would cause suspicion to fall on us. If we do not function at productive levels, we could face termination, and I, for one, would prefer to ascend. I have waited a lifetime to do so and grow weary of the waiting."

"We could take turns. One of us work on the scans while the other scans books and boxes searching for anything that would give us a clue as to what this creature is."

"You know that it could take years and years to find what we'd be searching for…if we do at all…and I will not be around for many more of those years," A9021 said, sadness tinging his tone. "Once I ascend, it will all be left to you, and there are simply too many documents to go through alone, in search of this one unknown."

"Then we best not waste any more time. We have a creature to identify," a75b99r84GE exclaimed, excitement in her tone.

"I would offer another word of caution," A9021 stated, saddened to potentially dampen her enthusiasm. "Let's not delve into the picture boxes further…for now. The task of locating information on this one picture is already an overwhelming notion. We do not need to add to the weight, nor waste precious time, getting lost in more and more images of the past."

"May I keep this?" she asked, pressing the picture to her chest, as if fearful that if she released her hold, it would vanish.

A9021 nodded, a small smile on his face, "just do not let anyone know…ever…that it is in your possession."

a75b99r84GE returned his smile, "No one will know. I just…there's just something about it that fills me with joy, and I look forward to learning what its designation is."

"As do I, little one."

As they stood to resume their tasks, the moment settled like dust on ancient tomes—fragile, delicate, and unforgettable.

A9021 turned away first, his movements slow, not just with age, but burdened by the weight of rules bent and questions newly born. Yet behind his tired eyes flickered something rare, something new: a spark not easily extinguished.

a75b99r84GE remained still, clutching the picture as though it contained not just an image, but a secret echo of a world long past, filling her with a longing of a world to which she desperately wanted to belong. In that silent photograph, frozen in time, she saw more than a creature—she saw hope.

The kind that can undo entire systems.

7.5 years later

a75b99r84GE lingered on the steps of the imposing archives building, her gaze fixed on the antiseptic sprawl that surrounded her, untouched by chaos or comfort. The exhaustion from the day wasn't just physical—it was existential, settling deep into her bones like a permanent ache. Still, she stood there, unmoving, as she did at the end of every cycle. A silent ritual. A compulsion. As if by staring long enough, the world might offer something *more.*

But it never did.

The buildings that lined her field of vision loomed like tombstones—uniform, colorless, stripped of individuality. Each one a silent monument to a civilization that had, at inception, traded vitality for efficiency. The inhabitants moved along the pavement with mechanical precision, their faces void of expression, their trajectories unchanging; a sight she'd overlooked as a youngling, now glaring at her in its apparency. There was no laughter here. No spontaneity. Just the sterile rhythm of existence.

The cobblestoned walkways were lifeless beyond its human inhabitants. No trees to rustle in wind that never blew. No birdsong to interrupt the silence. Foliage, wildlife—concepts so foreign to her that even the memory of them, captured in the fading images stored within the archives, felt like hallucinations. And yet they *ached* with reality.

She now understood what her predecessor had tried to warn her about—that the more one *knew*, the more unbearable it all became. But she hadn't listened. Curiosity had drowned out caution. And now she was ensnared—haunted by the vibrancy of a world that no longer existed; suffocating in the gray monotony of the one in which she lived.

In this realm, every object, every action, every breath served an austere function. There was no music, no celebration, no sense of wonder. Pleasure was not forbidden—it was simply not there in the hearts and minds of its inhabitants. No one was admired. No one was missed. The system endured, cold and exacting. Nothing more. Nothing less.

With her eyes shut tight, she abandoned the antiseptic present and let her mind unfurl into something brighter. In her imagination, the sterile world melted away, replaced by a vivid utopia: buildings embraced by winding paths of reddish cobblestone, their façades awash in a riot of color—ochres, aquamarines, soft coral pinks—no two alike. Towering trees flanked the walkways, their leafy canopies brushing the sky like living paintbrushes, daubing the heavens with streaks of green beneath an impossibly blue dome.

At the heart of it all, a magnificent fountain shimmered, its basin carved with intricate shapes that seemed to shift when looked at too long. Water arced gracefully into the air, catching sunlight and fracturing it into miniature rainbows—jewels suspended in motion.

And there, just in front of the fountain, stood *the creature*—its fur golden and thick, tail sweeping like a soft banner in the breeze. It looked exactly as it had in the faded photograph A9021 had once given to her all those years ago. They hadn't known what it was then—only that it wasn't human, and that it was beautiful.

She could still remember the moment they discovered its identity. After endless years lost in the quiet hush of the restricted wings, she'd unearthed a stack of ancient books labeled *ANIMALS*—each one thick with dust and mystery. Together, they had flipped through every fragile page, breath held in awe as unfamiliar creatures stared back at them—striped, scaled, feathered, horned. It felt like opening windows to dreams never dreamed.

And then, there it was.

Page 237.

The same deep eyes. The same stance. The same alert, noble posture. A *German Shepherd.*

A9021 had stared at the page for so long that a75b99r84GE thought he might never speak. When he finally did, it was a whisper: "We found it." His hand trembled slightly as he traced the name printed beneath the image. And though he smiled, there was a weight behind his eyes—as if knowing this would change him forever. It had done—for both of them.

A few months after that captivating day, he was taken away by the sentries, arms raised in solemn devotion, believing he was finally ascending to the realm of the wise ones. And then she was alone…with her work and with the memories of their time together. Those memories flickered like sunlight on the imaginary fountain's surface. As she opened her eyes, the Shepherd remained—watchful, loyal, tail still wagging gently—as if it remembered her too. Then it faded with the rest of her imaginings.

But she still heard everything within that scene softly, as it slowly drifted away. The air hummed with the soft rustle of leaves and distant, joyous calls of creatures that had never existed in her world but felt familiar just the same. The allure of it—the color, the sound, the *aliveness*—wrapped around her like warmth she'd never known. A world not just beautiful, but breathing. And in this fleeting sanctuary of her own making, she *almost* forgot what she was supposed to be doing in that moment.

The image of the water fountain shattered her reverie like a dropped glass. Heart hammering, she sprinted down the steps and across the courtyard, the weight of the daydream still lingering in her heart and mind. From the corner of her vision, a sentry shifted—its unblinking gaze locking onto her with clinical precision. Her pace faltered, heart stuttering in sync with her steps as she forced herself into a brisk, regulated walk. Any deviation from routine could warrant questioning…or worse. She couldn't afford that. Not now.

Her immersion in the archives was beginning to unmoor her. Once-rigid habits were slipping, her schedule unraveling thread by thread. She'd nearly missed her water ration the day before. That thought alone was enough to make her legs pump harder as she took the final steps two at a time, bolting into her quarters.

With a gasp, she shoved the bucket beneath the spigot just as it sputtered to life, coughing out her pre-measured allotment of water. Relief flooded her system, but it was laced with guilt. How many more times could she risk losing focus? Especially today. It was Sunday. Bathing day. The one ritual she looked forward to.

Once, years earlier, she'd attempted placing the bucket before leaving for the archives—an act of subtle rebellion—but the memory of her space being breached, her belongings disturbed, had quickly killed the thought of ever doing so again. Boundaries, both physical and internal, were enforced for reasons she could only guess at.

The stove clicked as she set a pot of water to heat. From the hidden fold in her jumpsuit, she withdrew the photo of the German Shepherd and placed it carefully on the table—her daily rite. The creature's brown and black fur seemed to shimmer in the dim light, as if it might leap free from the frame.

But there was only so much a single image could offer; only so much knowledge. Was it kind? Dangerous? Her chest tightened. A face that serene had to be gentle…didn't it? Yet ignorance gnawed at her—a hunger for knowledge, for contact. She would give anything just to *know*—to press her hand to living fur, to hear its breath.

The water hissed on the stove. She pushed the picture aside and turned back to the bowl, pouring the hot water over her meal ration and stirring it until it thickened. The scent was barely there, the taste even less. As she ate, she reached for her cup—only to realize she'd forgotten to fill it. A grunt of frustration escaped as she rose and dipped the cup into the bucket. Back at the table, she sat with a thud, shoulders sagging under the weight of a life that didn't feel like living.

The walls of her quarters pressed in around her. So sterile. So *silent*. Her throat tightened, and moisture gathered at the corners of her eyes. She swallowed hard, but the lump didn't move.

The dog's eyes stared back at her, full of life, of presence. She reached for the photo again, brushing trembling fingers over the glossy surface. What would its fur feel like—silken, dense, comforting? The not-knowing was a wound that wouldn't close.

She shut her eyes. A single tear fell, then another. Soon, they traced warm lines down her cheeks. When she opened her eyes and looked down at her hand, she found that it had been soaked with the salty liquid, and a strange wonder overtook her. These, she'd discovered in her daily research, were tears. *Her* tears. She'd known sorrow, but never like this—never so viscerally. She wiped them away quickly, smearing the briny droplets into her drab gray jumpsuit.

Her gaze dropped to the garment. So plain. So, uniform. Only after discovering color in archived photographs, had she realized how bleak their world had become. Even comfort had been sacrificed for efficiency.

With a sigh, she rose, rinsed her bowl, and placed it carefully on the shelf above the heater. Carrying the bucket to the bathing area, she winced as the concrete floor sent a chill through her bare feet. Summer was fading, the evenings becoming cooler.

She shed her jumpsuit, letting it fall in a soft heap around her ankles. Beneath it, her body was lean and symmetrical, sculpted by design. She reached for her washcloth, dipped it in the water, and squeezed a small amount of the no-rinse body wash onto it. As she drew it across her skin, slow and deliberate, sensation bloomed—warm, immediate, impossible to ignore.

She lingered, running the cloth over parts of herself usually shrouded in the fabric of compliance. Each pass awakened her—skin prickling, nerves humming. Goosebumps rose on her arms, shivers rippling along her spine. She closed her eyes. Her lips parted. Water slipped across her collarbone and down the length of her back in tender trails.

There was power in this. In simply *feeling*.

When she was done, she hung the cloth carefully, then knelt beside the bucket, dipping her head fully into its quickly-cooling contents. She then retrieved her head, her thick black hair darkened by the saturation of water, clinging to her scalp. She lathered it gently, carefully, wary of using too much shampoo. There was only so much water, and the ratio of shampoo to water was carefully assessed to ensure a complete rinsing.

As suds built, her mind wandered—again to a world she had never known, where water was not rationed, where people bathed freely beneath cascading streams, causing her chest to ache with longing.

She rose slowly to her feet, careful to keep her sudsy hair centered over the bucket, which she lifted. She moved a step over to the sink, lifted the bucket, and poured the remaining water over her head in a slow, silken curtain. Ensuring all sections were rinsed entirely, watching as soap and dream slipped away together.

Wrapping her hair in her towel, she walked naked through to the outer room, returning the bucket to its place by the heating unit, then as she dried her hair, she scanned the room for any signs of disorder. After she was satisfied all was as it should be, she returned to her antechamber, climbed onto her cot and curled beneath the thin blanket.

Sleep came easily now.

In her dreams, she ran. Wildflowers bowed beneath her feet. The sun was warm, the wind sweet. And beside her, tongue lolling, eyes bright, a German Shepherd bounded freely—neither artifact nor mystery, but companion.

Longings

The scent of the field still clung to her as she opened her eyes. Of course, there was no scent. No field. Only the sterile blink of her sleep-cycle light and the faint vibration of the air filter unit embedded in the ceiling. She closed her eyes again, grasping to hold tight to the images and sounds for just a few seconds more; to wrap herself in the contentment she felt. There had been laughter in the dream. Hers. Something she hadn't experienced since she was a youngling.

Too soon, the images dispersed like smoke in the wind, and the sounds faded away. She rubbed the sleep from her eyes, adjusting to the reality of her cramped quarters. Every morning—more so of late—the transition from sleep to wakefulness became more jarring and less looked forward to. The world within her dreams was creating an ache that lasted long after she woke.

a75b99r84GE swung her legs over the side of her bed with a jerkiness borne of frustration, then pulled them up again when her feet contacted the cold concrete flooring. She reached over and pulled on her booties, then with a heavy sigh, stood and stretched, forcing herself to push the remnants of the dream from her mind.

She dressed in silence, fingers moving with practiced precision. The suit was gray. Everything was gray. Mirroring her mood of late.

The walk across the courtyard was the same as it was every day, but something was…different. Inside her.

The archives greeted her with its usual quiet—a comfort…once. Rows of terminal ports, preservation vaults, digitization screens, and the mainframe, which glowed its patient green.

She walked along the dusty, narrow row she was currently working in, her fingertips lightly grazing the spines of the countless volumes lining the shelves. The air was thick with the musty scent of aged paper and ink, a comforting aroma she had grown to cherish over the years. She immediately reached for one of the books, its location marked by the slim scanning rod resting atop it, the silent sentinel indicating where she had paused in her labor the previous day.

With practiced ease, she settled onto a sturdy, well-worn stool she had taken to carrying with her every day, a faithful companion for several years now. She initiated the power on the scanning rod, its gentle hum breaking the stillness. With a reverent touch, she opened the book to the page she had last explored, the delicate rustle of the paper echoing softly in the quiet.

As she began to move the rod slowly along the surface of the page, her eyes scanned the material with eager curiosity. Her gaze lingered on the intricate images and illustrations that adorned some of the pages, her eyes wide with wonder at the stories they told and the knowledge they held.

It gave her a sense her of something. Of *age*. Of *time*. Of *before*.

As with every day, she was suddenly transported back as page after page was scanned into the mainframe. The text flowed into the database, creating a bridge between eras that had long since parted ways with the present. Each word she scanned was like whispering into the ear of the future, telling tales of the past.

As she scanned, the routine had her mind wandering from the pages before her, back to her dream; back to the fields of green. It was as if her dreams, of late, were trying to remind her of something lost, something crucial that she couldn't quite grasp while awake.

She completed that book and pulled at a box containing some loose-leafed pages. She set it on the floor and carefully retrieved the first one. Her eye immediately spotted something different and she paused her scanning. She cocked her head, trying to decipher what she was seeing.

The writing was sparse, just a few words scattered across the surface. It reminded her of the small, cherished picture of the German Shepherd she kept closely guarded within her jumpsuit, a little secret she carried with her. However, this image was much larger and depicted a different scene. She immediately recognized three figures as humans: one was tall, a male towering above the other two with a presence that dominated the image. Another was medium in height, her features softened by a joyful expression. The smallest figure, who appeared to be a youngling, crouched low to the ground, wrapping his arms lovingly around a creature similar to her German Shepherd—but this animal was distinct: longer in the body and shorter in stature, its light brown fur gleaming softly, and its floppy ears adding an endearing touch. The female human knelt beside the youngling and the creature, laughter illuminating their face, a moment of shared joy captured in the stillness. The man stood slightly behind, observing with a gentle gaze, a guardian over this tender scene. All of them were smiling, their happiness palpable and infectious, a snapshot of pure, unfiltered joy.

Smiling.

She stared. Something about the configuration—there was no utility in it. No task being performed. The humans were simply…together. Present. There was a cohesion to them that resisted her categorization. She was glad that the scanning rod held sole control over categorizing the data she uploaded, for had it been left up to her, she would have been stuck. Inputting something completely nonsensical, such as Unit Type: Unknown. Relationship: Unclear. Activity: Unclassified.

She paused, her fingers lingering on the edge of the yellowed page, reluctant to set it aside. The image held a certain charm, a captured moment that seemed to glow with life. Still, she gently placed it down, driven by the hope that another treasure like this lay nestled amidst the other loose-leafed pages tucked within the old, weathered box. The anticipation of uncovering more forgotten moments spurred her curiosity, urging her to scan more quickly.

Eight pages later, she pulled out another image that left her puzzled. This time, there was no youngling. Instead, it was dominated by only two people: a man and a woman. Their bodies were so closely intertwined that they seemed to merge into one form, their eyes closed in an expression of mutual serenity. Their arms were draped around each other in a way that suggested a strange kind of closeness and connection that she couldn't quite grasp. Their lips met delicately, in a gesture that hinted at layers of feelings beyond her comprehension, yet the sight stirred something profound within her—a sense of wonder and an unfamiliar depth of emotion.

She blinked.

She hadn't realized that the image had such a visceral effect on her, until her breath left her lungs too fast leaving her momentarily reeling.

She desperately searched for something written that would describe what she was seeing. Was it captured incorrectly? Had there been a mistake that wasn't corrected quickly enough, causing the image of the two people to appear fused as one? After a few moments, gazing at it intently, she drew her conclusion: the gesture was *intentional*.

She sat up straighter. She did not understand. Her pulse elevated.

She powered off the scanning rod, placing it in its case. She couldn't focus on productivity just now. She didn't want to. She preferred to absorb all she could about the image.

Her fingers glided over the outlines of the figures in the picture, as though by feeling them she might unravel the mystery they held; perhaps even grasp the emotions it conveyed—and she had no doubt that it was filled with emotion. Their faces showed pleasure, and their embrace conveyed an intentional closeness. Every aspect of it was saturated with emotion. And it confused her to her core.

The more she observed, the more a faint echo of longing stirred within her, a yearning for something undefined. Her fingers trembled slightly as she traced the image one final time.

It should have been enough to scan it, to log it, to move on. But she couldn't. The picture was not just data. It was a question that she could not answer. One she feared she *wasn't meant* to answer.

She slid the image into the lining of her jumpsuit, tucking it beside the German Shepherd. Her hand lingered there a moment; the warmth of the two images pressed against her chest like hidden embers.

She had already crossed a line when she chose to keep the first image. But this felt different. More dangerous. Because this time, it wasn't just about holding on to a piece of the past. It was about stepping into it. She needed to know what that gesture meant—what they had felt in that moment, wrapped so tightly around each other. She needed to feel it. To understand.

To *replicate* it.

The thought came unbidden, wild and impossible—and yet, once it appeared, it refused to leave.

She stood slowly; the picture still warm against her skin. Her heart—once so even, so controlled—now thudded with something urgent and new. The ache inside her had become more than curiosity. It had become *longing*.

And longing, in her world, was not without consequence.

Directive: Terminate

"Guardians of order, assemble," the commander's voice thundered, a resonant wave tearing through the pervasive speakers. Each word ricocheted off the icy steel and concrete walls of their stark utopia, carrying an authority as unyielding as iron that seeped into every concealed corner of their domain. The sentries, ever watchful in their roles, tore their piercing gazes from the monotonous rhythm of the populace. With a chilling uniformity and mechanical precision akin to a grand clockwork mechanism, they marched towards the towering garrison command building.

Upon crossing its formidable threshold into its austere interior, they formed a flawless concentric circle around their commanding officer—a towering figure who stood at the epicenter of power. This was their monthly briefing—an interruption to their ceaseless surveillance lasting precisely thirty minutes.

In theory, chaos could erupt during their absence—citizens could flood the streets, dance on rooftops, scream into the silence.

But they never did. They didn't know how.

Fabricated with suppressed emotion, and conditioned since younglings to value nothing but productivity, they lacked even the language for any emotional activity. Spontaneity was foreign. Joy and laughter were unheard of. Emotion was simply…inefficient. It served no measurable yield. So, the realm remained orderly and productive, despite the temporary absence of the sentries. It would seem that with the realm functioning in such perfected harmony, the need for sentries would be just as useless as emotions, but they did serve a purpose, because perfection was never truly ever perfect. Cracks inevitably appeared.

Thus, the sentries' primary function was to detect those cracks. Any deviation and citizen identifiers were marked for a month-long observation. If the decline persisted, their identifier was placed on the termination roster and sent to Dr. Kishida-Guan for final approval.

Two exceptions bypassed this process entirely. First: younglings. Until their transition from study phase to productive phase, they fell under the jurisdiction of their instructors, who held unilateral authority to terminate based on classroom behaviors and academic excellence. Second: any citizen whose actions suggested that a month-long observational period might endanger the fabric of society due to rapid degradation: emotional outbursts, sudden unpredictability, and, worst of all, falling below productive levels. These were not seen as anomalies—they were treated as contagions.

In such cases, termination was immediate. No review. No appeal.

The commander of the sentries was different than those within his ranks. He was fabricated earlier, prior to the introduction of suppressed emotions. He was also Dr. Kishida-Guan's personal liaison with the citizens. A majority of communications between the citizenry and the holy ones went through him, giving him a special position within the realm—much like the holy ones, themselves. On the day of emotional insurrection, when the Chancellor and holy ones determined emotions were becoming a liability, it was the commander who'd seen to the termination of those deemed too far gone. On that fateful day, it was announced that future fabrications would have emotions suppressed but, more importantly, the commander was given a choice: self-regulate his own emotions or self-terminate. He'd chosen the prior option, pushing himself hard to ensure that he faced his duties with little sympathy or empathy. And if he did feel for a citizen, he did all he could not to show it. Today was such a day.

Foregoing any formalities, he summoned one of his sentries to step forward with a stern command. The perfect circular formation was disrupted as the summoned sentry advanced towards his superior. His fellow sentinels remained unphased; their faces etched with stoic indifference—a chilling tableau of unwavering obedience.

"There are numerous issues we need to address in this meeting," the commander began, "but I have decided to focus on your recent lapse in attentiveness first."

If these watchmen had been wired for feelings, the allegation would have elicited a unified intake of breath, a ripple of disbelief through their ranks. Yet, their faces remained as impassive as ever—indifference was ingrained in their very blueprints; they were not engineered to exhibit concern. Nonetheless, the stinging indictment ignited something within the indicted—a flare of astonishment—an unusual emotional surge in an entity devoid of any recognizable emotional framework.

If these apathetic beings were somehow rebelling against their genetic programming and cultivating nascent emotions, it would wreak greater havoc on their society than the current deterioration in the fabrications that was causing a reduction in productivity.

"You stand before me to answer inquiries on why you have begun failing in your duties as prescribed by the holy ones. Do you accept, or deny, that your attention of late has been less than what it should be?"

SEN7954 paused momentarily before responding with an affectless voice, "Commander, I have noted my attention straying recently by minor distractions while observing our citizens. Trivial details that I wouldn't normally notice—like a citizen's gait or movement—have begun drawing my attention more frequently, for periods which could be deemed prolonged."

"Noticing a citizen's shift in behavior is not cause for alarm, as it is in your genetic makeup to be hyper-vigilant, marking their designation for further observation, if required, and then notifying me of any abnormality that needs approval for termination. So then, if you are simply observing, as you should, why would you be standing before me now?"

"My attention does not just shift to a citizen, momentarily, in order to monitor and report, if needs be," the sentry began. "Rather, I have found my gaze lingering when I should denote the abnormality and return to scanning the citizenry."

"Provide me an example."

"The sudden, frenzied sprint of a75b99r84GE down the stone steps towards her residence was when I first recognized that my curiosity could be piqued. Moreover, I found myself alarmed and disheartened, as she perceived my gaze fixed on her, since she decelerated abruptly as though...I find myself grappling for an apt description of her reaction."

"Apprehensive?" the commanding officer provided, the commanding officer, although he could not say for certain without having witnessed the offense. He merely offered a possibility for expediencies sake.

"Yes, that could be it," SEN7954 conceded, although he didn't fully grasp the depth of that human emotion; was having difficulty latching onto his own emotional state of late. So unfamiliar was he with what feelings entailed, that he had no choice but to accept that he, too, was possibly degrading on a cellular level.

"But your own conduct was also deviant," His commander pointed out as if reading his sentinel's mind. "You allowed yourself to be sidetracked for over half a minute during which something potentially significant could've transpired elsewhere, unnoticed."

"Do you not agree that the archivist's peculiar behavior justified my distraction?"

"Justified your attention long enough to mark her identifier and report the behavior. By your own account, that is not what you did," the officer retorted with a biting edge to his voice. "And questioning your superior—that too is an anomaly. It is these accumulative abnormalities that has you standing before me now. And did you witness anything further after marking her for observation? Anything that you, perhaps, failed to report?"

This time SEN7954 hesitated.

"Speak up!" the commander snapped.

"I did."

"Well?"

"It had been several weeks, but the same citizen did something which I cannot even begin to comprehend."

"Something which, had any other sentry noticed, would have been brought to my attention immediately so that I could have determined whether it warranted immediate termination or whether it needed to be taken before the holy ones for further contemplation. Yet you did what?"

SEN7954's eyes fluttered rapidly before confessing, "Nothing. I did nothing. But in my defense, I admit that the behavior of a75b99r84GE was so startling that I was shocked into immobility…" he trailed off when he saw the anger blazing in the commander's gaze. So startled was he, that he didn't even question how the commander knew of the second offense, when he'd not reported it.

Standing in front of his superior, he felt an unfamiliar wave of resignation wash over him, coupled with a budding curiosity. What had triggered this newfound awareness within him? Suddenly, he was noticing nuances and beginning to question everything: his existence, his duty…his leaders? This awakening had come too late for him. He'd been branded as a threat which meant…

"You will present yourself for termination immediately. As for the archivist—her behavior has been documented and I will address her termination with Dr. Kishida-Guan."

SEN7954 fought back the surge of raw emotions that threatened to rise from the depths of his soul, overwhelming him like a tsunami. With practiced ease, he fashioned his face into a mask of unyielding stoicism, only betraying a hint of tension through the slight tightening at the corners of his mouth.

The commander gave a rigid nod towards the sentry stationed across from him, whose gaze was as cold and piercing as an arctic wind. The sentry's icy stare seemed to slice through SEN7954 like a razor-sharp blade.

In his hand, the sentry held a rod which was as long as his arm and as menacing as an executioner's axe. The rod gleamed ominously under the stark lighting of their environment, its potential for harm evident in its very design.

From behind him, another sentry approached with measured steps. In his hands he carried a small bucket filled not just with water but also with impending doom. Each ripple on the water's surface seemed to echo SEN7954's mounting dread.

The sentry placed the bucket at SEN7954's feet with a thud that resonated forebodingly in the silence.

"Prepare yourself," the commander stated, his back straight as the rod being wielded by the executioner.

Bending down slowly, every movement deliberate and weighted by the gravity of what was about to occur, SEN7954 retrieved a sponge from within the bucket. Water dripped from its saturated surface, like tears falling from mournful eyes; each droplet created miniature splashes that sounded like whispers of last goodbyes. He pressed it against his jumpsuit over where his heart beat steadily beneath—an organ blissfully unaware that it would soon be stilled forever. The fabric drank up the water eagerly, darkening quickly under its influence until it clung wetly to his skin.

With a nod so subtle it could have been missed by an unobservant eye, SEN7954 signaled his readiness to meet fate head-on to the executioner standing in front of him.

The executioner snapped the switch on the rod with a chilling finality, unleashing a surge of energy that buzzed with a deadly intensity, its soft humming more terrifying than any roar.

The end of the electrified rod was pressed against the wet fabric covering SEN7954's heart. A jolt of fifteen hundred milliamps coursed through his body like a bolt of lightning, turning his veins into highways of pain. His body convulsed violently, each spasm a grotesque dance of death under the harsh light. Then, just as suddenly as it had begun, it ended. The executioner pulled the rod away and SEN7954's body collapsed to the ground in a lifeless heap, another victim claimed by this merciless ritual.

"Place his remains outside and summon the transporter to carry his carcass to the incinerator," ordered the commander. His voice echoed around the room, cold and emotionless as if he were discussing a mundane task rather than a man's death. The executioner, his face hidden behind a mask of indifference, gave a curt nod in response.

He passed off his weapon to the other guard who also took charge of the now inessential bucket. The executioner then moved with measured steps to SEN7954's side. He knelt down on the cold metallic floor and ceremoniously removed the sentry's stun gun, then unzipped and pulled off his jumpsuit, leaving the nude body displayed in front of his comrades. The executioner bundled up the items and passed them to the sentry holding his rod and bucket, who, with an air of resigned duty, retreated towards the shadowy rear of the room where only whispers dared venture.

The executioner then stood and moved to the deceased's head and wrapped his gloved hands beneath SEN7954's arms. With a sharp tug, he began dragging him through a sea of watching figures that parted like waves before him. The crowd was silent; their eyes followed but their bodies remained still as statues, closing ranks behind him once he had passed.

"Understand this well, each and every one of you," the commander's voice echoed ominously through the room, his words a chilling reminder wrapped in cold authority. "No individual is exempt from the finality of termination. It can—and will—befall anyone who fails to uphold the stringent standards of focused productivity our Chancellor and holy ones' demand." His tone was as merciless as their mandate, a grim testament to their dystopian reality.

He paused for a moment, allowing the weight of his words to settle over them before continuing. "Now, let us return to our immediate task at hand. The data I've received from each of you have marked forty citizens whose behavior patterns are deviating erratically or whose productivity is plummeting at an alarming rate compared to their projected trends." As he spoke, he raised an arm encased in polished armor that gleamed under the harsh light—a symbol of power and control. With deliberate precision, he punched in a code on his wrist-mounted interface. A holographic chart shimmered into existence before them, casting eerie blue light across their faces.

The chart listed the alphanumeric identifiers that were now marked for something far worse than just further observations. These were identities now destined for termination; lives soon to be snuffed out without remorse or regret. "These identifiers are being uploaded to your terminals," he stated with ruthless resolve. "Locate and inform them they are summoned to appear at town center at the first of the month," he added with an air of finality that brooked no argument or delay. "You are dismissed." His last words hung heavily in the air as the sentries began exiting the building one by one under dimmed lights reflecting off polished floors and steel walls.

Realm 1482's commander inputted another sequence into his device, which transmitted the list of condemned citizens for final judgment so that Dr. Kishida-Guan could offer the final say. If he did not reply before the first, commuting the sentence of any of the forty identified, that sentence would be carried out without delay on the first of the coming month.

Only once, that he could recall, in the last decade, had the holy one stopped termination against a single citizen, when she was but a youngling, intervening in the instructors' governance. Now, nearly nine years later, that same individual was marked again: a75b99r84GE. He was curious whether, this time, the holy one would intervene and save this citizen whose behavior was becoming more erratic than he'd ever borne witness to in his centuries-long existence.

Early the next morning, engulfed in an ethereal halo of holographic screens, Kishida-Guan found himself lost in a labyrinth of intricate calculations and reams of data. His eyes darted across the floating digits, a symphony of information that only he could decipher. The sterile silence of his lab was punctuated when his assistant, rigid with tension, stormed into the room. "Doctor," she began, "I implore you to examine this month's termination requests from the commander of the sentries." The words she spoke implied a sense of urgency, those her tone was calm and flat. She thrust a sleek tablet towards the doctor, her arm as straight and inflexible as a steel rod.

The doctor released an exasperated sigh that seemed to echo through the stark lab. His gaze hardened as he shot his assistant a stern look that could freeze mercury. Were the assistant capable of interpreting such a look, she would have lowered the tablet and left the room. She didn't. She merely stood and waited in silence.

"Review of this material isn't required of me for two more days, so leave it on my desk. I will go over it before the allotted time." He commanded with a tone as sharp as shattered glass. It didn't dawn on him that the list was being presented early for a reason, nor could he have discerned that from the assistant's voice.

"Sir…" The assistant tried again, but her voice trailed off under Kishida-Guan's piercing glare, which stated he didn't want to be interrupted further; however, the assistant, acting out of character, refused to retreat.

Seeing the assistant's persistence, the doctor snatched the tablet from her with an air of palpable frustration. His eyes skimmed over the ever-increasing list of alphanumeric designators scheduled for termination review until they landed on one particular identification, ending GE. This was why his assistant had interrupted him. He readily understood the urgency…now.

He drew in a deep breath to steady himself before turning back to his assistant who was tasked specifically with monitoring a75b99r84GE—an assignment executed impeccably so far, especially as she'd had very little to report. Their specifically fabricated genetically enhanced was performing above and beyond all others, instilling confidence in the holy ones that their mission—when the time arrived—would go off flawlessly. But now…

An unsettling sensation gnawed at Kishida-Guan's gut; he wanted desperately to dismiss this anomaly as a simple error, but errors were not characteristic of his meticulous sentries. He took another moment to compose himself before addressing the grave matter at hand.

"Thank you for your diligence," he acknowledged solemnly before continuing, "I'll communicate directly with the sentries' commander from this point. You are relieved until further notice."

The assistant nodded curtly in acknowledgment, reclaimed her tablet, and retreated from the lab, passing another scientist who had just entered.

Kishida-Guan watched as his fellow scientist, 41GB, approached him with a what would pass for a look of confusion spread across her features. "What has occurred?" she inquired, her voice steady, belying the concern she so attempted to mimic, as the doctor gestured for her to come nearer.

"Patience," he replied, his fingers swiftly punching out an urgent message to the commander. Once the coded missive was dispatched into the ether, he turned to face his colleague. "a75b99r84GE is demonstrating peculiarities that are causing concern," he admitted, his voice heavy with apprehension. "She was included with the commander's monthly termination requests, which, I must say, is getting longer with each passing season."

41GB's tilted her head and widened her eyes at this unexpected news. "It's distressing enough that forty more citizens are rapidly degrading early into their production stage, but even more so that our genetically enhanced fabrication is also—"

"She's not deteriorating," Kishida-Guan interjected hastily. "Quite the opposite actually. According to the report," he continued, pulling up the list of inculpated that he'd transferred to his own tablet with the tap of a button just prior to returning the assistant's tablet to her. "She's performing exceptionally well. According to this report, the thirty-nine others are displaying degradations; however, in the case of a75b99r84GE, it isn't her productivity at stake here; it's her behavior that has attracted attention from the sentries."

"Behavior?" 41GB echoed.

"Yes...behavior. Well, that's the commander's notation. Apparently, one of his sentries, who has since been terminated, failed to acknowledge, mark, or report a75b99r84GE's unusual behavior as well as other small infractions, so the commander decided to surveil the sentry's monitoring behavior by tapping into his helmet's visor. It was only because of this effort, that the commander became aware of both the sentry's failings and a75b99r84GE's concerning behaviors."

"So, the sentry responsible for failure to mark and report has been terminated. What of our GE? What behavior was she caught doing that would warrant a call for termination? She hasn't yet been terminated, correct? This would set our progress back sixteen years."

"Emotional behaviors," Kishida-Guan stated succinctly.

"How can that be? Our fabrications are created with emotions highly suppressed and are taught throughout the youngling years that any sign of emotions surfacing is to be ignored and repressed under threat of termination. It is a rare event that anyone chooses to allow their emotions to surface, let alone engage them in public. Anyone wishing to emulate those with emotions, such as yourself, can certainly do so without risking actual emotional interference."

"You certainly are a prime example of that, aren't you?" Kishida-Guan queried rhetorically before quickly shifting the topic back to their genetically enhanced, "Anyway, I spoke with a75b99r84GE nearly a decade ago when she was beginning to demonstrate emotions, which had her questioning her instructors. I thought I impressed upon her, at that time, the importance of masking her emotions; the necessity of fitting in with those around her. Apparently, something has happened since then, as I hadn't received further negative reporting, which has caused her emotions to surface yet again…even more unashamedly."

"But I do not understand," 41GB inserted. "Even the very few who have displayed emotions have not done so with overwhelming displays; rather, it has generally reared itself through small expressions or gestures. So then, why are a75b99r84GE's emotions exploding with such volatility?"

Kishida-Guan grimaced and shook his head slowly before responding, "If I had an answer…"

"You must understand we cannot afford to create another genetically advanced at this stage—"

"I know, we are so close…we need to evaluate the situation ourselves before making any hasty decisions," interrupted Kishida-Guan firmly, reaching for his communication tablet.

"And if termination becomes an unavoidable option?"

The doctor paused mid-action, visibly burdened by the weight of their predicament. He massaged his temples against the tension that was steadily building, causing wrinkles to form on his forehead like crumpled parchment.

"If it comes to that," he said slowly, "we may have to consider undertaking the mission ourselves."

"We are well past our prime. Our bodies and minds, despite enhancements, would not withstand—"

"I'm painfully aware!" Kishida-Guan snapped back. "But we stand at the precipice of humanity's end and are so close to finalizing that which we need to implement to set things to right. If our genetically enhanced's emotions have become a liability and we must terminate her, then I may need to make the trek myself."

"At the risk to your life," 41GB interjected, "the loss of which will benefit no one in this realm. Perhaps, before we jump to hasty alternatives, which are not true alternatives at all, we determine what sort of emotional instability we are dealing with and see if it cannot be rectified. We are ten years from project completion, so if another genetically enhanced needs to be fabricated, we will only be delayed for a little over a decade. Surely, humanity will survive…"

"Its not a risk I'm willing to take," he interrupted, then fell silent, his brow knitted in thought.

In the midst of his contemplation, an unassuming ping from his tablet broke through the silence, signaling a response from the commander of the sentinels. "I requested that the commander escort a75b99r84GE to us," he stated, his tone flat. "Until they arrive, let's try to unravel the mystery surrounding her behavioral…glitch…for want of a better word. I have a suspicion that's gnawing at my insides that I'd like to confirm before taking action…" he trailed off and swiveled towards his computer terminal, fingers flying over the holographic keys in a flurry of motion. A series of complex commands later, he brought up her data on an expansive screen that dominated the room. The genetic blueprint of their subject, known as a75b99r84GE, filled the screen with cryptic symbols that danced and flickered like ancient hieroglyphs—each one hinting at a destiny yet to unfold.

Upon seeing that Kishida-Guan was scanning the GE's genetic template, 41GB moved closer, "You think that the issue lies in her genetic makeup, rather than her ability to self-regulate?"

"The inability to self-regulate could also prove to be an issue with her genetics, and if that were the case, that would indeed pose a significant problem."

"Because it would mean that even a genetically enhanced is prone to degradation," 41GB concluded.

Kishida-Guan shook his head. His eyes narrowed and his voice took on an ominous tone as he added darkly, "Or perhaps our geneticists meddled with her design and unintentionally ignited this malfunction." He gestured towards a specific segment of her genetic map marked by unique modifications—a glaring omission was clear: there was no trace of an emotion suppressor inserted during inception as per standard protocol. He looked over at his colleague, his face a mixture of anger and concern.

Thanks to groundbreaking strides, their supercomputer could scrutinize each individual's genetic makeup and predict their prime productivity years with pinpoint accuracy. It also broke down the genetic template into an easy-to-decipher log in order to quickly pinpoint abnormalities.

"What would make them to that?" 41GB asked, scanning the section pointed to by the doctor.

Kishida-Guan sat back, his lips compressing as he recalled his conversation with the geneticists, years earlier. They had asked why he was opposed to genetically enhancing all future fabrications as a potential remedy to the current issues of degradation plaguing their citizenry. After that conversation concluded, he'd eavesdropped on their conversation and noted that they intended to defy his command not to alter fabricated design; had sent a sentry to ensure compliance. But that was after they'd already been given the blueprint for his genetically enhanced.

He turned, again, and pulled up his directive for a75b99r84GE's fabrication. A quick scan confirmed that he hadn't specifically denoted 'suppressed emotions' as a part of the genetic makeup. Had they decided to include emotions, he wondered, because he had not specifically requested those emotions be suppressed? He'd never needed to state it specifically before; however, he admitted to himself, he'd never requested a genetically enhanced before.

Another thought struck him that if he hadn't taken it upon himself to probe deeper into her genetic modifications, then this first genetically enhanced being fabricated by them for a specific purpose might have been hastily branded as defective and terminated without further thought or consideration.

He shook his head in frustration. While he may not have specifically noted the suppression, the geneticists had still failed in their duty by presupposing his intentions. They were culpable for the current behavioral issues plaguing their genetically enhanced, which now placed their future plans at risk.

As if 41GB knew that Kishida-Guan was mulling over information surrounding the geneticists, she spoke up, "Should we have the geneticists begin fabrication on a replacement GE…just to be on the safe side?"

"No," Kishida-Guan replied softly, thoughtfully. "In fact, I intend to suspend production of all fabrications until after we have completed our mission."

"But that won't be for another decade or more. Our citizens are degrading—"

"At a rate of less than…" he paused to retrieve the current data, "four hundred citizens a year. And since the current fabrications are degrading at a rapider rate than the older fabrications, it is simply a waste of what genetic material we do have to keep churning out defective workers. No, instead, we will wait until we have fresh genetic material to work with. In the meantime, I will have the Chancellor send out a request to one of our sister realms for the fabrication of replacement geneticists. Those new geneticists will have completed their youngling study phases a few years before the onset of our project, thus will be in place to begin work with the new genetic material once it's been replenished."

"But how will they get here to begin work? We do not have an interconnected transportation system between realms. And if we find ourselves in dire need of replacement workers before then? We have never communicated directly with other realms, nor, as I just stated, is there a method by which to bring workers in from another realm…unless you have information of which I am unaware."

"That will be for me and the Chancellor to concern ourselves over. Not for you to try to sort out. Now, let's pull up the video footage of the town center for the time stamp related to a75b99r84GE's emotional disturbance. I want to see for myself just precisely what it was that discombobulated a sentry so much that he ended up getting terminated. It will also aid in my determination on whether our current geneticists have deviated from their prescribed duties."

Entangled

As the last threads of daylight surrendered to the encroaching night, a75b99r84GE found herself held captive on the cool concrete floor of her compact sanctuary. The single light above her, bathed her in a soft, golden glow, its light weaving intricate patterns across her bare, damp skin like an artist's brush on canvas. Normally, she would have meticulously arranged every object in her room with precision and sought refuge in sleep by now. But this night, she was transfixed, her gaze ensnared by the two pictures she had secreted away from the archives.

The image of the two humans caught in some form of latching hold upon each other, had been a silent witness to her evening's endeavors. It watched over her as she ate at the table and observed quietly as she dried herself after bathing. The beloved photo of the German Shepherd was there also, but it was this new picture that had her perplexed, and unable to draw her gaze away, refusing to release its grip all evening.

When necessity demanded that she avert her gaze—such as when washing her hair—she did so as briefly as able; however, her mind remained fixated, enmeshed within their mysterious hold. A compulsion to unravel this enigma, frozen in time. The German Shepherd picture had once been a puzzle too and had taken years to sort until the mystery of its identifier had resolved that particular enigma. Now, it was a companion; a link to a past time that she longed to be a part of.

In this new picture, she had a new obsession. Not identifying an unknown creature, because those within the image were definitively human. No—now it was the behavior of those two humans that confounded her. Why were they bound together by their arms; their bodies molded to one another, and their faces touching at the lips. The expressions visible did not appear to relay distress rather the opposite—they seemed content in the action.

She'd spent the remainder of her work day attempting to locate anything that would identify this gesture, and while she came close with one monochrome image within a book under a label of 'family unit', it was not quite the same. Yes, it did have humans, but not captured in the same form of entanglement. In the monochromatic image was a man, woman, and a youngling that the label stated was a 'young girl', and an unfamiliar tiny entity nestled in the woman's arms, identified as an 'infant'.

It was the infant that baffled her in this picture. Why did the woman need to hold it in such a manner? Because it was so small? The notion of such a teeny defenseless human thriving despite its clear non-productivity was exceedingly confusing to her. After all, in her society, she had never seen anything so small. Her first encounter with humanity was as a youngling, when she entered the dormitory with other younglings and immediately began her study phase.

Had she ever been that small? The question struck her with a sudden ache, as if her body remembered something her mind could not. A hazy impression stirred—an echo of something once known but now a ghost wandering the halls of her mind. A brief vision flashed: an overwhelming sensation of softness, of warmth— something cocoon-like, a quiet space that felt strangely...*secure*. It was a place she inhabited before being taken from that security and dropped into a sterile dormitory as a youngling.

Then, just as quickly, the memory slipped through her mental grasp, evaporating like mist under the weight of the present. In its wake, there was...nothing. No trace. Just the sterile blankness of a past that she wasn't certain ever existed for her. And she let it go, because it wasn't truly what interested her at that moment.

Although that particular image had intrigued, it was the one of the man and woman that she now held in her hand which had her enraptured. This man and woman; their bodies entwined in such a way that they appeared as one entity—an enigma that left her utterly bewildered.

After what seemed an eternity, she released a long, frustrated sigh, then laid the picture beside the other on the floor. Her legs were stiff as the she stood to finish towel-drying her hair, which she did with a groan at having her attention taken away from the pictures.

She quickly replaced her towel on its rack, then turned and swiped up the pictures, then moved to recline on her bed covers, an unknown ache coursing through her body. Her finger hovered at her lips, tracing the soft curve, willing herself to feel what they felt, but her skin offered only warmth, not revelation. The gesture, though inexact, lacked what the mystery of the photo enticed. The *meaning*. Her mouth was just a mouth. And there was not another mouth with which she could replicate the gesture.

She then envisioned being encased by another body as depicted in the photo. The imagined weight of another body against hers sent a jolt of electricity through her limbs—a sudden, burning ache, low in her body, that she had no name for. Was this what it meant to be…touched? A soft murmur seemed to emanate from the photo—a phantom symphony of whispers caught within its crinkled edges, luring her towards its concealed secrets.

With a sigh heavy with exasperation, she rose from the bed and crawled beneath the blanket—her body humming with alien desires to know, to feel. As sleep began to pull at her consciousness, she cast one final longing glance at the photos that she'd placed on the floor beside her bed, before succumbing to sleep's seduction— her dreams haunted by riddles of its symbolism.

Dawn found a75b99r84GE dragging herself out of bed—craving clarity to banish the fog shrouding her mind. The room was draped in melancholic gray light seeping through the window above—a mirror reflecting her scrambled mental state. Her body felt weighed down as if filled with lead as she dressed—grappling with remnants of a restless night. She reached down and picked up the pictures, tucking them in the inner pocket of her jumpsuit, then went about her morning routine.

Shortly before six-fifteen, she stepped from her room and walked downstairs; she opened the door to the outside and shards of ice-like morning air assaulted her face. Taking a deep breath, she exhaled slowly—gathering herself before plunging into another day's monotony. Lost in this haze, she bumped into another citizen on his way to work.

Regaining her balance, she blinked rapidly—trying to focus on this unexpected encounter. His gaze met hers with an indifference that shocked her—a hollow void where emotion should reside. It was something she should be used to, raised as she was among the emotionless. But the last time she'd truly looked into eyes so devoid of feeling was as a youngling, when she'd tried to talk to c479956cf. Even then, at just six and a half years old, she noticed his blank gaze but hadn't understood it—just as she hadn't when younger still, trying to play with unresponsive classmates. For the last ten years, all of her interactions had been with those who had emotions but worked hard to hide them: A9021, Dr. Kishida-Guan, and her instructors.

Now, after spending so much time in the archives, poring over what it meant to be human in the 'before time'—in the era before emotions were suppressed—her own reality was beginning to crash down on her like a flood. It wasn't just a disorienting wave; it shattered her sense of self, leaving jagged edges that cut through her understanding, making everything she had been taught seem hollow and distant. Each moment felt like a violent collision, forcing her to confront the raw, aching void that stretched between the humanity she had learned about and the cold, sterile existence she inhabited.

She looked up at the man she'd collided with, an urge to apologize welling up within her, but it was swiftly stifled. Instead, she seized this chance encounter as an opportunity to experiment; however, when a75b99r84GE remained standing in front of him, the man took a step to the side and started to walk away, but she dashed around in front of him. He looked down at her, completely unphased by her action—no irritation, agitation, curiosity—he simply moved to step around her again. Once more a75b99r84GE moved swiftly into his path. She didn't yet know what she was wanted to accomplish, but had decided that colliding with him was an opportunity that she didn't want to let pass.

She studied the line of his jaw, the blue of his eyes, the static stillness of his breath. Could he tell she was trembling? Would he even care if she were. The fact that he moved to go around her again, told he didn't…couldn't. She, again, moved into his way, as a voice within her—older, quieter, not quite hers—whispered…*touch him.*

She no longer tried to fight her urge, though she was vaguely aware that her actions were likely being monitored by a nearby sentry and she risked severe repercussions if it was determined that her actions were a sign of degradation. For her, it was now or never.

Curiosity and longing overwhelmed any caution that attempted to surface and, with a hand quivering like a leaf in the wind, she reached out tentatively towards him. A small gesture just to see what would happen. Her fingertips grazed his cheek in an almost imperceptible caress; an electric current surged into them— both exhilarating and terrifying.

Her heart pounded wildly against her ribcage, its rhythm echoing in her ears as though it were a drum heralding impending doom. Yet the man standing before her remained eerily still and unaffected; his face devoid of emotion. She knew it was irrational and wholly untrue, but she took his stillness as permission to continue her experimentation. The intoxication of the touch, though light and fleeting, flooded over her senses, sending waves of sensations that made her head spin. She'd never felt someone's skin in this way; could never recall ever being touched at all.

Suddenly, an image flashed across her mind—the couple entwined within each other's grasp—filling her with a sudden yearning so intense it left her breathless. She found herself drawn to him like a moth to a flame. She bridged the short gap between them and her arms encircled his rigid form, and for a breathless instant, she felt…everything. So much so that the absence of a response didn't matter. To her, she no longer felt alone.

The moment was short lived however, for just as she began to lose herself in this moment, the man stepped backward, pulling her along with him until her grip loosened and she fell to her knees. Her knees scraped the cobblestone and she gasped. With no concern for her wellbeing, the man moved around her and walked away. She waited for gasps of alarm, for anyone to acknowledge what had happened, but the world continued as if she didn't exist. Passerby swerved around her like water splitting stone. And suddenly, it wasn't just his inadvertent rejection she felt, it was the silence of an entire world unwilling to see her.

She felt humiliated, not because she'd drawn attention to herself, but because it was only she who seemed to be cognizant of the fact that she'd fallen in the middle of the walkway. Everyone else passing by, merely ignored her presence, all too focused on where they were going. She glanced about her and her gaze fell on a sentry stationed about twenty feet away. He noticed her; was, in fact, watching her very intently, but he didn't make a move towards her. Unlike the people passing by, there was something in his stance that said he felt something. But because of his visor, she couldn't tell what that something was: anger, curiosity?

She stood and brushed at her pant legs, then turned toward him. Could she dare approach him?

Just as she was trying to decide whether she should do so, or just head on to the archives, the loudspeaker system screeched to life and the commander's voice bellowed: *Guardians of order, assemble.*

What a75b99r84GE didn't know—couldn't know—was the choice that was made, just moments earlier, behind that sentry's visor. SEN7954 had watched her actions and a startling curiosity flared within him. Then he'd seen her fall and for the briefest of moments, had wanted to go to her…but he didn't know why. His actions, in parallel with hers, had driven him to make a grave error in judgement. Instead of reporting, he had *felt*. That single second of human hesitation sealed his fate. Before the day ended, he would be terminated and his identifier recycled to a new fabrication; a new sentry. His replacement.

a75b99r84GE's touch upon another citizen had instigated that. Her need to *know*, to *feel*, had reached out and cracked the lid to the well on that sentry's emotions.

And now the system had her in its sights.

Not to understand her.

To decide what to do with her.

"Look closely at the replay of a75b99r84GE's behavior yesterday morning," Kishida-Guan stated, his calm tone belying the turmoil swirling within him. Now…" he paused to press a button, pulling up another video, "watch the consequences of this infectious behavior." Those in the room with intact emotions, gasped in unison, as they watched the termination of one the sentries. The gasp wasn't because of the action, for they'd seen many terminations over their lifetimes. Rather, it was because of the accusation leveled by Kishida-Guan—that the sentry's execution was a direct result of a75b99r84GE's emotions and indirectly because they, the geneticists, had opted to think and act in opposition to the holy ones.

"Imagine the damage to our society had you two not been stopped sixteen years ago; had I not eavesdropped on your seditious conversation and sent a sentry to guard your actions from that day forward. If you two had flooded our society with these emotional genetically enhanced, not only would you have depleted the remainder of our genetic materials, we would now be having to contend with the spread of this infectious behavior, leading to the termination of more citizen workers than we're already facing each month," he continued, the accusatory tone getting more pronounced with each word. He shook his head, continuing with a heavy sigh, "Had I known the difficulties that the genetically enhanced would face, the havoc she would wreak…" he paused, then continued, amending his thought, "no, it isn't because she is a genetically enhanced; it's because you chose not to suppress her emotions." The voice of Kishida-Guan reverberated through the antiseptic, chrome-splashed room, shattering its typical silence like a dropped glass vial.

His towering silhouette stood as firm as a steel column, his face an unyielding mask hiding the storm brewing within him. He confronted the two rogue geneticists from his realm with eyes that were icy slits of scrutiny, scanning their faces meticulously for any trace of remorse or attempts at justification. Silence was their only response—a damning confession in itself.

"For over sixteen years she has lived among our citizens," he spat out with increasing ferocity. "Did it not occur to you that her unchecked emotions could lead to catastrophic outcomes? Clearly not, otherwise we wouldn't find ourselves knee-deep in this crisis today! Now I'll let you enlighten me as to the reasoning for your blatant disregard for our standard protocols: did you observe her over the years, hoping she would validate your absurd theory that all our citizens should be genetically enhanced; given emotions? If I hadn't stationed a sentry in your laboratory, what chaos might you have unleashed? Well? Speak up! Have you no defense?"

G13654 stole a quick glance at G9983, her eyes pleading for him to take charge due to his seniority. But G9983 remained disturbingly mute; fear and resignation painted on his face like an abstract canvas of dread. She couldn't blame him, for they had flagrantly defied orders and made a unilateral decision with far-reaching implications. It didn't matter how they felt at that moment of choice, because it was now, sixteen years later, that the consequences for those actions were now coming due. As G9983 chose silence over defense, G13654 drew in a deep breath and summoned every ounce of bravery she possessed to explain their rationale.

"In absence of specific directives for this genetically enhanced entity related to her emotions," she began, her voice steady despite the palpable tension hanging in the air like an ominous fog, "we took the liberty to include them."

"Yet, at no other time has it been necessary to include this directive. Why? Because it's part of the protocol. And unspoken expectation that should not need to be included in any directive I hand down."

"Yes, but at no other time had you ever requested a genetically enhanced. This was our first GE fabrication and we saw it as a chance to push boundaries—"

"Without checking with me first," Kishida-Guan interrupted. His penetrating gaze fell on G9983, the elder and de facto leader of the genetic facility. The scrutiny seemed to crush his already hunched shoulders further, but he remained too shell-shocked to utter a word.

"I was the one who suggested not suppressing the GE's emotions due to lack of directive to do so," she confessed in an attempt to defend her co-worker; her voice unwavering despite her heart pounding against her ribcage like a trapped animal. "I interpreted your directive to mean that his genetically enhanced was meant to be distinct from standard fabrications. As both my colleague and I were created before emotional suppression became standard practice and have led stable lives, we hypothesized that it could potentially benefit the genetically enhanced."

Kishida-Guan remained silent for what felt like an eternity, his gaze swinging between them like the pendulum from Poe's *Pit and the Pendulum* deciding which body to halve first. "Your assumptions are flawed," he finally responded in a manner that startled the geneticists, as his seething gaze contradicted his calm speech. "There is nothing that would indicate that emotional inclusion would cease the deterioration of our citizenry. Quite the opposite, if this latest incident is an indicator. Also, I would question whether you have led stable lives. If you, yourselves, weren't in some way deteriorating, you would not have gone against standard protocol; then discussed intentions to take it a step further by disregarding future directives. I clearly recall stating during our discussion years ago, that proceeding with alterations to fabrications was not authorized; that the holy ones and I were working on plans to resolve the issues facing our citizenry."

"But a75b99r84GE is functioning well beyond the standards placed for normal productive levels; and if you were in fact devising a remedy for the deterioration issues facing recent fabrications, why has there been a steady increase in the need for terminations over this last sixteen years?" G13654 protested, boldly, defiantly, which had G9983 cringing visibly, and taking a step away from her.

That seemed to snap Kishida-Guan's measured, deliberate calm. His lips curled into something that resembled a smile—but it was the sneer from a man who made it clear that G13654 had made the decision easy for him. "You are correct," he said, voice like ice cracking across a frozen lake. "There *has* been a steady increase in terminations, and today, that number rises by two."

He stepped over to his desk and pressed a button on the console. Within seconds, two sentries silently entered the room, their black visors reflecting the sterile lights above. "Take them away to be terminated."

G9983 and G13654 did not resist. There was no point. No words could unmake the betrayal; no pleading could undo what had already been set in motion. They moved as if caught in a slow, merciless current, toward the final and irreversible consequence of their actions. G13654 wept openly—not only for herself, but for G9983, who had once dared to hope for more. Together, they had spent countless hours whispering of ascension, imagining the day they would lay down the burdens of productivity and cross into the sacred realm of thought, of legacy.

Never had they let themselves consider the possibility that they might be *denied* that future altogether. The loss was a jagged thing, ripping through their composure. G9983 stumbled from the room, barely able to move under his own power, as if the weight of failure—the weight of dreams now turned to ash—had been chained around his ankles, dragging him down with every shuffling step.

a75b99r84GE, who'd been retrieved from the archives and led into the room just before the second video began—which showed the termination of the sentry—stood frozen in place as if witnessing a snowy avalanche; one which threatened to engulf everything and everyone it touched, herself included.
But what rooted her to the spot, more than the violence, was the dawning horror that their conversation was about her.

Kishida-Guan had hinted, when she'd first been summoned before him ten years ago, that she was different—that she'd been fabricated for a purpose. But she had never imagined the true extent of it; couldn't fathom the consequences for those who had dared to create her.

A sick heat flooded her chest, choking the breath from her.

She had always known she was different from the others in their homogenous, hollow society. But today, that knowledge was not whispered or suspected—it was hammered home in a brutal, public execution.

And for the first time, a75b99r84GE was forced to confront a terrible truth: Her existence was not a triumph. It was a crime. And those responsible for her fabrication were now facing their sentence; which left her wondering what precisely that meant for her.

Kishida-Guan signaled towards a sentry who nudged a75b99r84GE forward. Terror gripped her throat like a vice as she locked eyes with Kishida-Guan, his gaze an inferno of rage threatening to consume her. He stepped forward and gripped her elbow, waiving away the sentry, then guided her toward his work area.

As she ascended the steps to the dais, a75b99r84GE's mind raced. Each step felt like a mile, each second stretched impossibly long as she processed the grim fate of her creators.

Once they reached his work space, Kishida-Guan released her elbow and motioned for her to sit. He then turned his back to her, facing a large, opaque screen that flickered with intermittent streams of data. His hands moved with practiced ease over the controls, adjusting settings and inputting commands that remained a mystery to her.

The silence that filled the space was suffocating. a75b99r84GE could still hear the distant echoes of the sentries' movements below, a haunting reminder of what was occurring just out of sight. Her heart pounded against her chest; each beat a drum of war against the calm demeanor she struggled to maintain.

Kishida-Guan finally broke the silence, his gaze fixed ahead, as if the very act of looking at her might disrupt the delicate balance of his own emotions. "Your actions yesterday were unexpected and rather disturbing," he began, each word considered and stripped of warmth. "Though you were just a child when we last crossed paths, I held onto the hope that you'd follow my guidance—"

a75b99r84GE found her voice, though it wavered like a leaf in the wind. "You mean...to blend in, not stand out."

"Exactly," he replied with a nod that seemed to echo through the room. "It's reassuring to know your memory is sharp; however, your recollection implicates you in yesterday's events. Can you explain why you thought it acceptable to conduct yourself as you did in the town square on your way to work? Your actions not only delayed your own productivity but also disrupted another worker and left a sentry so compromised that termination was necessary. Now I must decide what course of action to take concerning you."

"But didn't you say that I was fabricated by you and the holy ones for a specific purpose—"

"Do you think you're irreplaceable? That we can't fabricate someone else who isn't burdened by emotion?"

"Then why didn't you replace me when I first stood before you in this office ten years ago? You knew then that I was made with emotions."

"No," Kishida-Guan interjected firmly. "Back then, your solitary disruption was merely something to observe—a potential problem akin to those affecting other citizens yet manifesting differently. Not through diminished productivity, but through emotional upheaval. I believed if you understood emotions were not to be cultivated or encouraged, you'd strive doubly hard to suppress them and prevent any recurrence."

"And for ten years, I succeeded."

"Until yesterday," he said softly yet sharply, "when your breakdown surpassed anything I've witnessed before. So now I'm left pondering what should be done with you as we edge closer to completing our project and approach a training date less than eight years away…" His voice faded into contemplation. "For transparency's sake, replacing you isn't really an option; since the Chancellor and I discussed the issue facing our realms and have decided to place a hold on fabrications until we find a solution for what's causing the degradation."

"Not that you could, even if you wanted to. You terminated the geneticists."

That reminder seemed to momentarily unnerve Kishida-Guan, causing a slight shift in his typically impermeable demeanor. His eyes narrowed, processing the implication of her statement before regaining composure, "I would not be so smug. Terminating you is not off the table…at least not for me. While working on a replacement might set our project back decades, I believe it's an option worth considering. Your emotional state is not to be trusted." Before a75b99r84GE could counter, he continued, "however, there are those who believe that your emotions might serve a purpose, when the time comes."

"Then why was it necessary to terminate the geneticists?" a75b99r84GE gasped in horror.

"Because they overstepped their bounds," Kishida-Guan stated curtly, with an icy edge. "Now, listen carefully, because I'm going to lay something out for you, and you'd better engrave it in your memory; because the next time you're brought before me for any other reason than to start your mission training…let's just say, we won't be having a polite conversation. And if that doesn't move your emotions to take my rather blunt threat to heart, then perhaps this will. You were fabricated because the citizens of this realm are degrading at an alarming rate. Many aren't even getting past their youngling years, as you witnessed firsthand. The fate of humanity hinges on whether our project mission is a success, of which you're meant to play an integral part. In between the now and the then, it is imperative that you learn to mask your emotions; to emulate those around you. Or…as you recalled in brief "blend in, not stand out." I cannot have you influencing others into acting rebelliously, otherwise it could completely disrupt the delicate balance of our realm. A balance already teetering on the edge of an abyss. Do you want to be the cause for the downfall of humanity?"

Kishida-Guan's words landed like a sledgehammer, leaving a75b99r84GE reeling to the point where she could do no more than shake her head.

"Good. Then might I suggest that you harness the emotions you're feeling over this situation right now; and use that harness to guide your actions moving forward. To ensure that there are no more incidences, a sentry will follow you daily, closely monitoring your activity and behavior for the slightest deviations. I do not expect to receive any reports from that sentry."

a75r99b84GE nodded in silence and Kishida-Guan nodded to the sentry who moved in behind her. Without a word, she stood and followed her guardian from the room, without a backwards glance; her body a study in silent acquiescence. No flicker of disobedience marred her face. No tremor betrayed the fury tightening in her chest as Kishida-Guan's words from long ago reverberated through her mind:

"You must learn to wear the mask that everyone has on naturally, even if yours feels heavier by virtue of your awareness of it."

And so, before reaching the courtyard, she ensured that the mask was firmly in place; but behind that mask, something fierce and feral clawed at her soul leaving it bloodied.

She lifted her chin as she entered her apartment building, a spark of defiance beginning in the pit of stomach. Those who ruled the realm could force her to control her emotions, but they would never command the fire taking root in her soul.

Seven grueling days elapsed since a75b99r84GE was hauled into the austere confines of Kishida-Guan's office by an implacable sentry, and Kishida-Guan's lethal threats still echoed in her ears.

Each dawn since, she woke to a spectral light seeping across the opposing wall, a silent herald of another day's arrival. The prospect of rising from her bed to face another battle against escalating emotions gnawed at her spirit. It was a war within herself that left her feeling as if she were walking up a sharp incline daily, with chains strapped to her ankles.

Yet, this internal struggle wasn't her only adversary. As she navigated the sterile streets to work each day, she wrestled with an insatiable urge to shatter her isolation and reach out for human contact—a forbidden touch that would bring her dire consequences. This yearning pulsed within her heart like a relentless drumbeat growing louder every day, making it increasingly arduous to don her emotionless façade.

A quick glance over her shoulder at the sentry who accompanied her everywhere made it slightly easier to suppress those rising urges. His very presence was oppressive, leaving her feeling that each step she took was monitored; each breath surveilled. It was as though he could read the slightest wavering in her composure, ready to report any infringement to Kishida-Guan.

She was utterly drained by this relentless charade—the incessant act of pretending emotional numbness while desperately craving to feel alive inside. She was aching for Kishida-Guan to reveal her true purpose so she could finally put an end to this agonizing facade. He had hinted, in passing, that someone believed her emotions would be valuable for the project she was designed for. She wished fervently that this person wielded more influence over Kishida-Guan, perhaps persuading him to allow her to explore her emotions, to master them in a healthier way so they wouldn't be so utterly stifled. But no one, aside from the Chancellor, wielded more power than Kishida-Guan. He hadn't dismissed the idea of emotions playing a role in her future mission, yet he was steadfast in his insistence that they remain suppressed until then. He emphasized that, in a world where duty and performance reigned supreme, delving into human emotions was like tiptoeing through a minefield—any miscalculation could unleash disastrous outcomes.

A sudden grip on her shoulder jolted a75b99r84GE, sending a cascade of fear through her like shards from a shattered glass. Her heart thumped erratically, each beat echoing in her ears with the urgency of an alarm bell. Her muscles tensed, bracing for the worst as dread coiled around her spine like a snake ready to strike. She was paralyzed by the thought that the sentry might have detected some flaw in her gait, and if she dared to turn and face him, it would seal her fate. Her body went rigid, every nerve on edge, as if waiting for a verdict that could end her life.

"Is this your feeble attempt at emotional control? I expected better," came Kishida-Guan's voice, slicing through the air like a razor-sharp blade, laying bare her vulnerability.

a75b99r84GE turned to meet his gaze, taken aback by the presence of a holy one here, in the town center. In all of her sixteen years…she paused the thought realizing that he could have been wandering about daily and she—nor the other citizens—would likely have noticed…or cared. They were all just automatons mechanically going about their daily lives.

"Am I not even allowed to be startled?" a75b99r84GE retorted petulantly then proceeded to draw deep, calming breaths through her nostrils when the sentry took a step in her direction.

Kishida-Guan waved the sentry back, then responded, "Startled, sure. Emotionally reactive…I'd say it should have been far less pronounced, I must say. You've had an entire week to practice."

"Perhaps it would have been best if my emotions had been suppressed, then I wouldn't be struggling with this. Isn't there a way to do that? Reverse the process?"

"If there were," Kishida- Guan replied, his tone exasperated, "I would've done a week ago. But as a genetically enhanced, surely you can find a way to make it happen."

"I've been trying!" she snapped back, and tears pricked her eyes. "And I was doing just fine until you essentially threatened me last week. I may have been struggling, but I wasn't keenly aware of my differences until you pointed them out and then demanded that I control what feels incontrollable!"

Neither of them realized that a75b99r84GE was going through a phase of heightened moodiness because of hormonal changes, a common occurrence in teenagers. However, in her society, emotions were suppressed and any emotional expression was repressed, making such experiences nonexistent.

"Perhaps we should take this off the streets," Kishida-Guan replied, latching onto her elbow and guiding her towards the archive building.

"Why?" a75b99r84GE retorted, "it isn't as if anyone around us cares about what's happening."

"No, but, again, we know that your behavior can have a negative influence on some, and I'd rather not terminate citizens when we're in short supply with no current way to replace them at the moment. Now, let's get inside. There's something I want to show you, which is why I'm here. It may help you understand why emotions are so dangerous to a society."

After they entered the archival building, Kishida-Guan quickened his pace toward the rear, an area that she'd never ventured because A9021 had stated it would take her decades just to clear the shelves nearer to the front of the building, and he hadn't been wrong.

After a near-ten-minute walk, Kishida-Guan stopped before a massive door and pressed in an amazingly long alpha-numeric code into the antiquated-looking pad to the side of the door.

"It occurred to me," he started, while still punching on the pad, "that after our conversation that my I failed you," began Kishida-Guan as he halted abruptly and turned towards a75b99r84GE, "by not letting you know that the trials for the project are still years away."

"You told me that," a75b99r84GE replied softly, sniffling back the remnants of her emotional outburst as curiosity gained a hold on her.

"No, I intimated it," Kishida-Guan clarified, "but I didn't state outright that we're still facing at least seven years more before we even bring you in to begin the trial phase. That's the other reason I'm here. I cannot stress enough," he continued after a deep breath, "the importance of gaining control over your emotions. If you cannot, then you will be no good to us in this upcoming mission. Do you understand what I'm telling you?"

"If I cannot suppress the emotions that I was never meant to have, then I will be terminated," a75b99r84GE replied in a near-whisper.

"Precisely," Kishida-Guan confirmed with a clench of his jaw before unlocking turning a knob on the heavy door that they stood before.

"But…" a75b99r84GE ventured again, "why does someone else think that my emotions will serve the mission? Why are you so certain they won't?"

"I'll show you where my certitude comes from," he replied in a tone of resignation that confused her. But her curiosity, as he led her into the room, pushed her questions to the recesses of her mind.

"I think this is a good place for your mission to officially begin…albeit prematurely," he announced as they ventured deeper into the room filled with antiquated equipment, clothing, jewelry, and weaponry—each item shrouded in layers of dust and forgotten memories. "Specifically, to demonstrate to you why emotions are suppressed in our society and why it's so important that you learn to harness yours. If, during our mission, I deem them of importance, I will allow you to remove that harness. That is the best I can offer you at this moment."

"What can a room full of old relics teach me about emotions?" a75b99r84GE asked skeptically.

Kishida-Guan paused, his fingers tracing the edge of a massive sword that lay atop a scarred wooden table. "These are not mere relics," her murmured, turning to face her with a seriousness that rooted her to the spot. "They are reminder of how emotions, unchecked and rampant, led to the downfall of previous civilizations."

He picked up a faded photograph from a nearby box and handed it to her. It showed a large crowd, faces contorted in rage, buildings aflame in the background. "Emotional outbursts led to wars, destruction, chaos. Our society was built from the ashes left by such emotional indulgences. That is why they must be controlled—"

"But can't emotions be a good thing? Surely not all emotions lead to this level of destruction." a75b99r84GE queried, dragging her gaze away from the picture she was holding. Even though she leveled her gaze at Kishida- Guan, her mind was drawn to other pictures she'd come across in her job, displaying emotions that appeared far removed from that in this picture. Pictures that showed laughter and contentment.

"Emotions, regardless of their nature, possess a fierce potency—as you well know." Kishida-Guan skewered her with a piercing gaze, a sharp reminder of her recent emotional upheavals. "Indeed, they give rise to love, yet they equally breed hatred. One cannot embrace pleasing emotions without also grappling with their darker counterparts. Our mission in crafting these new realms was to forge unyielding stability; to prevent history from repeating its darker times that were always ignited by the unbridled fervor of the masses. Still, images alone cannot begin to explicate the true depth of that which I'm trying to convey."

He turned, beckoning her to follow. As they moved further into the room, a75b99r84GE felt an overwhelming sense of history closing in around her, each item whispering secrets of a tumultuous past. Kishida-Guan would occasionally stop by a relic to illustrate lessons on the dangers of unchecked emotions.

"This," he said, pausing before items of rusted metal, "is called armor and belonged to the leader of a nation whose passion for his country drove him to make devastating decisions with regard for consequence. His emotions clouded his judgement, leading to needless wars."

"What's war?" a75b99r84GE queried, eyeing the items with open wonder.

"It stems from the emotion of anger causing humanity to fight and terminate each other in extremely brutal manners."

Observing her persistent look of confusion, Kishida-Guan shifted her attention to another relic, its surface glinting softly under the ambient light. "It's best if I demonstrate," he said, his voice calm yet insistent. "Before you can truly learn to harness your emotions, you must first grasp why this mastery is crucial." His gaze was steady, almost probing. "To emphasize its importance, you need to understand the different kinds of emotions, and the most effective way is to observe them in action." Each word was deliberate, as if building a bridge to deeper understanding.

"This was our society before," Kishida-Guan segued while pulling out a set of circular items from a nearby box. He then went quiet as he manipulated the circles onto the relic. a75b99r84GE watched in fascination, completely oblivious as to what the item was or what it could do to demonstrate emotions to her in the manner implied by the doctor. After a few more minutes of apparent struggle, Dr. Kishida-Guan completed the set up and then pressed a button, which caused the two attached circular items to begin spinning slowly and a bright light to appear at the front.

"Don't look at the machine," Kishida-Guan instructed. "Look at the wall over there."

a75b99r84GE turned and immediately gasped, her legs giving way beneath her. She fell onto her knees watching in rapt attention at the wall which appeared to come to life with moving images flashing by slowly, depicting a spectrum of human emotions. There, etched by the glow of the projector, was an old man smiling, his arms open wide as younglings ran toward him. The image vanished replaced by another: a man and woman screaming at each other in the middle of a rain-drenched street. Then another: a female, curled up on her side, tears streaming; wailing in profound sorrow. Each scene switched until one appeared that caused a75b99r84GE to leap to her feet and race toward the wall: a man and woman embracing, their lips touching.

"Please, stop the image from leaving!" a75b99r84GE cried, turning back to Kishida-Guan, herself on the verge of an emotional meltdown. Kishida-Guan's gaze narrowed, but he paused the projector.

a75b99r84GE turned back to look at the couple, whose movements were now frozen. She reached up to touch the man's face, "what is this called?" She whispered, choking back tears from her voice, unable to grasp that the photo that she treasured had come to life before her eyes.

Kishida-Guan walked up to stand next to her, observing her, noting each flicker of emotion that flitted across her face. "That's how people express love for each other," he explained, his own voice barely above a whisper.

"Love?" a75b99r84GE queried in awe.

"It's one of the pleasant emotions…" Kishida-Guan began, but then stopped. "Our predecessors led lives brimming with emotional nuance. While this brought them immense joy at times, it also resulted in profound suffering and turmoil. This is what we wanted to avoid at all costs. We want humanity to continue without being torn apart by emotions that easily spiral out of control."

"But how can 'love' be something we don't ever want people to experience?" she asked, unable to tear her gaze away from the image.

"Because love cannot be isolated…" He paused; his eyes clouding with frustration because he knew she'd stopped listening to him. He turned and strode back to the projector. With a swift flick of his wrist, the image vanished into darkness. a75b99r84GE gasped, her fingers instinctively clutching at the cold emptiness of the now-bare wall where moments ago the picture she so cherished had come to life.

Kishida-Guan returned to her side with determined strides, seizing her arm and spinning her to face him with an urgency that left no room for resistance. Her breath caught as she was forced to lock eyes with him, the intensity in his gaze burning like a wildfire. "Love inevitably draws upon other emotions—both good and bad. Joy, jealousy, anger, despair…these all come with it. Did you not hear what I've said to you this whole time? Emotions are volatile and serve no purpose in a society which was designed to function on productivity."

Her breath hitched in her throat, the echo of the vanished image still burning behind her eyelids. She tried to cling to the lingering warmth it had stirred within her, but it was already slipping through her fingers like ash. Kishida-Guan's grip tightened, anchoring her in the cold, stark present. His eyes, fierce and unyielding, searched hers as if willing her to understand.

"Love," he said, "teaches longing, teaches need. And when it is threatened, it births anger, violence, and despair." He did not speak with bitterness or regret. He spoke as one reciting a formula, a truth so deeply embedded in his mind that it had hardened into law.

a75b99r84GE swallowed hard, blinking back the sting in her eyes, but the yearning in her chest did not dim. If anything, it flared brighter, reckless and hungry. Even as Kishida-Guan spoke of devastation, she found herself mourning something she had never even known—and already knew she could never let go.

As he steered her in silence toward the door, Dr. Kishida-Guan's gaze was distant, his thoughts far away. He had led her through the archives with a singular purpose: to show her the consequences of unchecked emotions. To convince her that not suppressing her emotions could be dangerous, not just to herself, but to the very fabric of their society. But now, with each step, a hollow sense of failure gnawed at him.

He had spoken the words—those truths he knew to be vital—but they had barely scraped the surface. Her fascination with the emotions, that spark in her eyes, hadn't been the acceptance he expected. Instead, she had embraced them, just as she had embraced the image of love. It was a rebellion, silent but unmistakable, as if she had already begun to see what he had tried so hard to eradicate from her mind.

A bitter taste curled in his mouth. He had tried to make her see reason, tried to break through the emotion she was so desperate to feel. But all he had done was feed her curiosity. His heart tightened; an emotion he couldn't suppress no matter how much he wished it. He had failed her, and in doing so, he may have failed them all.

As they neared the exit, his fingers tightened briefly into a fist, the motion betraying a tension he hadn't intended to show. He forced his hand to relax, but the effort left him feeling more vulnerable than he cared to admit. His voice, when it came, was low and strained, the weight of unspoken frustration hanging between them. "We are far from finished here," he said, his gaze locked forward as if trying to distance himself from the truth he was about to share. "Though I failed to make you see why your emotions must remain in check, you will still be expected to control them. Just as I am now—fighting against them every moment. I am the example you must learn from."

His words were edged with more than just authority; there was a quiet admission of the battle he faced within himself. He wasn't merely speaking of what was expected of her—he was grappling with the truth that, despite his own attempts at control, his emotions were a constant threat. And yet, it was this very struggle that he had to make her understand: he wasn't merely a teacher in this. He was a living warning.

As they exited the archive room, he secured the door behind them with an air of finality that echoed through the silent corridor like a far-off gunshot.

a75b99r84GE trailed behind him silently down the long hallway, her mind awash with images from history—the laughter, tears, rage, and joy so alien yet strangely alluring. Could these suppressed facets of human nature be more than remnants to be controlled? Could they enrich? Her thoughts were interrupted by Kishida-Guan's stern countenance; she would comply with his request if it meant staying involved in this mysterious project that promised further insights into the before time.

"I'll leave you to your tasks for today," he stated as they parted ways at the end of their journey through time and memory. "After all, I wouldn't want my presence to impede your productivity." His voice was firm but not unkind as he added: "Heed my words carefully—there are years ahead for preparation—but ensure that you do not falter when it matters most—for humanity's sake."

a75b99r84GE's gaze lingered on him for a moment longer as she watched him walk away. Kishida-Guan's words echoed in her mind as he exited the archives. They were not just words of warning. There was something deeper in them, something raw that he couldn't quite suppress—an admission of his own inner battle. He wasn't merely telling her what to do. He was struggling with his own emotions, acknowledging that his control over them was always in jeopardy. And yet, *he* presented himself as the model for how she must behave. He wanted her to suppress what she was feeling. To fight against what had begun to stir within her, even though he himself fought similar battles. If he could successfully harness his emotions, couldn't she? For the betterment of humanity?

The moment that Kishida-Guan returned to the lab, 41GB pounced, "Were you able to impress upon her—"

Kishida-Guan interrupted with an icy certainty: "I've sufficiently impressed upon her the necessity of quelling any budding emotions within her."

"While I continue to disagree with the importance her emotions may play in our mission, I do agree that, in the interim, she must learn to control them," 41GB stated.

"And I don't see how you can possibly think that emotions—volatile, unpredictable nuisances that they are—could possible aid in what we're trying to accomplish." Kishida-Guan fired back, then sighed heavily. "But it doesn't matter right now. All that matters is that she doesn't hinder what we're trying to accomplish; especially as the Chancellor has made it clear that he is prepared to see our society die," Kishida-Guan spat, unintentionally, then closed his eyes, trying to reign in the emotions that had nearly overwhelmed him during his time at the archives.

The sudden revelation did not go unnoticed by his fellow holy ones.

71PQv approached, "when did he express this to you and why did you not reveal this to us?"

"The day he gave us the go-ahead to complete our project, he asked why we shouldn't just let society die," Kishida-Guan stated, fighting to keep the disappointment and bitterness from his tone.

41GB added, her tone mimicking one of concern, "We have dedicated our entire lives to achieving perfection in our society, and then pouring every ounce of effort into overcoming the challenges we face because of the degradation of our genetic templates. But because our Chancellor cannot fathom the possibility of success in reversing this setback, he wants to throw away all that we've accomplished? It's madness that he does not have faith in the holy ones."

Kishida-Guan faced his colleagues, a somber look on his face. "Whether this is just a minor obstacle or an insurmountable challenge, I prefer to find hope in our abilities to resolve this critical threat to our society's future. The Chancellor's drastic admission remains a mystery to me, and I confess that my trust in his leadership was broken the moment he shared that belief. At this point, we could be wholly successful and he may still wish to see humanity end."

His fellow scientists regarded him without expression, unable to share in his emotional turmoil.

"What action do you suggest, doctor?" 41GB asked without inflection.

"I am not suggesting any specific action," Kishida-Guan replied. "I'm merely voicing concern that the success of this project must be indisputable so the Chancellor has no reason to act on his worries."

Observing silently until now, 71PQv finally spoke with clinical precision, "It is essential that we not only achieve success but also present it unequivocally. We must ensure every variable is controlled, leaving no room for doubt or uncertainty in the leadership's perspective."

That night, Kishida-Guan sat in his private quarters, staring out into the darkened sky, his mind consumed by thoughts of the project—and of a75b99r84GE. She had shown a vulnerability, an emotional depth, that neither 41GB nor 71PQv could fully comprehend. They saw only a potential asset to the mission, a tool to be shaped; though 41GB seemed to believe that her emotions could prove a useful tool—without really expressing why she believed that. But Kishida-Guan was suddenly beginning to see that potential utilized for a different purpose.

Her emotions could serve me, he thought, a dangerous gleam in his eyes. *With the right manipulation, I could make her my ally, my pawn.* His hand clenched around a glass of water; his knuckles turning white. The path ahead was clear. The Chancellor's rule was fragile—weak, even—and Kishida-Guan was not content to sit by and let it crumble on its own. He would hasten its collapse. And when the time was right, he would step into the void left behind, not just as the one who had saved them, but as the one who had always held the power.

A small, dark smile crept onto his lips as he thought of the possibilities. *Soon, I will make them see the truth. Soon, everything will change.*

7 years later

"Against the odds, we've triumphed," 71PQv declared, placing his hand on 41GB's shoulder. "For nearly twenty-five years, we devoted every waking hour—every moment of our lives—to this monumental endeavor."

If this statement had come from someone with a trace of emotional awareness, it would have erupted with jubilation, perhaps accompanied by ecstatic cheers. Instead, it was delivered with cold precision, prompting only solemn nods from the gathered scientists, acknowledging the magnitude of their success.

"While we've conquered the mechanical portion...we now face the moment of truth," Kishida-Guan interjected, his voice steady but thrumming with a barely contained excitement. "We will see if it functions as intended. The future of our society hangs in the balance. This first test trial involves inanimate objects, but the stakes will soar when we prepare to transport a living being. Every eye must be laser-focused on this test run, ensuring absolute perfection. Every piece of data must be meticulously monitored from start to finish. The slightest hiccup could halt our progress; failure is not an option. Everyone to your stations. Let's initiate trial run number one. 41GB, place the object on the platform."

41GB, with a swift, purposeful motion , moved towards the designated platform in the center of the laboratory. The object in question, a simple metallic cube, glinted under the harsh white lights as she set it down delicately, ensuring its position was exactly centered as per the specifications.

Kishida-Guan, his eyes scanning the room, nodded once sharply. "Begin the sequence," he commanded, his voice echoing slightly in the vast, sterile chamber.

From behind their consoles, technicians sprang into action, fingers dancing over keypads with practiced ease. Screens lit up with streams of data—temperature readings, energy outputs, spatial coordinates—all flowing in a steady stream as the machinery hummed to life. The air tingled with electricity; a physical manifestation of the tension that gripped everyone present.

As the sequence progressed, a low hum grew to a resonant thrumming. The cube began to vibrate slightly on the platform, surrounded by a shimmering field of energy that seemed to warp the very fabric of space around it. Kishida-Guan's hand hovered over an emergency shutdown button, ready to act at the first sign of anomaly.

Seconds felt like hours until finally, with a sound like a sigh of relief from the universe itself, the shimmering field stabilized and then slowly dissipated. The cube appeared unchanged to the naked eye.

"Status report," Kishida-Guan demanded crisply.

A technician nearby, responded promptly. "The object has been successfully transported and returned.

"But I didn't even see it disappear," 71PQv countered. "Review your data to confirm."

"Data confirmed," the technician replied after a few seconds.

"How far away in time did we set the trial for?" 41GB asked, leaning over the technician's shoulder to view the data for herself.

"Just a few seconds," the technician confirmed.

"Okay, readjust for a time jump of thirty minutes into the past. That way we can easily account for actual movement and collect data from a longer interval. After all, if anything is going to go wrong, it won't be in a matter of seconds," Kishida-Guan directed. "Inform when the recalibration is complete."

The technician turned back to her console and began the recalibration process, her fingers tapping swiftly across the holographic interface. The rest of the team watched in silence.

Kishida-Guan paced slowly back and forth behind the console team; his mind filled with possibilities and potential pitfalls. "While the recalibration is taking place, the rest of you double-check all safety protocols. While we're working with an inanimate object at this time, it won't be long before we're doing test runs with a person. This isn't just about proving we can do this—it's about doing it right," he reminded sternly.

Minutes ticked by as all of the technicians worked. Finally, the technician making the recalibration looked up from her console, giving a slight nod indicating readiness. "Recalibration complete. We're set for a thirty-minute jump into the past."

Kishida-Guan stopped pacing and turned towards the platform. He drew in a deep breath to steady his nerves then gave the command to commence, "Initiate sequence."

The machine restarted, and though the hum hadn't changed, it somehow seemed more foreboding, as if it recognized the greater stakes involved. The cube began to vibrate intensely, its edges blurring as the energy field enveloped it fully. Finally, the energy field peaked and the cube abruptly vanished from the platform. This time, there was no doubt that the cube had been yanked away through time.

The technicians monitored their screens carefully, eyes darting between numbers that represented energies and dimensions that humans were not meant to meddle with. Time seemed to tick by too slowly as they waited for the cube to return from the past.

Just as the tension with Kishida-Guan was about to erupt, the time portal reengaged, the hum filling the room again, and withing seconds the cube reappeared, exactly as it had been before it left—and without any fanfare. The only person capable of reacting emotionally did so by simply drawing in a deep breath of relief.

71PQv turned back to the technicians, "Review all data for anomalies. Ensure that there are no discrepancies between the cube's pre- and post-jump condition. We need absolute confirmation that the object returned exactly as it was sent, down to the atomic level."

Technicians buzzed around their stations, running diagnostics and comparing the results. The air around Kishida-Guan was charged with a mixture of anticipation and anxiety, as he awaited the final assessment. The success of this trial one would pave the way for the human trials. As time ticked away on humanity, mistakes and failures were not an option.

After an intense period of scrutiny, one of the technicians spoke up, her voice steady despite the immense pressure. "All data indicators confirm that the cube is identical in every measurable way to its original state. There is no deviation in material composition, no temporal distortions observed, and energy signatures are consistent."

Kishida-Guan allowed himself a small nod of satisfaction, "Excellent."

"Might I suggest that for our second trial, we attempt a longer leap with something organic?" 41GB queried, while her eyes continued to review the data stream.

"I concur," 71PQv interjected. "While this first trial was a success, by all measures, we must satisfy the true criterion: whether a lifeform will survive the jump."

"Precisely. This is a new area of exploration for our scientific team, and while we did our best to construct the unit based on research materials, we cannot be certain of our efforts unless we test it using the materials for which it was designed," 41GB elaborated.

Both turned to Kishida-Guan for approval of the next steps.

He paused, considering their suggestion. It was an important step, because they couldn't risk running a trial with a75b99r84GE at the onset, because they didn't have a replacement should the test fail, "I agree this is a necessary step; however, with fabrications on hold, we must select an individual of little import, preferably from an area of operations already saturated with productives. That way, if there is an issue, their loss won't be felt long term. Agreed?"

41GB and 71PQv nodded.

"Very good. While the recalibrations for organic time travel are taking place," he began, nodding at the technicians to begin work, "I'll let you two locate…one or two people, do you think?"

"We should have two," 41GB interjected. "If the first is in anyway unsuccessful, then we'll need to recalibrate and try again."

"Let's get to it then. I'll be in my office. Inform me when we're ready to proceed."

Kishida-Guan left the lab, his footsteps echoing in the silent corridor as he headed to his office. The lab remained a hive of activity with technicians and scientists scurrying to prepare the next phase of the experiment.

Meanwhile, 41GB and 71PQv departed the lab to locate two individuals who would act as the subjects for the next phase of trials.

"I'd suggest we find our volunteers from among the academics," 71PQv began, as they made their way across the cobblestone courtyard.

"Because we have not produced any new fabrications in the last seven years, and therefore there are no new younglings in need of instruction," 41GB concluded correctly.

"Precisely."

"I concur. There are four instructors and we only need two. If we lose one…or both…it will not affect the ability to train new younglings, once fabrication production resumes."

By the time 41GB and 71PQv returned with their two organic test subjects, the laboratory technicians were set to with their recalibrations.

A quick call summoned Dr. Kishida-Guan from his office. "I take it that everything is set to commence?" he queried.

"Yes," replied the lead technician, her hands poised over the control console. "Recalibrations are complete and all systems are primed for a trial with the first organic subject."

"Acknowledged," said Kishida-Guan, who then turned to face 41GB and 71PQv who stood by with the two chosen subjects. "41GB, guide the first subject to the platform."

Acknowledging the risk without fanfare, the septuagenarian male impassively followed 41GB in silent acceptance of the mysterious task he'd been selected to complete.

"Stand in the center of this platform, and do not move," 41GB instructed, then turned and walked back to stand next to her colleagues. "Medical personnel are standing by."

"Initiate sequence," Kishida-Guan instructed.

Once again, just as they had with the cube, all eyes were on the pod as it hummed back to life. The energy fields flared around the platform, encircling the subject in a vortex of shimmering light.

His figure blurred momentarily, then stabilized as the technicians worked fervently to monitor every parameter of the experiment.

The hum crescendoed and then, quite suddenly, the man vanished. The silence that followed was tangible, a collective holding of breath until the portal would decide to unveil the fate of their first living trial subject.

Minutes passed—each one stretching longer than the last—until finally, the energy field reactivated. The hum filled the room once more, and with it came the reemergence of the figure on the platform. He stood there, seemingly unchanged, blinking slowly as if waking from a deep sleep.

"Status report," Kishida-Guan called out immediately, his voice firm with anticipation.

The lead technician quickly scanned her data, her eyes flicking across various screens before responding. "All vital signs are stable; he appears to have returned in perfect health with no temporal anomalies detected."

A murmur of relief escaped Kishida-Guan who then nodded, allowing himself a moment's respite from his rigor. "Prepare for immediate medical examination. We need to ensure there are absolutely no underlying effects."

71PQv approached the platform cautiously, "Are you experiencing any anomalous effects?" he asked the subject.

"I am...unharmed," the man answered, his voice as monotone as one would expect from someone who lacked the ability to express emotions.

"Very good." 41GB documented his response before signaling for medical personnel who quickly escorted him for thorough testing.

Kishida-Guan considered this first organic trial run a success. "I'll go and inform the Chancellor of the progress," he stated, then lifted his wrist to punch in the command for the sentries to retrieve a75b99r84GE.

With the first organic trial completed and success confirmed, the laboratory settled into a focused calm. They had achieved more than a scientific milestone—they had opened a doorway through time itself. And through that doorway lay the only chance their dying world had left.

A sentry navigated through winding corridors with practiced efficiency and silence towards a75b99r84GE's quarters. His mission was clear: bring her to Kishida-Guan for what could potentially be a landmark step in human survival—a leap into uncharted territories of time itself.

a75b99r84GE had only returned from work and had placed her bucket for her evening water ration when the door to her living quarters slid open with a hiss. Her emotions, a part of her that she had learned to suppress over the last seven years, skipped with both anticipation and unease. The sentries' presence did not require words; their purpose was always unmistakable.

"Kishida-Guan requests your immediate presence in the laboratory," the sentry announced, its voice devoid of any intonation.

With a sigh of relief, a75b99r84GE was glad she hadn't been caught showing emotions, which would have led to her termination. She cast a longing look at her bucket of water.

"Given that I'm unsure about how long I'll be away, could I have my dinner before I leave?" she inquired, her stomach growling audibly.

The guard briefly left, presumably to get permission for the request. Upon returning, he just nodded and then turned his back to the entrance.

a75b99r84GE went back to making her dinner and then sat at her table to eat it quickly. When she finished, she stood and quickly set about tidying the room then addressed the sentry again, "Do I need to bring anything with me or will I be returning this evening?"

Again, the sentry moved away to consult with someone unseen. When he returned, he announced, "Bring nothing. The time you will be away is currently undetermined; however, accommodations have been arranged near the laboratory."

"That must mean that Dr. Kishida-Guan's project has been completed," she murmured to herself, her voice barely audible over the rush of excitement bubbling up inside her like a fountain of joy. Her grin stretched across her face, a wide, jubilant expression that seemed to light up her features. However, she quickly lowered her head, letting her hair fall forward like a curtain, ensuring the sentry wouldn't catch sight of her exuberant reaction.

Once she was sure her mask was securely in place, she raised her head, signaling her preparedness to the sentry. He turned on his heel and began to stride away, fully confident that a75b99r84GE was trailing closely behind him.

As they walked, her mind whirled like a storm—fixated on the enigmatic project Kishida-Guan had cryptically mentioned years ago. The implications for her future loomed large, a shadowy specter of possibility. She grappled with the crushing weight of being specifically fabricated for something so monumental, torn between the insatiable curiosity that propelled her forward and the paralyzing fear of the unknown challenges that lay in wait.

Upon entering the laboratory, she was instantly affected by the severe environment—characterized by the stark white walls, the mechanical hum of the equipment, and an observable distractedness among the gathered scientists and technicians. A scientist then approached her. "You are a75b99r84GE and I am 41GB. I have been selected by Dr. Kishida-Guan to be your facilitator through this process; however, we cannot begin until the doctor returns. He will return shortly. He's gone to notify the Chancellor of our progress before we proceed. Do have a seat over there, out of the way. We'll summon you when all is in readiness."

The halls were silent as Kishida-Guan made his way to the Chancellor's chambers, his steps echoing through the corridors of power. The gravity of their nearing achievement weighed heavily on his mind, but so did the potential consequences of introducing a75b99r84GE to the unpredictable variables of the before time.

He stopped at the large door and punched in a code which would signal, to the Chancellor, his arrival before the door would even begin to slide open and permit his entry. A few moments later, the doors opened with a hiss and he stepped inside.

The Chancellor, the eldest of them all, whose body had long deteriorated with time, was no more than a head floating in a preservation solution, wires protruding from the brain to the mainframe of their society. It was from this mainframe that he was able to keep apprised of all that happened within the society—of all of the realms—and to communicate with those few holy ones who were permitted time in his presence.

"You have completed the time machine and have succeeded with the initial trials," the disembodied voice stated before Kishida-Guan could even offer his normal, respectful greeting.

"We have, yes. I wanted to keep you apprised of our progress and our next steps."

"Proceed."

"We placed a cube within the unit and sent it back in time a few seconds—"

"And it returned undamaged?"

"Indeed."

"And the next trial? I assume you are not risking the fate of humanity upon the execution of a single test of an inanimate object."

"Indeed. We selected to individuals from the populace to ensure that a person could travel through time safely. The test was also an unmitigated success…at least at the time of this briefing. All indications are that the person, who was transported back in time a mere half hour, returned physiologically unaffected. To be certain of the readings, however, I am having him undergo a complete examination by the medical staff."

"And yet you chose to apprise me of your progress prior to the conclusions of those tests."

"As the outcome of the actual test was successful, I decided to apprise you so that you are aware that all of the work accomplished over the last quarter century was well worth the effort. The test itself was a complete success."

"And your fabricated one?"

"She has been summoned to begin her own trials. The primary trial of importance is, of course, through time; however, as we are uncertain as to where, precisely, she will be going in the before time, we must also consider the travel through space a factor also."

"And you did not think to test both time and space before placing your fabricated one in the chamber?"

This gave Kishida-Guan pause. They had to guarantee that a person could navigate through space-time as effortlessly as returning to a specific moment in history. This would undoubtedly be more complex, demanding a precise and delicate balancing of the intricate variables within the time-space continuum. "We will, without a doubt, proceed with conducting an additional trial with the second test person, to ensure every detail is meticulously prepared. Given the monumental success we've witnessed so far, we are resolute in our confidence that everything will unfold exactly as planned."

"Explain to me, again, the purpose of sending this fabricated one back centuries in time."

"Our future is bleak. Those holy ones who've lived for more than a century will not be with us as long as you have been. For some reason, the longevity genes added to the genetic template have also begun to degrade. The fabrications that were being produced to fill the needs of society were beginning to degrade to the point that we were terminating citizens in record numbers. It also resulted in the termination of our two geneticists, which you know resulted in the cessation of all operations. No new citizens have been fabricated in the last seven years. If we do not send a75b99r84GE back far enough, before the inception of our realms; to collect clean genetic materials in which to reverse the degradation, then there will be no hope—"

"Hope? You speak of hope?"

"I'm not certain as to your incredulity, Chancellor."

"About a hundred years ago, you decreed that we must infuse emotion suppressants into our fabrications. This was because some individuals dared to challenge the structure of our society: they began perceiving the opposite sex in corrosive, unhealthy ways; they wielded emotional justifications as weapons to drag down their productivity...and countless other transgressions that threatened to hurl our society back to the chaotic era when emotions rampaged unchecked, and humanity was rebellious, apathetic, lustful, and uncontrollable. Now, you have vehemently proposed that, once we restart fabrication production, we eradicate emotions entirely—"

"I'm still uncertain as to where you're headed with this, Chancellor."

"What is the point of hope in a society stripped of all emotions? Why does it matter if these manufactured citizens cling to hope for their futures? They're nothing more than creations set to work, only to be coldly terminated. Hope was once the privilege of the elder members of society, those fabricated before the emotional suppression mandate took hold. It was a cruel, calculated hope—a false promise that if they were productive enough, they might ascend to the mythical realm of the wise ones. A deceit crafted to keep hope alive and productivity soaring. But with the next wave of fabrications being devoid of feelings, hope becomes utterly irrelevant. So, I ask you again, what purpose does venturing back in time serve? Is it merely to harvest new genetic material to replace what is decaying? Or is there a deeper motive, Kishida-Guan? Perhaps it's your ego at play, your refusal to accept that this centuries-long experiment with an emotionless society is collapsing into failure. We are spiraling downwards, regressing instead of advancing, becoming more like soulless machines than living, breathing beings. What is the meaning of perpetuating humanity when there is nothing left for them to aspire to?"

Kishida-Guan's brow furrowed as he considered the chancellor's pointed observations and questions. His heart raced, as his brain scrambled to form a logical response that would withstand that Chancellor's critical scrutiny. After a moment, he drew in a deep, confident breath and pressed on, "Chancellor, it is true that our society operates on a cycle of creation, labor, and termination. However, the degradation of our genetic templates threatens not only the efficiency but the very sustainability of our system. By venturing back to the before time, we can potentially harvest original genetic material that has not been subjected to our eroding cycles. This isn't merely a salvage operation—it's a necessity to prevent our society from crumbling into obsolescence. It is important for humanity to continue…" he trailed off, unable to voice a logical reason for why. The Chancellor didn't miss that hesitation.

"I'll ask again, why not just let humanity die? Is it ego?"

He paused, his gaze fixed on the floating head before him, its eyes seeming to pierce through the fluid that preserved its ancient wisdom. After a moment, he managed to gather his thoughts again, "Yes, perhaps there is an element of ego involved, but there is also hope. Not in the emotional sense that once plagued humanity with chaos, but in the strategic use of hope as a stabilizing anchor. If we can ensure continuous improvement in our people's health and capabilities without emotional distractions, would we not be elevating our society closer to its ideal? Isn't this pursuit of perfection the ultimate goal we have all strived for?"

The Chancellor was silent for a moment, processing Kishida-Guan's defense. The solution-filled chamber bubbled softly as if contemplating the weight of his words. Finally, it spoke again, its voice resonating through the interconnected systems that kept it alive. "I believe that you completely overlooked my point." The Chancellor continued before Kishida-Guan could counter again. "Very well," it conceded with a digital sigh. "Proceed with your plan. But do so with caution not to allow your own emotions to interfere with the outcome of this mission and mindful that what you are attempting could either be our salvation or our undoing."

With a nod of acknowledgement, Kishida-Guan exited toward the laboratory, his thoughts heavy. He had, in fact, not overlooked the Chancellor's point. He understood it all too well—a silent acknowledgement that their civilization's pursuit of emotional suppression might have cost them the very essence of what it meant to be human; but he also saw, in their society, the improvements in productivity which saw their realm functioning at a level of perfection that was unprecedented. Wasn't that perfection far more desirable to one in which emotions, uncontrolled and unpredictable, played havoc?

By the time he reached the laboratory, he'd convinced himself, again, that his path for humanity was far superior to anything the Chancellor and their predecessors ever imagined, or enacted. He waved his hand over the panel and the door to the laboratory swished open. His gaze immediately spotted a75b99r84GE seated off to the side, and air of barely-constrained patience etched on her face.

He shook his head, hoping she had learned to manage her intense emotions better over the past seven years since their last encounter. 41GB was sure those emotions would eventually prove useful, but until then, he had no interest in witnessing any emotional displays from his created one. He gestured for a75b99r84GE to accompany him to a private section of the lab meant for confidential conversations.

"Everything is nearly set for your initial trial." Kishida-Guan announced. "However, after my meeting with the Chancellor, we agreed that one more test is necessary before moving you to the next phase. I expect this final trial to be quick, so there's no need for you to go back to your quarters. You may observe, but remain out of the way. Do you understand?"

"I understand," a75b99r84GE murmured.

"Then let us move back to laboratory." He stood and headed back toward his colleagues. "41GB, retrieve the second subject. The Chancellor has requested one more trial run, through space and time, to ensure that there is zero complications." 41GB nodded and moved to a small antechamber to retrieve the second individual. "Have we heard back from the physician as to the condition of subject one?"

71PQv nodded, "I have the report right here. The subject shown no sign of defect resulting from the jump through time."

"That's good to hear. 41GB, prepare the second subject. Technicians, recalibrate the system for a jump back in time. A short interval of ten minutes should suffice. Also, you are to set the position in space to realm 4183—our sister realm."

As the team worked with precision and focus, the room buzzed with the energy of anticipation, every movement choreographed in the dance of scientific exploration.

41GB soon returned with the second test subject, leading him to his place on the platform within the small chamber. Although his expression remained placid, a75b99r84GE watched him intently, anxiety swirling through her system as a rate that caused her nerves to tingle uncomfortably.

Kishida-Guan oversaw the final preparations meticulously, occasionally correcting a calculation or calibration; ensuring that every setting on the elaborate console registered the required parameters perfectly. With a final check, he turned to the lead technician, "Are you ready?"

"All is ready,"

"Initiate sequence."

"Initialization in three…two…one…" the technician announced solemnly.

The machine hummed, its lights flickering rhythmically as it gathered temporal energy. a75b99r84GE moved closer, her eyes wide with curiosity…and alarm. The air around the subject shimmered slightly, like heat over pavement in the summer, and then he disappeared in a blink, leaving only a faint echo of displaced air.

Silenced reigned as everyone in the room waited for the subject's successful return. Moments felt like lifetimes. Then, ten minutes after he disappeared, the subject reappeared.

"Well?" Kishida-Guan barked, his voice slicing through the tense air, prompting 41GB to dart forward with an urgency that matched the escalating stakes. The first individual had merely swayed with mild disorientation, but this subject was different.

The moment he moved away from the center of the platform, he collapsed to the ground, his body folding like a puppet whose strings had been cut. A hollow thud echoed through the sterile lab, reverberating in a75b99r84GE's chest like a warning bell.

The technicians watched in utter silence, recording each movement with detached efficiency. No one spoke. No one gasped. Only Kishida-Guan's lips pressed into a bloodless line, anger and concern for his project boiling in his blood; and from the shadows near the wall, a75b99r84GE felt a terrible shiver pass through her — as if the room itself had exhaled its final breath.

This wasn't supposed to happen. The machine was supposed to be perfect. As perfect as she was supposed to be.

Her palms felt clammy against the rough fabric of her uniform, as she clasped a fist full of the material tightly. A thread of panic stitched itself into her spine as she watched the medical team descend on the unmoving figure, their faces composed, their movements efficient—but a75b99r84GE saw it for what it was. They were too late.

For the first time in her memory, a sharp, raw instinct overwhelmed her conditioning: *What if I'm next?*

The thought hit her with the force of a physical blow. She stumbled back a step, her heart hammering in a frantic, chaotic rhythm she couldn't suppress, couldn't control.

Around her, the room continued to operate, a symphony of cold, calculated procedure.

Inside her, something had cracked—and no force of training or design could undo it.

"It would appear that the second subject perished because his body was already degrading. Had we been aware of this deterioration, we would not have selected him to participate in the trials," Kishida-Guan spoke in a measured tone, but the failure of the second subject left him seething inside. "While I do understand that this was a shock to witness; as it was for me also, we must set aside any discomfort that we may be feeling for the good of humanity. It should also bring you some relief to know that subject one suffered no ill effects in the first trial run." Kishida-Guan concluded the long-winded speech knowing that he'd left out valuable information concerning subject one. The potential that the first subject had survived because they'd only gone back in time; whereas the second subject was shot through time and space.

a75b99r84GE sat across from Dr. Kishida-Guan in a tense silence, her mind tangled in chaos and her body shivering slightly as if a stun grenade had detonated next to her. She was not a stranger to death, so although the abrupt passing of subject two had been disturbing, it wasn't the sight itself that unnerved her. The real jolt came from the realization that she was destined to step onto that platform soon, and she had no choice in the matter. The thought of being fabricated by Dr. Kishida-Guan and the other holy ones for this very purpose—to traverse time and gather the genetic materials crucial for humanity's survival—left her torn between duty and a deep-seated desire to flee. Not that she had anywhere to go.

Her gaze finally drifted to the machine—the cold, metallic beast that had claimed a life—then her eyes shifted back to Kishida-Guan. "How can you ensure my safety, Doctor? Given what happened to subject two, it's clear that there are risks that we might not understand."

Kishida-Guan's eyes narrowed thoughtfully, his fingers steepled before him in a gesture that resembled prayer. "While your concerns are indeed valid," he began, his voice calm yet firm, "I've already explained that the deterioration of subject two was due to an unforeseen variable, something that does not pertain to your situation. Even so, the medical team will be conducting a comprehensive examination of your person to ensure absolute safety." His gaze was steady, reflecting a deep-seated confidence. "We have every assurance that the machine we engineered is without flaw. Nevertheless, to quell any lingering doubts, I have tasked the technicians with meticulously analyzing every component of it, along with reviewing the data from the space-time leap that led to the demise of subject two. Although any delay at this juncture is less than ideal, we will not move forward until all uncertainties about your viability and that of the machine are completely dispelled. Since there are no other ways to address your concerns, we'll conclude this conversation to allow the medical team to start their tests on you. I'll entrust you to their expertise while I attend to my own duties."

Without allowing for further discussion, Kishida-Guan stood and walked away, signaling to the medical staff to take over the care of a75b99r84GE. He then moved over to speak to his colleagues, "71PQv, I'll leave you to oversee the tests and analysis. 41GB, as the mentor I've assigned to a75b99r84GE, go with her and oversee her medical exams. Every test that can be run, down to the cellular level. I want it done. Understood? I need to go advise the Chancellor."

41GB and 71PQv nodded, and Kishida-Guan turned to exit the laboratory. He was dreading the upcoming meeting because the Chancellor had already begun questioning the effectiveness and importance of his project. Kishida-Guan envisioned a future of relentless productivity for humanity, a stark contrast to the Chancellor's divided perspective. The Chancellor saw there being only one of two paths open: either thrust humanity back into an era resembling the chaotic "before time," where emotions ran rampant, or let humanity wither into extinction. For Kishida-Guan, these options were unthinkable, an affront to his unwavering commitment to progress.

His brow furrowed deeply as he navigated the corridors toward the Chancellor's quarters, his mind ablaze with sudden, disquieting questions. Why did the Chancellor permit him to pursue a project so starkly opposed to his own beliefs? As the supreme leader, he possessed the power to crush Kishida-Guan's initiative with a single decree, yet he refrained, igniting a storm of suspicion within Kishida-Guan. Was the Chancellor merely biding his time, allowing the endeavor to spiral into chaos and self-destruction?

Were these suspicions arising now solely due to the flicker of doubt that ignited within him upon subject two's demise? He found himself tangled in uncertainty, questioning if he was unfairly projecting his own insecurities onto the Chancellor just because their perspectives clashed. Yet, a part of him couldn't shake the feeling that there was more at play, leaving him torn between trusting his instincts and acknowledging his bias.

In their centuries of life, never had there been a time in which the Chancellor's beliefs and actions hadn't aligned with his own. Now they appeared to be at odds over every aspect of humanity's future.

He compelled his mind to quiet the storm of uncertainty as he halted in front of the Chancellor's door. Taking a few deep breaths to steady himself, he entered his identification and stepped back, waiting for permission to enter.

The door finally hissed open and Kishida-Guan stepped inside. The Chancellor's office was stark and minimalistic, illuminated primarily by the pod in the center, which held the holy one's head and the glow of ambient panels that connected him to the realms of the world.

"Step closer, doctor. I understand that there have been complications with your project."

Kishida-Guan took a deep breath, steadying himself before he began to speak. "Yes, Chancellor," he acknowledged with measured calm. "In preparation for the pre-trial runs you requested, we selected two citizens from the general populace. Subject one emerged from his leap unscathed, but subject two tragically passed away shortly after completing his leap. Upon further examination, we discovered he had already been undergoing physiological deterioration, which likely contributed to his death. Despite this setback, I remain confident in the integrity of the unit itself." Kishida-Guan paused, pursing his lips as if trying to stop himself spouting something which could undermine his position further, and further erode the Chancellor's confidence in him. "I assure you; we are taking exhaustive measures to prevent such incidents from recurring. Our medical team is currently examining a75b99r84GE for any underlying conditions which might hinder her ability to perform in the manner for which she was fabricated."

The Chancellor remained silent for a few moments as if processing the information. After a short pause, he responded thoughtfully, "The purpose of your project is to restore that which we are rapidly losing, not to risk lives unnecessarily; especially, as fabrication production is currently on hold. So then, why did you not carefully vet the two subjects prior to running the trials?"

"I confess that maybe my enthusiasm to start this project might have outweighed my caution. After all, it took us twenty-five years to reach this point, and with our society deteriorating, I sensed that time was against us…" He paused, unsure of how to fully articulate his reasoning. Instead, he attempted to shift the subject subtly, while not overlooking the implicit warning in the Chancellor's tone. "I can only assure you, Chancellor, that my team and I are fully committed to ensuring the safety and success of this project, including all future participants."

"Very well, doctor, you may proceed. But be warned. Humanity already stands on a precipice; it does not need a push from its own saviors."

With these stern words, the Chancellor dismissed Kishida-Guan; however, the doctor didn't move. "You have something further you need to report?"

"May I pose a query?" Kishida Guan asked, his voice quiet, an uncertainty in his tone.

"You are wondering why I am so opposed to your vision for humanity," the Chancellor rightly guessed.

Kishida-Guan's eyes widened, startled. "Yes, Chancellor."

"Centuries ago, before you and I were created to become the overseers for the new realms, the world was divided into its own versions of realms, each ruled by a different leader. During times of greatest concerns, these rulers often gathered in an attempt to control humanity—in one way or another. One such effort was put forth, if memory serves, by a President Elizabeth Marker, who wanted to sterilize a majority of the world in an attempt to control the population. Decades later, a President Saltzer, along with other world leaders, determined that population controls would be best served by eliminating all those deemed incapable of contributing to the productivity of society. It's from these templates that our current realms were based on; but we took it a step further in that we determined that humans were to be fabricated within strict guidelines so to only serve the needs of society. Over time, humanity has been stripped of all that makes us human. Look at me, for instance. I exist as no more than a head inside of this liquid bubble; my brain used to monitor and oversee all of the realms: dictating policy and providing directives to ensure all citizens move through their lives at peak productive levels."

"If you do not believe that humanity is on the right track and should simply die off, why allow me to continue."

The Chancellor was silent for a long moment, as if weighed down by memories too ancient to name. A faint, weary sigh broke the stillness. "Because, my friend, I too hold onto hope." His voice, when it came, was almost fragile, a rare and aching glimpse into his lingering humanity. "I believe that your project holds merit in aiding in humanity's survival; however, if you and your team are successful in replenishing our genetic stores, I would like you to consider restoring that which makes humans…human. Make this not just a step towards survival, but renewal, a restoration of some of the essence we've lost. But I do confess that fear holds me back from gripping too firmly to my hope; worry that in your frantic attempt to hold onto our present way of life, you might overlook what could be possible. Therefore, I implore you to remain open to all possibilities and continue cautiously, thoughtfully, and thoroughly in every single step of your endeavor."

Kishida-Guan did not respond. He bowed low in respect, masking the fracture line that had begun to split his loyalties. He turned and walked away with measured precision, but behind his steady pace, calculations had already begun to unfold. The Chancellor spoke of hope and restraint, yet all Kishida-Guan could hear was the creaking of a dying leader—and the need for a new architect to seize the reins of power. The fire kindled within him was still small, but it would not remain so for long.

"We conducted three additional test jumps with subject one," 41GB explained, leading a75b99r84GE toward the time-travel unit. "He returned each time only mildly disoriented. Considering his age compared to yours, and the fact that he wasn't genetically enhanced for this mission, the results have been promising. There have been some slight fluctuations in the unit that we are closely monitoring…" She paused, choosing not to create unnecessary concern. "Please proceed to the platform. We'll start shortly."

41GB moved away, joining her colleagues, who were deep in discussion. After a moment, they dispersed and positioned themselves behind the technicians.

"Let's begin," Kishida-Guan announced with crisp authority. "a75b99r84GE, are you ready?"

A knot twisted tighter in a75b99r84GE's core. She was far from ready, but she forced herself to nod, suppressing the tremor of anxiety that threatened to surface. This was her purpose, she reminded herself—what she had been designed for.

Without further delay or fanfare, her trial run commenced.

The chamber was stark and humming, its walls lined with observation consoles that pulsed faintly in the low light. a75b99r84GE stood within the stabilizer ring, a thin band of metallic circuitry weaving like a crown around her ankles. Tiny threads of light crawled over her skin as the technicians, sterile and silent, prepared for the readiness trial.

Behind them, the holy ones watched intently. Kishida-Guan quietly instructed the technicians to proceed with the initiation sequence. Beside him stood 41GB, her posture impeccable, her face an exact mirror of calm, and 71PQv, whose eyes flickered across the readouts with enviable efficiency.

A low chime sounded—the final cue.

A medical technician approached and handed 41GB a tablet, causing Kishida-Guan to glare in frustration at the interruption. 41GB accepted the tablet, waved the tech away, and stepped back to scan the information.

a75b99r84GE inhaled sharply as the stabilizer activated. Reality itself seemed to shudder around her edges; the space-time channel unfurling like a thousand invisible threads grasping at her molecular form. For a breathless moment, she felt herself slipping—not bodily, but fundamentally—as if her consciousness were being unwoven, examined stitch by stitch.

Then, suddenly—

"Shut it down!" 41GB called.

Everything went silent. The lights snapped out, leaving only a single beam spotlighting a75b99r84GE. She felt a lurch in her stomach, the unique sensation of being nowhere yet everywhere at once. She had crossed into the stream of time, but only for a breath.

Kishida-Guan's voice was terse: "Why are you stopping the trial run? Reset sequence protocols immediately."

"Wait. You need to see this," 41GB interrupted, offering the tablet to Kishida-Guan.

A medic hurried over to help a75b99r84GE off the platform, unsure if the sudden stop was related to her well-being. She swayed but dismissed the medic with a wave.

Her heart pounded irregularly against her ribs, but she knew she wasn't harmed. "I don't think the cessation was because of me," she whispered. The medic nodded but continued to guide her away from the machine. Though uninjured, a75b99r84GE's hands continued to tremble because something had triggered the unexpected halt.

Ahead, the three holy ones had gathered at the control platform's edge, speaking quickly and quietly.

"I can make my own way now," a75b99r84GE said, pulling away from the medic. When the medic moved away, she slowed her pace and angled herself slightly to better catch fragments of the holy ones' conversation.

"...how certain are we that the degradations are related to the trials?" 71PQv asked, his voice stripped of affect.

"More importantly," Kishida-Guan cut in, "how certain are we that our genetically enhanced will face the same issues?"

"I think, to err on the side of caution, it may be necessary to limit the number of trials we subject her to," 41GB murmured. "She is the only genetically enhanced we have, and we need her to make multiple leaps before inevitable degradation forces termination protocols."

When Kishida-Guan spoke again, his tone was hard with frustration. "Her termination is a forgone conclusion; however, right now, I agree we need to proceed with as much caution as we can, but we cannot—"

"You really should be seated," the medical tech approached, interrupting a75b99r84GE's eavesdropping. She nodded and allowed herself to be guided to a nearby chair.

Her stomach twisted—not from fear of the trial, but from the heavy realization pressing against her bones: she was a necessary sacrifice. An expendable one.

Outwardly, she showed no sign of distress. Inwardly, calculations spiraled: probabilities, risks, contingencies.

41GB approached, moving with the grace of a holy one. Her expression was schooled into perfect neutrality, yet as she drew near, she tilted her head slightly—a near-emotional gesture.

"The emergency shutdown had nothing to do with the unit. You were completely safe," 41GB said, her voice modulated to a register meant to convey reassurance.

a75b99r84GE nodded once, obedient, daring not to betray what she had overheard.

"The recalibration sequence will be completed shortly," 41GB continued, studying her. "Rest until then. I'll come collect you when we're ready to proceed."

It was not encouragement. It was a directive. A brittle beat of silence stretched between them.

In a voice so soft it might have been mistaken for a glitch if she was a robot, 41GB whispered, "Do not be afraid."

a75b99r84GE's eyes flickered upward, meeting the holy one's calm gaze. She wondered, fleetingly, if those words were Kishida-Guan's, mechanically conveyed—or if, somewhere deep within 41GB, a flicker of genuine sentiment had dared to surface.

"I'm not afraid," a75b99r84GE lied, keeping her voice steady.

41GB offered a small nod, then turned and walked away without another word.

Left alone, a75b99r84GE curled her fingers tightly into her palms, feeling the delicate strain in the muscles beneath her skin. She had been fabricated to endure; to leap through space and time. Yet now, the defiance she had struggled to suppress for the last seven years reignited: she would leap, not because she was ready—but because there was no other choice. She could not allow herself the luxury of hesitation or doubt. Nor could she believe in the illusion of safety.

The dimly lit room seemed to close in around her, its walls not just structural boundaries but reminders of her confinement. She was crafted for a purpose—but now, the purpose felt like a cage.

From the shadows, data pads beeped and hummed, their screens glowing like bioluminescent creatures of the deep sea she had once read about in a faded book—a relic of the past. These devices monitored every quantum vibration of her being, preparing her for something no one entirely understood. The trial was more than an experiment; it was a bridge to a desperate hope.

Time stretched on as technicians scurried about, their movements swift and silent, adjusting equipment and checking monitors—a symphony of soft clicks and whispers. In her peripheral vision, she caught Kishida-Guan speaking intensely with 41GB and 71PQv. Their discussion appeared heated—at least on Kishida-Guan's part. The gravity of their decisions pressed against the room like a storm waiting to break.

She closed her eyes for a moment, to block out the activity and to try to regain her center; her balance. When she reopened them, 41GB was standing in front of her again, accompanied by 71PQv and Kishida-Guan.

"We're ready for you," 41GB stated, stepping back as a75b99r84GE stood abruptly, moving without prompting toward the platform. The holy ones followed.

Kishida-Guan, despite his age, managed to close the distance between them. "We're going to send you over to our sister realm, 4183," he said. "We aren't going to set a time limit for your return."

a75b99r84GE halted, causing him to nearly collide with her. She turned, eyes wide with surprise and apprehension. "There are other realms, like ours?" she asked, incredulous. "And what do you mean, you will not set a time limit?" Her emotions surfaced again, unconstrained.

"Will you please," Kishida-Guan hissed, voice low and exasperated, "get control of your emotions." His lips pressed into a thin line.

"With all due deference," a75b99r84GE retorted, "compared to you, I am still but a youngling. Yet you command me to control my emotions, when you struggle with them yourself." Her words were pointed; arrows aimed at his pride.

Kishida-Guan closed his eyes, gathering patience. "I only struggle when dealing with you," he admitted more softly. "Now, focus." He then turned to 41GB. "And you believe *this*," he gestured at a75b99r84GE, "will aid us? These emotions?"

"It will likely assist her blending in when she returns to the before time," 41GB clarified, calm. "Not now…but then."

Kishida-Guan shook his head, disbelief and resignation warring within him. He turned to address a75b99r84GE again, his tone, deliberate. "Since we must limit jumps, we'll carefully review the data before pulling you back. And since we're still mastering this technology, remain stationed where the transport drops you. It'll help us lock onto your coordinates when it's time to retrieve you."

a75b99r84GE's pulse still raced, but she managed a small, obedient nod.

"Good," Kishida-Guan said, satisfied, and turned away, signaling the technicians.

41GB clasped her elbow and led her to the platform once more. The metallic ring encircled her as she stepped onto the cold, unyielding surface. She marveled at the routine impersonal nature of it all—how something so simple could carry such monumental risk. The air was charged, molecules buzzing in anticipation.

"Remember," 41GB said in her measured tone, "your training is paramount. Trust your instincts, but follow the protocols we've drilled into you." She hesitated—then simply nodded, stepping back.

a75b99r84GE gave a short nod, though the gesture felt hollow in her bones. She shifted her gaze to the other holy ones one last time. No farewell. Only duty.

The platform began to hum beneath her feet.

This was not bravery. This was necessity. And she was the sacrificial lamb.

The stabilizer flared to life, swallowing her in a torrent of white light.

Without Sanction

a75b99r84GE felt herself falling through the fabric of time, layers of reality peeling away like pages from a book in a windstorm. It was an endless cascade of blurred images and sensations, each more fleeting than the last. Her body was both absent and omnipresent, scattered across dimensions yet pinpointed at a singular moment.

She tried to focus, to remember the details of her purpose, but the torrent swept away coherent thought. Still, amid the chaos, a single clear moment flashed before her—41GB's almost imperceptible nod of assurance—and then she was thrust through an unseen boundary.

As suddenly as it began, the destabilizing whirlwind ceased. The white light dimmed to reveal a new, yet familiar environment— one that she was hurtling toward rapidly. Realization set in—she was falling. As soon as that realization struck, she hit the ground. Grateful that the distance hadn't been that great. Still, the impact left its mark, jarring her senses. For a breathless instant, panic threatened to rise—*Where am I? Had the transport failed?*—but she pressed her nails lightly into her palm, anchoring herself. Scan. Assess. Survive.

Her legs buckled under the sudden force, and she stumbled forward into a crouch. The ground was so similar to her own realm's that, for a moment, she wondered if her mind hadn't played tricks on her; that she hadn't actually traveled anywhere. The sudden appearance of a sentry approaching, disabused her of that notion.

"Unidentified citizen. Remain where you are," he commanded. "Stand, slowly."

She followed the instructions, making sure not to provoke the sentry into acting before asking questions. As she faced the command, she immediately observed that this sentry looked quite different from those in her own realm. He wore a high-tech uniform that gleamed with an iridescent shimmer under the sunlight. Another detail that stood out was his cautious approach toward her, some form of weapon firmly held in his extended hand. She wasn't precisely certain of her assessment, as she'd never seen anything like what he was wielding before, but something in his mannerisms led her to conclude that whatever it was could easily terminate her on the spot. She froze, barely drawing breath, for fear that any sudden movement would lead him to act with aggression.

When he moved to within a few feet, he stopped. "Unidentified citizen. Identify yourself!"

She wrestled with her thoughts. Panic clawed at the edges of her mind. She counted, barely mouthing the numbers—one, two, three—while her nails dug slightly harder into her skin. Forcing herself to steady her breathing, she tore her gaze from the sentry's piercing stare...*Say something—anything!* After the short battle with her will, she finally responding, her voice barely audible to her own ears, "My designation is a75b99r84GE."

"Where did you come from? You are not in the database." The sentry's voice was laced with a sharp edge of confusion, a tone that sliced through the air, challenging her presence with an intensity that made her question if the inhabitants of this realm were programmed to suppress their emotions as those in hers. Yet, the sentry's demeanor was unnervingly calm, lacking any trace of the emotional turmoil that churned within her. She wrestled with her thoughts, tearing her gaze away from the sentry's piercing stare, forcing herself to confront the precariousness of her situation with renewed urgency.

a75b99r84GE had never thought on her feet so swiftly as she did at that moment. Her mind buzzed with urgency as she replied, "I've only just graduated into the productive phase. There was an unexpected glitch at graduation, which explains the delay in registering me into the database." Her voice carried a hint of pleading, adding to the authenticity of her fabricated tale. "I was just on my way to the archives when I stumbled and fell. I believe I've injured my leg," she continued, her tone a perfect blend of vulnerability and earnestness. "Would you mind if I just sat here for a short while, until I feel able to move?" The ground beneath her was hard and unforgiving, but it provided a momentary refuge in her act of deception. Plus, the warning given by Doctor Kishida-Guan had chosen that moment to slam into her mind: *"…remain stationed where the transport drops you. It'll help us lock onto your coordinates when it's time to retrieve you."*

Not knowing how long the holy ones intended to leave her stuck in realm 4183 only made her anxiety worse. She couldn't just sit on the cobblestones in the town center without attracting even more attention. And what would she do when the locals finished their work and went to their living quarters? How could she explain that she had no living quarters to go to? She pushed those thoughts aside, realizing it was pointless to worry about something that hadn't happened and might not ever happen. For all she knew, the holy ones could be tracking her signal to bring her back home at that very moment... she hoped.

That hope began to wane when the sentry rejected her proposal, "You will follow me!" He gestured with the item she perceived, correctly, was meant for terminations, indicating that there would be no further discussion. Assessing the cold tone in his voice and the unwavering menace of his stance, she complied without further argument.

He turned and immediately began walking in a direction she recognized as it was similar to the one which housed the sentries in her realm. She'd never actually been inside that building and couldn't stop the curiosity that began to outpace her trepidation.

Navigating the cold, oppressive corridors of the foreboding structure, she was overwhelmed by the crushing atmosphere of control that seeped into every corner. How could a building exude such a suffocating presence?

Their journey ended at a formidable door that slid open with an almost imperceptible hiss the moment the sentry stepped up to it. He stepped aside and silently commanded she enter. As soon as she stepped inside, the door hissed closed. She spun back, her heart skipping a beat, knowing that she was well and truly trapped. Would the sensors back on her realm be able to penetrate the walls within this fortress in order to retrieve her? She began drawing in deep breaths in an effort to calm her runaway nerves again. She closed her eyes for a moment and decided that she needed to focus on something other than whether she was going to get out of there.

She chose to examine the room she was in, but the sparse furnishings—consisting only of a single table and chairs at the center—meant her survey was brief. Consequently, her thoughts shifted towards evaluation.

Was this a place the sentries brought people when they wanted to speak to them prior to termination. She'd only seen a few people in her realm led away by sentries rather than immediately terminated. Now, she wondered if this was why? Was she only being held here until the sentry got authorization to terminate her? Again, to bring a halt to her runaway thoughts, she forced herself to focus on something else—although in this room devoid of…everything…finding something else to focus on was difficult.

She observed the plain walls and the metallic table that glinted coldly under the stark artificial lights. This space clearly valued practicality over comfort, embodying the realm's core principle: utility devoid of emotion. It wasn't any different from her own realm. She pondered whether the sentry quarters back home resembled this one.

Her muscles trembled with nervous energy as she made herself sit on the hard chair, determined to keep her nerves in check. She dug her fingernails deeper into her palm this time, feeling the dull sting, focusing on it. It was real. It meant she was still present.

What if they had already decided to terminate her? The thought struck like a hammer, and she gripped the chair's edge harder, fighting the terror back into the corners of her mind.

Taking deep, slow breaths, she focused all her mental strength on calming her emotions. She knew that showing any sign of emotion now would not help her and might even worsen her situation.

As the hours crawled by with excruciating slowness, she felt an overwhelming pressure closing in, testing her endurance to its breaking point. Her mind, a chaotic whirlwind, had nothing to anchor it, spiraling into a frenzy of questions and frustrations about why she hadn't been rescued yet. Each passing minute gnawed at her sanity, leaving her teetering on the edge of despair.

In a fervent whisper, she chanted to herself with unyielding determination: *nothing has gone wrong with my lifeline back to my own realm.*

She jumped when the door slid open and an elderly woman strode in. She was clad in a brilliant white utilitarian gown that draped over her skeletal body loosely. Her paper-thin skin, wrinkled heavily with time, hinted that she was as old as Kishida-Guan. Her authoritative stride and purposeful demeanor, however, bore no signs of age and she immediately commanded respect as she seated herself across from a75b99r84GE, whose first thought was that this woman must be one of this realm's holy ones.

"I am Dr. Petrov," she declared without mincing words, "State your purpose and origin." Her voice was stern but laced with an undercurrent of curiosity which she couldn't quite conceal.

a75b99r84GE responded, unable to hide the slight tremor in her voice, "I am here to observe and report—"

"By whose decree, and how did you infiltrate our realm undetected?"

"By decree of the Chancellor, and the holy ones in my realm; however, I'm unsure if I can disclose the method. I suggest you reach out to my realm's leaders for answers. If you can." It suddenly occurred to her that realm 4183 might be completely unaware of her mission? Was Dr. Kishida-Guan's project meant to assist all realms; were all realms even in need of assistance? How interconnected—or isolated—were each of these realms? That internal question set off a spur of other questions bouncing about in her mind: just how many realms were there in her world? Were they all identical in nature or were some more aligned with the before time? How many held holy ones? Did they all bow to the Chancellor as the creator and overseer? Most importantly, were the citizens of this realm degrading as they were in hers? If not, couldn't she simply request to take back some of their genetic materials? That would certainly solve the issues facing the people in realm 4182.

Her gaze returned to Dr. Petrov, who was staring at her intently, her gaze, murky with age, radiating an unsettling intensity that sent chills down a75b99r84GE's spine, freezing her thoughts. Dr. Petrov's face subtly shifted when she realized that a75b99r84GE's attention had refocused, and she took that as consent to continue the interrogation. Leaning back in her chair, fingers knitted beneath her chin, she scrutinized the unusual visitor with a clinical detachment that belied the storm of thoughts brewing within.

"It is highly irregular for someone to arrive unannounced, claiming direct authority from the Chancellor," Dr. Petrov murmured skeptically. "And why would our holy ones authorize such an invasion?"

a75b99r84GE sensed the change in atmosphere; the room seemed to shrink around her, heavy with suspicion and unspoken threats lurking behind every word spoken henceforth. "I understand your apprehension," she replied calmly, "The holy ones I speak of are those in my realm. May I propose establishing a verification link between our realms? It could provide necessary clarity."

Dr. Petrov considered this before rising from her seat—a silent cue for a75b99r84GE to follow suit. "Come with me," she instructed tersely, "and I must warn you that any attempts to leave without authorization will not bode well for you." She turned and lead them out of the room and down another series of sterile corridors.

As they navigated through endless passageways, a75b99r84GE observed their surroundings keenly—the starkness was familiar yet it carried an undercurrent of severity far more pronounced than in her own realm.

They halted before an imposing metallic door adorned with various security clearance symbols. Dr. Petrov punched in a series of codes, and with a succession of electronic beeps, the door slid open, revealing a sprawling room bustling with individuals in lab coats amidst screens and blinking lights—an apparent nerve center not dissimilar to the one from which she'd leapt hours earlier.

Dr. Petrov gestured towards a console at the far end of the room. "From which realm do you hail? I will verify your purpose with the Chancellor."

a75b99r84GE nodded, though a tight knot had formed in her chest. She pressed her nails into her palm again, wincing when they found tender, broken skin. Willing her voice to stay steady, she replied. "I'm from realm 41—"

The air shifted—sharply—and before she could finish, the world tilted violently.

Sting of Return

There was no sensation of falling—only an agonizing tearing, a violent wrenching of every particle in her body, as though the very fabric of the universe sought to rend her asunder. The platform slammed into her back with a force that expelled the air from her lungs, leaving her gasping and disoriented. Harsh, sterile light blazed into her eyes, searing her retinas with its intensity

She slowly rolled over and instinctively tried to push herself up, but her hands slipped from beneath her. She fell again, her face nearly colliding with the platform. She looked down back at what had caused her to lose her grip and immediately noticed the blood, smearing the floor of the unit. She lay flat, bringing her hands up to look over her palms. Blood stained her palms from the crescent-shaped piercings where her nails had dug deep into flesh.

Footsteps echoed in a calm, rhythmic pattern, letting her know that the holy ones must be approaching. There was no urgency, no concern—only the relentless, measured march of duty.

"Physical injury observable," intoned 41GB, devoid of any trace of emotion.

"Neural agitation, rising," added 71PQv, his gaze briefly flicking to the monitors tethered to the platform, cold and analytical.

With immense effort, a75b99r84GE managed to lift her head slightly, every cell in her body screaming in protest. Yet, the true scream remained internal—a desperate, swelling panic that she knew she must smother beneath a veneer of control.

"I—was discovered," she gasped, her voice raw and shredded from the ordeal. "Lead away from the insertion point."

Dr. Kishida-Guan's shadow sliced through the glaring clinical light as he crouched beside her, exuding an air of ancient composure. His gaze narrowed slightly, the only indication of deeper contemplation. "You will provide a full account once we get you tended to," he stated, his voice low and nearly gentle—if she didn't clearly hear the iron behind it.

a75b99r84GE's arms trembled violently as she attempted once more to push herself up. Her bloodied palms more vivid red smears on the cold floor, a testament to her struggle. Suddenly, a fierce urge to sob surged within her, threatening to break free. *Push it down*, she commanded herself. *Control it.* Yet, her body betrayed her, tiny spasms rippling through her—a shudder of breath, a twitch in her battered hands.

41GB moved with methodical precision, applying neural stasis and pain-reliever patches to her temples without ceremony. The small, cold discs clicked into place with a finality that was almost comforting. "These will ease pain and side effects temporarily," 41GB informed her, before stepping back to allow the medical technicians to proceed.

a75b99r84GE's vision began to swim and blur from the effects of the patches as the medical staff carefully lifted her from the platform, her body now limp and unresponsive as she slowly lost consciousness. They carried her from the stark confines of the laboratory.

"We lost track of her," 71PQv stated as he watched the medical techs carrying a75b99r84GE away.

"This is of grave concern," 41GB added.

"There needs to be a way for us to keep track of her once she leaps. We know she's not going to remain stationary in the before time. It's a contingency we should have thought of already."

"We were focused on getting the time travel unit operational," 71PQv inserted.

"This is a new area, foreign to all of us," 41GB continued. "We couldn't have possibly thought of everything at the onset."

"Well now that we've thought of it," Kishida-Guan snapped, turning to face 71PQv, "get on it! And you," he continued, turning his attention to 41GB, "stay with a75b99r84GE until she's recovered. I want to know all that transpired on her leap. Do you both understand?"

41GB and 71PQv nodded, then turned and wandered away, leaving Kishida-Guan standing there fuming; chastising himself that he hadn't foreseen this issue.

As Kishida-Guan paced back and forth with his hands clasped behind his back, the soft hum of the lab's machinery intermingled with the distant clinks and clacks of technicians scrambling to revise protocols. His brow furrowed deeper with each pass, reflecting not just concern but a keen discontentment with the unexpected outcome.

"I should have seen this," he muttered under his breath, stopping briefly to glance at the blinking monitors from the medical lab showing a75b99r84GE's vital signs stabilizing. "We prepare for so many variables, yet it's always what you don't prepare for..." He trailed off, shaking his head.

In a corner of the lab, hidden from immediate view, 71PQv stood silently observing his superior's distress. He noted that Kishida-Guan always prided himself on his ability to anticipate and control, but today had proved that even his was not infallible.

His then glanced down at his processor as it churned through data at a frenetic pace, simulating possible future scenarios in rapid succession with the new parameters fed in to determine how to maintain location of their subject. As the simulations continued, he quickly determined that there would be no way to locate a75b99r84GE through the unit itself; that they would need to invent yet another device that she would either need to keep on her person or that would be injected beneath her skin. Either way, he knew one thing for certain—Kishida-Guan was not going to be happy by the further delays. And this *would* cause a significant delay since, just as with the time-travel unit, none of the holy ones, nor the other scientific technicians, had experience with this type of work.

Determined to regain control over the situation — and perhaps provide some solace to Kishida-Guan — 71PQv headed back to his workstation. His fingers flew over the console, typing commands and querying databases for any precedence or similar devices that could aid their new necessity. The screen blipped with a flood of information, datasheets on tracking technologies used in various other applications and times past. None exactly fit their unique requirements, but each piece added to his understanding.

"Perhaps," he murmured to himself, "a combination of these could be tailored to suit our needs." He still wasn't certain how to address this issue with the doctor, but at least he had the beginnings of a viable plan. He moved in Kishida-Guan's direction, just as 41GB approached from the other side. She'd returned from overseeing a75b99r84GE's medical care. Her face, as always, was unreadable, but her pace was brisk, as if it were her way of demonstrating the urgency and gravity of their predicament.

They both arrived at Kishida-Guan's side simultaneously and glanced at each other in silent acknowledgement that they'd wait to speak until the doctor was ready to listen.

Kishida-Guan paused in his pacing, noting the arrival of his colleagues. He gave a slight nod, a silent permission for them to speak. "Updates?" he demanded succinctly, his voice hardened with a mixture of anticipation and dread.

71PQv took the initiative, clearing his throat lightly. "We are considering new technologies to ensure we can maintain location tracking on a75b99r84GE during her missions." He hesitated for a moment before adding, "The proposals involve a blend of existing tracking systems, adapted specifically for our needs. We might need to design something that she can carry without knowledge or a way to embed it discreetly."

Kishida-Guan's eyes narrowed slightly as he processed this information. "How long will this take? We cannot afford more delays." His fingers twitched impatiently at his sides as he awaited an answer.

"It will require invention and testing," 71PQv responded earnestly. "But I believe we could have a prototype ready for field trials within a few weeks."

41GB added, "I will oversee the integration tests personally to expedite the process." Her tone was firm, leaving no room for doubt about her dedication to resolving the issue.

Kishida-Guan sighed deeply; the lines of responsibility etched deeply into his face reflecting his internal struggle with the pace of progress versus the necessity of precision. Turning to face both of them fully, he said, "Is there any way to facilitate things quicker? Each second that we delay, we risk more than just this project—we risk the future of humanity itself." He emphasized each word with a sharpness that conveyed the weight and pressure he was feeling.

"Not without potential errors which could risk the entirety of our endeavors," 71PQv stated.

"Very well. How is a75b99r84GE faring?" he inquired after drawing in a few calming breaths. "Where did the blood come from? Was she injured on realm 4183?"

"The blood appears to have come from self-inflicted wounds to the palms of her hands," 41GB explained. "The whys of this action will remain unknown until she wakens from the induced sleep we put her in. As this is her first trial leap, a thorough scan has revealed her to be in excellent condition with no indication of degradation. Her disorientation upon arrival back here was likely due to the effects of temporal displacement."

Kishida-Guan nodded slowly, absorbing the details with a heavy frown. "Keep her sedated for the time being. It will assist in her recovery, especially since she appeared emotional volatile upon her return."

"What of the detailed report you requested?" 41GB asked.

"I decided a reporting of her encounters on realm 4183 are irrelevant to our continuing project. What happened there is insignificant. Her return to the before time is where our focus will be greatest. We will, of course, have her relay what happened, but not in any official capacity."

"Will you be updating the Chancellor?" 71PQv asked when Kishida-Guan fell silent again.

Kishida-Guan hesitated for a moment, his eyes narrowing as he considered the implications. "Not yet," he finally said. "I will brief the Chancellor when we have solid progress or if an urgent issue arises. For now, our focus must remain on the creation of a tracker so to ensure we can retrieve a75b99r84GE when the need arises."

With a firm nod to both 41GB and 71PQv, he signaled the end of their discussion. "Proceed as planned. Keep me informed of every step." His tone left no room for argument, and he turned away, his mind clearly already racing with the next phases of their project.

As Kishida-Guan walked away, a mixture of determination and concern marked his stride. The numerous micro-delays were causing a multiple of setbacks and he felt each one as a stone around his neck, weighing him down. They needed to get this project back on firm tracks. The future of humanity demanded it.

41GB and 71PQv exchanged a glance as they watched Kishida-Guan walk away, mutual understanding passing between them. They both knew the stakes were high and failure was not an option. With a nod to each other, they turned to go about their respective tasks with renewed vigor, each driven by a sense of duty that went beyond personal ambition.

In another part of the facility, a75b99r84GE lay in a quiet medical bay enveloped in darkness, her breathing steady but shallow under the influence of sedatives. The medics moved around her silently, monitoring her vital signs and administering care with clinical efficiency.

Outside the bay, 41GB paused to observe through the glass. She watched as a75b99r84GE's chest rose and fell in a steady rhythm, her face serene yet utterly void of emotion—an eerie calm that belied the tumultuous experiences she had undergone. The patches on her temples glinted faintly under the dim lights, their medicinal purposes providing scant comfort to the viewer, knowing the brutal reality they masked.

Turning away from the glass, 41GB let out a slow, controlled breath. Her expression remained impassive, but the weight of their predicament was palpable in her rigid posture and the tight clasp of her hands behind her back.

Just then, 71PQv approached, his footsteps silent yet urgent. "I have initiated the design phase for the new tracking system," he reported succinctly. "We are exploring several advanced technologies including subdermal implants and quantum entanglement devices to provide constant location data without affecting the subject's bodily functions."

"Good," 41GB responded. "Ensure that it is discreet and foolproof. The last thing we need is for the technology to fail at a critical moment or to be detected and tampered with."

"I understand," 71PQv nodded, his features set in grim determination. "The balance between efficacy and safety is delicate. I'll proceed with maximum caution."

"I'll continue monitoring a75b99r84GE but am at your disposal should you require assistance." 41GB offered.

Deep within the core of the facility, machines hummed and minds raced, but outside the sealed glass of the medical bay, a stillness settled—an uneasy pause as if bracing for another storm. As 41GB and 71PQv parted ways once more, a subtle tension lingered in the air. They were running out of time, out of margins for error. And in the dark cradle of sedation, a75b99r84GE remained unaware that when she woke, she wouldn't be given rest—but another mission, perhaps even more dangerous than the last. The weight of her role—as a singular pawn on a vast chessboard controlled by the holy ones—was both an honor and a burden.

As the facility exhaled into its temporary stillness, her dreams stirred. Faces turned toward her, half-formed by memory, half-invented by longing. A German Shepherd leapt through a sunlit field. A man touched her cheek, then vanished. The images looped again and again—laughter, tears, heat, chaos.

In sleep, the past whispered to her.

Back at the lab, Kishida-Guan approached his colleagues, "Is a75b99r84GE fit to proceed?"

"I take it that the meeting with the Chancellor did not go well?" 41GB asked, knowing it was unlikely that Kishida-Guan would tell her about the conversation's contents either way. He tended to keep those discussions guarded.

"It was…enlightening," Kishida-Guan replied curtly, marking the turbulence within. "We proceed as planned. Prepare a75b99r84GE for the next trial run immediately."

Silence fell over the room for a moment before 71PQv, who had been quietly observing the exchange, stepped forward. "She's ready physically, but mentally and emotionally…I urge caution. We still have no clear understanding of what triggered her collapse."

"The transmission location prototype is ready to test?" Kishida-Guan asked, ignoring the concerns voiced. 71PQv nodded. He then turned to 41GB, "Are we ready to move forward with the training on the before-time holographic simulators?"

41GB's reply was measured. "We're still painstakingly piecing together believable scenarios from archival records. It will likely take several more weeks before we have a few holographic simulations robust enough for her to run through."

"Might I suggest that we send it through, alone," 71PQv interjected before Kishida-Guan could respond to 41GB's update; his mind focused solely on the prototype. "If we receive a viable signal and can retrieve it without issue—"

"That does seem a logical first step in testing the prototype," 41GB interjected. 71PQv nodded, then both turned to look at Kishida-Guan, whose lips seemed to be perpetually in a compressed state of frustration.

"The test will only confirm its viability at the insertion point, correct? Since it's a stationary object and can't move on its own?" he queried.

"I'm confident that if we can successfully lock onto and retrieve it, it will function equally well when in motion," 71PQv assured.

"And these tests will verify its effectiveness through layers of skin?" Kishida-Guan inquired further.

"I understand your point," 71PQv responded. "I'll encase the prototype in a material that mimics human skin to ensure we can track it even when enclosed. The aspect of movement will need to wait until a75b99r84GE conducts her trial leap. I suggest she holds the device initially, so we won't need to remove it if tracking issues arise."

Kishida-Guan nodded, his gaze narrowing with impatience. "Alright, let's proceed with what we can. Since we can't start holographic simulation training, we'll conduct a *single* trial leap with the prototype to ensure its viability. But, let me remind you both, these trial leaps aren't just for amusement. We need to assess a75b99r84GE's capacity to endure multiple leaps to determine whether she experiences any physical or mental degradation. We can't achieve that, nor our ultimate goals, if we keep delaying for the slightest reasons. We are now three months behind our schedule, which brings humanity closer to extinction."

The conversation came to an abrupt halt when a75b99r84GE entered the room, apparently dressed and ready to go, "You do not need to concern yourself over my wellbeing, as I am more than prepared to proceed."

41GB approached, "a75b99r84GE, your courage is commendable, but we must also consider your safety. After all, if you were to have an even more intense experience as when you returned from realm 4183, it could jeopardize all we have fought to achieve. The anomalies you experienced during that last simulation—could they not be indicative of something we have overlooked?"

"The most I can do is to keep you apprised of how I am feeling after each leap so that you may monitor me and use that information to potentially improve further leaps. We cannot allow ourselves to stagnate because of unknowns related to my mental or emotional condition. If I am able to continue, then I must do so. I cannot fail, for our world would be doomed, and every moment we delay in rectifying that which plagues our people edges us closer to irreversible decline."

Kishida-Guan observed the interaction, his thoughts conflicted. While part of him admired a75b99r84GE's dedication, another was concerned over this glacial attitude that she'd developed soon after waking in the medical bay. It seemed she was purposely attempting to appear even less emotional than his fellow holy ones. He recognized it was a facade, but he couldn't understand the reason behind it. Was she worried that his patience for her emotional outbursts had worn thin and that he might terminate her if she kept behaving so uninhibitedly? While it was something he knew he needed to monitor with her, he decided that now wasn't the time. They needed to get things moving again. "Okay, since a7599b84GE is ready to go, let's do the trial run with the prototype and review the data as quickly as able. I want her on that platform in half hour."

71PQv nodded and proceeded to collect the prototype chip that he and his fellow technicians had designed for implantation into a7599b84GE. If all went well, it would enable continuous tracking, allowing the system to locate her regardless of how far she strayed from the insertion area. He swiftly located a sheath to replicate the thickness of skin for encasing the device, which was as small as a grain of rice, and then positioned it on the platform. Together, the assembly was double the size of the prototype. "Ready to proceed," he announced.

"Adjust the jump to take the device back a hundred years. I need to confirm it operates correctly and as close to the time period in which we want her to return. Use our realm as a target, since we already know that the unit can transport between space and time effectively," Kishida-Guan instructed, prompting the technicians to quickly implement the necessary changes. "Initiate when ready."

"Initiation in three…two…one…"

The platform started its usual humming, buzzing with an energy everyone could feel. The air rippled as the stabilizer ring activated, its light so bright it almost hid the small device from view. The technicians focused on their screens. In just a few moments, there was a flash, and the prototype vanished. Silence filled the room as everyone watched the monitors closely, but as the minutes passed, there was no sign that the prototype had arrived at its intended destination.

The room was a sea of impassive faces, but Kishida-Guan's features were taut with anxiety. "Any signal yet?" he barked, unable to contain his agitation as he paced relentlessly behind the monitors, his gaze darting frantically.

"The device traveled a great distance…" 71PQv began, but was interrupted by a sudden beeping sound.

Everyone in the room turned towards the source of the noise—an alert from the tracking console. 71PQv quickly checked the data, his fingers tapping rapidly across the screen. "It's there," he finally announced. "The signal is not as strong as I'd like it to be, but it is stable. It has successfully arrived in our realm, a hundred years in the past."

Kishida-Guan moved closer to view the monitor himself, "And the retrieval. Is the signal strong enough to bring it back."

"Initiating retrieval protocols…now," 71PQv stated, as his fingers danced across the controls.

All eyes were fixed on the screen displaying real-time feedback from the retrieval process. A tense minute passed, and then another, until finally the signal strength increased and the platform engaged.

"Good," Kishida-Guan exhaled sharply, his relief evident though his face remained stern. When the prototype reappeared, he exhaled an audible sigh. "Full analysis. 71PQv, as soon as the trial run is concluded with a75b99r84BE, I want you working on a way to boost the signal strength. We don't need anything interfering with our ability to retrieve her."

71PQv nodded, then left to retrieve the prototype while 41GB moved over to where a75b99r84GE sat, her gaze glued to the platform.

"Everything is nearly set for your leap," she announced, "We've done all we can do to this point to ensure your safety. You must trust in the preparations we have made. Dr. Kishida-Guan is personally overseeing the input of your coordinated jump so to ensure zero errors. See? Personal attention to every detail." She moved out of the way to allow a75b99r84GE to view the space where everyone seemed busy with preparations. Kishida-Guan was sitting in the spot usually occupied by one of the technicians.

After a few minutes of preparation, 71PQv consulted with the technicians and then turned around to announce, "All systems are ready. Please step onto the platform." Everyone's attention shifted to a75b99r84GE, who suddenly felt self-aware. She took a deep, calming breath and let 41GB gently guide her by the elbow to the chamber.

71PQv approached her, saying, "No matter what you go through physically, it's crucial that you do not let go of this." He extended his hand, waiting for her to open hers to receive the chip.

"Wouldn't it work just as well if I kept it in a pocket?" she asked, glancing at the tiny, rice-sized pellet in her palm, now stripped of its outer casing.

71PQV shook his head slightly. "It has been tested with a skin-like covering, not a fabric one. I think there's a higher likelihood of it slipping from your pocket than you holding it tightly in your hand. Furthermore, although we haven't confirmed this yet, we believe the chip needs to be in direct contact with your body during the leap for optimal data transmission and reliability. Moreover, since the chip will be implanted under your skin before your actual leap back in time, it's best to test it under those conditions which closely replicate its actual use."

"Do you have any additional questions or concerns before we begin?" 41GB queried.

a75b99r84GE swallowed hard, tightening her grip on the small chip. It's cool surface barely registered against the warmth of her palm. "No, I think everything's clear," she responded, her voice a bit steadier than she felt inside.

41GB offered a curt nod and stepped back, allowing space for the final preparations. a75b99r84GE edged closer to the platform, each step measured and deliberate. The metallic ring awaited—silent yet ominous—as it had so once before.

She could feel Kishida-Guan's eyes on her, heavy with expectation. The hum of the machinery swelled around her as technicians moved fluidly through their last checks, their faces a blend of focus and fatigue.

"Remember, keep your hand closed tightly around the chip during the leap. It's crucial that we get this right," Kishida-Guan called out from his station, his tone clipped. The urgency in his voice did little to ease the knot of apprehension tightening in her chest.

With a final nod to everybody in the room, a75b99r84GE stepped into the center of the platform. The familiar buzz of energy prickled at her skin as the stabilizer ring activated, casting an eerie glow that seemed to pulse with its own heartbeat.

"Initiating jump sequence in three...two...one..." Announced one of the technicians.

The floor beneath her vibrated subtly at first then with increasing intensity as the machinery propelled her beyond the confines of their realm and time itself. She clenched her fist around the chip, focusing all her concentration on not letting go.

She closed her eyes against the glaring light, focusing inward. The world dissolved into a kaleidoscope of colors and sensations. Streaks of temporal energy wrapped around her like ribbons in the wind. Time stretched, pulled at its seams by the demands of their technology. Then, with a sudden jolt that seemed to snap everything into place, it ceased.

Her eyes snapped open and once again, she was plummeting through the air, hurtling towards the unforgiving cobblestones below. Her chest constricted with panic as her body braced for impact, but it came quicker than expected. With a bone-shaking thud, she slammed into the ground, pain exploding from her tailbone like a shockwave. She drew in deep breaths, trying to will the painful throbbing away.

After a few minutes, she decided to test her ability to stand, but each muscle quivered as she tried to gain her balance and so she sat back down, deciding to give herself a few minutes to recover from the jolt her body had sustained. She cursed the relentlessness of the temporal shift, desperately wishing there was a way to land on her feet instead of being flung through space—even if it was only a short distance; although, she was certain that this second time was a bit of a longer drop.

Finally, slowly, she rose, testing her legs' tenuous hold on stability, but her head began spinning with a disorienting dizziness that threatened to topple her again. She sank back down to the ground, a frustrated sigh escaping her lips.

Dr. Kishida-Guan wanted her to move away from the insertion point, to assess the chip's capability beyond mere stationary function, but until the world stopped tilting dangerously, she refused to gamble with fate.

Thought of the chip caused her heart to skip a beat and she quickly unfolded her grip, sighing in relief when the chip lay in the center of her palm. It was coated in her perspiration, which had her questioning whether this would affect its efficacy. Had this contingency been taken into account? She shut her eyes and closed her hand around the chip again, then began taking in slow, calming breaths. She couldn't allow herself to focus on something which was completely beyond her control, so she focused on calming her body and mind.

Once the dizziness subsided, she chose to observe her surroundings until she felt confident enough to move. The place seemed familiar, but something didn't feel right. She decided that she wouldn't be sufficiently able to determine what was wrong until she managed to move. Carefully, she stood up, steadying herself. She closed her eyes for a moment to gauge her equilibrium, then proceeded with a careful step. When she was certain she wasn't going to collapse, she opened her eyes and began walking slowly along familiar paths, but the cold, clean lines of the architecture provided no comfort. *Had they truly ever done?* she wondered.

She didn't really have a mission set for this test run, so had no reason to wander around exploring. After all, this was her realm, only a century removed. She merely needed to move far enough away from the insertion point to test the technicians' capability of tracking and retrieving her from any place, any time.

She stopped walking and slowly rotated in a circle, taking in her surroundings as if seeing them for the first time through a lens that stripped away all illusions and revealed the heartless core underneath. The surroundings were recognizable, yet somehow different.

There were only a handful of citizens, far fewer than she would have anticipated being here a century ago. Those whom she could see wandered aimlessly, moving with a strange, mechanical precision—like cogs in a soulless machine. Each step seemed intentional, yet led nowhere. Their eyes were vacant. Their presence felt accidental. Though it was similar in her own time, these individuals, if possible, seemed even more oppressed.

How could time collapse in reverse? She wondered. How could this place—eroded and hollowed—possibly precede the seamless, humming world she had just left behind? It made no sense. The decay wasn't ancient; it was advanced. This couldn't be the past. It felt like something falling apart in real time.

And yet…wasn't this what Dr. Kishida-Guan had feared? A slow, forward slide into dissolution, masked by the illusion of progress. Not a civilization evolving. A civilization unraveling.

As she looked more closely at the buildings, unease coiled in her chest. A filmy layer of grime dulled the once-pristine surfaces; streaks of corrosion crawled across metal facades like veins. These structures were never like this in her time. They were sterile, polished, whole. A mirror of the world's order.

Before she could begin to make sense of it all, a flicker of movement arrested her thoughts. Her gaze snapped to the shadowed space between two buildings—something had shifted in the dark.

There—just at the edge of her vision—a figure began to unfurl from the darkness, as if the shadows themselves were giving birth to it. It didn't move so much as it emerged, one hesitant step after another, as though uncertain of its own right to exist.

a75b99r84GE's pulse quickened—not from fear, but from the almost electric curiosity that seized her. She had been briefed that contact was possible, even likely. But not this. Not like him. This anomaly stood apart from the others—not aimless, not hollow. He had intention.

He shuffled forward; his movements deliberate but strained. There was something disturbingly familiar in the way his body moved—a cautious stoop, a dragged foot, a kind of muscle memory from a time long buried. As he stepped into the waning sunlight, she could make out his features—or rather, the remnants of them. His face was a map of erosion: skin paper-thin and mottled, stretched across a skeletal frame that spoke of endurance rather than survival. The bones of his skull pressed like whispers from beneath his flesh. But it was his eyes that anchored her. Not just with their intensity— but with the strange feeling that they weren't entirely alive. They glinted with something ancient, something that felt aware.

Recognition flickered across his face. Then disbelief. Then horror. His expression cycled like a system caught in a loop—until, finally, something settled.

"You should not be here," he rasped.

His voice was brittle, like a sound pried loose from a rusted hinge—but it vibrated through her like a warning embedded in her core.

"I…I'm just observing," she replied, the words stumbling from her lips. She didn't usually falter. But under his gaze, her clarity fractured.

"Observing?" he repeated, this time more to himself than to her. His expression twitched—processing, rewinding. "You're here already. Of course. Of course you are." He glanced around sharply, not with fear, but with the wariness of someone remembering too late…something. His gaze swept over the aimless citizens in the distance, then returned to her with an intensity that made her feel pinned in place.

He stepped in, voice low. "Who sent you? Did I send you? I already sent you?" Then, softer still, almost reverent in its dread, his hand stretching outward towards her, but his gaze glazing over as if seeing past her: "This is not a window. It's a wound."

He looked at her again not with confusion, but with the weight of someone speaking to his own mistake. "You play with time like it's a toy," he said. "It is not. It resists. It remembers."

a75b99r84GE's breath hitched as a strange vibration rippled through the air. The man took a step forward, as if to say more—his face a lattice of recognition and regret—but whatever words followed were stolen.

She didn't see the portal open.

She *felt* it.

Like the pull of a deep tide that she hadn't realized was rising. Her body convulsed, spine arching as the air around her folded inward. The man's expression twisted into something that might've been panic—or perhaps guilt—as her vision blurred and sound warped into a static hum.

He reached out. Too late.

She was gone.

****

Back inside the lab, the silence was abruptly shattered. A technician turned from his console; his voice flat, unmarred by the urgency his words should have carried. "We've made an error in our calibrations."

The holy ones froze.

Kishida-Guan's eyes snapped toward him. "Explain," he ordered, already striding forward.

The technician blinked once, slowly, and gestured to the display. "The system indicates a forward leap to the year 2478, not the designated target of 2278."

Kishida-Guan halted. "That's impossible."

"Apparently, it's not," the technician replied. "It is the recorded output of the leap."

"I saw who was seated at the console," 41GB said suddenly, her gaze drifting toward Kishida-Guan. "Wasn't it you, doctor, who keyed in the final sequence?"

He faltered for just a moment—too brief for most to notice, but 41GB was not most. Kishida-Guan's jaw tightened. "I may have done. I don't recall."

"It doesn't change the fact that she was sent too far…in the wrong direction," 41GB stated.

208

"I do not know how it happened," the technician replied, staring forward as if waiting for a command that hadn't arrived. "But the data confirms it."

Before anyone could respond, 71PQv stepped in, physically shifting the technician aside. "We've overloaded this system for weeks—calibrating, recalibrating, pushing timelines through a matrix that barely stabilizes for one target year before we shift again. We've been reckless."

"Reckless doesn't begin to cover it," Kishida-Guan muttered, pacing. "This means a75b99r84GE is now operating inside a timeline fifty years past our extinction threshold. A time where she should not, cannot, exist."

"She may be in contact with remnants of a dead world—or worse," 41GB said, her voice almost tentative. "She could be facing something that outlived us."

"Why haven't we retrieved her?" Kishida-Guan snapped. "She should've been pulled the moment the error was detected."

"I'm initiating the extraction now," 71PQv said, fingers flying across the console. "Anchor locked," he said, tension bleeding through his otherwise measured voice. "Initiating pull now."

The generator began to vibrate, a low hum growing into a sharp pitch. The lights around the chamber flickered as the portal's center pulsed erratically.

Kishida-Guan stood motionless, watching the waveform collapse. "Hold it steady. Don't lose her!"

Everyone turned as the air within the containment chamber shimmered, bending around a central point. Light fractured—then condensed—and with a sudden snap of force, she was there.

a75b99r84GE collapsed to her knees on the platform, breath ragged, eyes wide and unfocused.

For a heartbeat, no one moved.

Kishida-Guan stepped forward but hesitated, his gaze locked on her face. Something had shifted. The expression she wore wasn't confusion. It was calculation.

Recognition.

But she wasn't looking at Kishida-Guan. She looked past him.

"He seemed to be waiting for me," she said softly. "As if he knew."

Whatever will had kept her conscious slipped—her body crumpling as if time itself let her go.

A Step too Far

Kishida-Guan was the first to arrive in the medical bay the moment he received news that a75b99r84GE had regained consciousness. Unlike before when he appeared concerned for her wellbeing, even if it were second to the overall arch of the mission, he seemed not to care in the least whether she was suffering any ill effects from this leap.

"Report," he demanded briskly, his gaze scanning her eyes for any signs of physical or psychological marring.

"The chip…did I lose…" she gasped, her gaze falling to the palm of her hand, now empty.

"The chip is safe," 71PQv confirmed, and a75b99r84GE sighed heavily in relief. "Excellent work maintaining your grip."

"Tell us what you saw," Kishida-Guan demanded again. "Give us your report!"

"Something went wrong, only I'm not certain what that something is," she replied, her voice airy with uncertainty and the residual effects of disorientation. "There was a man," she continued, trying desperately to collect her wits and her thoughts. "He appeared from the shadows, a specter amidst the phantom of humanity…" her words began to slur, and she fought against her eyes drifting closed. The ceiling above her blurred into a thousand fractures, like the broken skyline she'd left behind. A low, keening sound echoed in her ears—it took her a moment to realize it was her own breath. *Don't let it fall,* a voice inside her whimpered, but she couldn't grasp what *it* meant—the past, the future, or herself.

"What was administered to her?" Kishida-Guan asked urgently, directing the question to a nearby medical technician. "Did you give her a sedative?" The technician nodded in response and resumed his work, unbothered by Kishida-Guan's anxious reaction.

His voice, so sharp and unyielding, shattered across a75b99r84GE's somnolent senses—and for a heartbeat, it wasn't Kishida-Guan at all, but the hollow-eyed man from the broken future, screaming wordlessly into a crumbling sky.

"She's making little sense," 41GB interjected. "Perhaps we should wait to question her after the medics have had the opportunity to scan her for decline. She doesn't even know to *when* she went, and it's obvious that she needs rest. She's been through quite the ordeal."

Kishida-Guan nodded sharply, his expression a mask of steely determination that revealed nothing. His eyes were cold and unyielding as he turned on his heel, the motion decisive and commanding, an unspoken declaration that the discussion had reached its abrupt end, at least for now.

Through the haze of sleep's calming grip, a75b99r84GE felt a hand on her shoulder. "Rest now," 41GB murmured, her calm tone an imitation of comfort. "Tomorrow will be another day."

Those words lingered in a75b99r84GE's mind long after 41GB had departed, echoing through her consciousness as she drifted further into oblivion. In the depths of her induced slumber, fragmented visions of the man from the shadows haunted her dreams. His words replayed like a broken record, each iteration layering more weight upon her chest: "You play with time like it's a toy...It remembers."

When morning light filtered thinly through the medical bay's shielded windows, a75b99r84GE awoke with a start. Her body felt leaden, every movement an effort as if she were swimming against an unseen current. The room was silent except for the soft electronic hum of machines monitoring her vital signs.

She lay motionless for several minutes, allowing her mind to settle as she tried to gather the scattered remnants of her last mission. The man's face—etched with a haunting expression that shifted from recognition to sheer horror—was slowly dissolving from her mind's eye, like a painting blurred by rain. She strained to remember his words, but they too started slipping away, dissipating like wisps of fog caught in a morning breeze. No matter how hard she fought to regain hold, the memories kept escaping her grasp, leaving her feeling more disconnected and less certain of what had actually transpired during the leap.

With a frustrated grunt, she attempted to push herself up, but her muscles protested with a sore stiffness, the aftermath of her temporal journey still lingering in her bones. The door opened quietly, and a medic walked in, his expression one of clinical indifference as he approached her bed.

"Morning," he said, his expression flat as he checked the monitors before turning to look at her directly. "How are you feeling?"

"Sore. Stiff. Still mildly disoriented," she murmured. "And there's a heaviness…like I'm still not fully here."

He nodded, making notes on his tablet. "Despite the obvious impact that the time travel is having on you in the moment, your recovery times are remarkable. The sensations you are feeling should pass within a few hours. Are there any other symptoms that I need to be made aware of?"

She shook her head, which took considerable effort. "Are you privy to information about my leap? Where I actually went?"

The medic paused, "Nothing beyond the post-medical analysis."

a75b99r84GE gave a hesitant nod, then whispered, more to herself than to the medical tech. "I keep catching glimpses of...something...there's a man...he said something important. At least, I think it was. But I can't quite grasp hold of it."

"If you can remember, do so," Kishida-Guan demanded in a voice sharp as a blade. She hadn't even heard him enter the room; his presence as silent as a shadow slipping across the floor.

Flanking him were 41GB and 71PQv, their expressions unreadable, like sentinels carved from stone. She knew all too well what their appearance signified; it was time to report. Yet, her mind was a battlefield, thoughts scattered and elusive, resisting the command to coalesce into coherent memories.

When she remained silent, Kishida-Guan began pacing at the foot of her bed, "You didn't go back in time as intended," he began, trying to remain calm but still expressing an extreme agitation. "We know where the mistake was made, but I'm more interested in hearing about where you actually ended up. It seems that you encountered a period of time that should not exist according to our predictions and estimations. So please, tell me everything you saw when you arrived."

a75b99r84GE's response was quiet and direct, seemingly ignoring his request. "Where did I go?"

Kishida-Guan pursed his lips, annoyed that she wasn't following his directive—the topic he wanted her to focus on. "You were supposed to go back in time, but due to an error during calibration, you were sent one hundred years into the future instead. Now that I've answered your question, please focus on what you observed."

a75b99r84GE closed her eyes and tried to sort through the jumbled memories. "I've been trying to remember, but—"

"Try harder!" Kishida-Guan demanded. "What…who…did you see? Was our realm still standing?"

a75b99r84GE closed her eyes, willing herself to concentrate with every fiber of her being. "The realm, yes. Still standing…barely. There was a man. Warned me that we should not…" her voice faltered as she fought desperately to grasp hold of memories that had begun dimming the moment she awoke, scattering further to the recesses of her mind, and then, finally, were completely out of reach. "I'm sorry. It's gone now. I can no longer see…" she trailed off, closing her eyes again against the anger emanating from Kishida-Guan's gaze.

Kishida-Guan's frustration was palpable, his fists clenching at his sides as he attempted to maintain his composure. "Very well," he said, his voice a controlled calm that belied the storm of thoughts raging within. "Perhaps later we'll be able to find a way to coax those memories from you. For now, 41GB will brief you on the next part of your training."

41GB spoke up, "As soon as you're cleared, we'll begin running holographic simulations to prepare you for your assigned leap to the before time. It will give your body a reprieve from the stresses of time leaps."

71PQv spoke up, "That will be acceptable, as we should postpone further jumps until we have the opportunity to run a full neural panel on her to ensure that she's operating at full capacity, especially since she is obviously experiencing lapses in memory recall…" he trailed off when he saw the storm clouds building on Kishida-Guan's face.

"Do I need to remind you that our time, the opportunity to save humanity's future, is limited—"

"Not if what a75b99r84GE saw is indeed accurate," 71PQv interjected.

"What did she see? Tell me! She certainly cannot!" Kishida-Guan replied, his tone less than patient. "For all we know the jump so far into the future played havoc on her mind. Or what she experienced, what she saw, was so traumatic that her mind invented the whole thing. Our best…our only…option is to attach a recording device to her. Set it to begin recording automatically after a preset time so that nothing is missed during her jumps again. We thought that her genetic enhancements would protect her against time travel…" he trailed off, shaking his head in frustrated bewilderment.

71PQv waited a moment to ensure the doctor had finished his tirade, "While the thought of a recording device sounds plausible, it would be wholly impractical, as it would need to send a signal through time. If that is even a possibility, it would take far too long to develop the technology; far longer than I'm certain you are willing to wait."

As if to distract her from the debate being conducted at the foot of her bed, 41GB place a hand on her shoulder, "a75b99r84GE, are you feeling improved?"

a75b99r84GE's eyes flittered over, her gaze slightly unfocused. She shook her head and then nodded, "I'm sure that I will be fine, once the fog lifts fully," she murmured.

"Try to focus. Is there anything that you can recall from this last jump? Anything that was said to you by the man you encountered?"

a75b99r84GE closed her eyes again, as she tried to claw back the fleeting images from her mind's recesses. "He said…something…I'm sorry…I can't remember. It's just gone."

41GB nodded. "Alright. Don't strain yourself further now. Rest is what you need."

Turning away from the bed, 41GB walked towards her colleagues, who'd continued their discussions while walking out of the medical bay. The uncertainty of a75b99r84GE's condition was something she felt needed to be addressed, even over potential monitoring device invention. "We may be pushing her too hard," she said directly, cutting through their conversation.

Kishida-Guan turned slowly to face her; his eyes hard but his voice steady. "This project is bigger than any one individual, 41GB. You know what is at stake here."

"Yes," 41GB responded, maintaining her composure despite her rising anxiety. "But at what cost? We are manipulating time itself, altering human capacity—"

"To save humanity," he interjected sharply. "Do not lose sight of that."

41GB paused, choosing her next words carefully. "Understood. But consider this: If we break her in this process, if we lose her to madness…or worse…what does that say about us? About our humanity?"

Kishida-Guan's expression relaxed a little, though his eyes still showed signs of inner turmoil. "She'll be working through the simulations over the next month or so, allowing her body enough time to heal. I won't approve any additional trial leaps to ensure her ongoing well-being. Her next leap will be to the before time. Meanwhile, she'll have ongoing assessments to confirm she hasn't suffered any lasting physical or mental harm. Does that satisfy you?"

41GB gave a nod of approval and changed the subject. "I concur with 71PQv that halting our progress to try to create a new device would be irrational since it's unlikely to work."

"It was just an idea," Kishida-Guan blurted out, his voice tinged with frustration. "I just can't stand being left in the dark, not knowing what she's seeing! It could be of monumental importance…" he trailed off, then turned and walked away from his colleagues.

41GB and 71PQv exchanged a look, their expressions unreadable yet hinting at shared concerns. They understood the pressure Kishida-Guan was under, even if they themselves couldn't feel with that same intensity; however, they also recognized the risks of pushing a75b99r84GE too far, too fast. If the project to save humanity's future was the end all, be all, then a75b99r84GE was their most pivotal asset.

She was the singular thread anchoring the unraveling hopes of their world—a creation fragile enough to shatter, yet strong enough, they hoped, to carry everything they had left across the abyss of time.

A week following her recovery, a75b99r84GE was abruptly thrust back into the demand of working. From her previous discussions, she anticipated embarking on an exploration of civilization from the before time through holographic simulations, a looked-forward-to time that had sparked an uncontainable excitement within her. However, on the eve of the simulations, the three holy ones visited her with news of a slight alteration to her training schedule. Dr. Kishida-Guan explained that the upcoming weeks would be devoted to rigorous training designed to fortify both her mind and body. Their concern stemmed from the physiological and mental effects wrought by her two preceding leaps. Yet, Kishida-Guan appended the training regimen with an intriguing caveat.

"After all," Kishida-Guan remarked, with a contemplative air, "you do not know the challenges you'll be exposed to in the before time." Thus, she was immersed in virtual simulations that rigorously tested her problem-solving acumen, strategic thinking, physical prowess, and emotional resilience. The simulations were so vividly realistic that she often felt as if she were genuinely living through them.

In one particularly harrowing simulation, she found herself ensnared in a blazing inferno, the building around her moments away from catastrophic collapse. With quick thinking and resourcefulness, she managed to carve out an escape route just as the roof disintegrated and crumbled. The ensuing explosion and scorching heat that chased her exit were so lifelike that she collapsed on the ground, instinctively shielding her head.

She was thrust into one punishing scenario after another. Each demanded every ounce of her wit, strength, and agility, pushing her physical and mental endurance to its brink.

However, each simulation lacked one crucial element: emotions. It seemed as if the holy ones either didn't consider them significant, or, in the case of 41GB who was in charge of creating them, did not understand the importance well enough to know how to incorporate them. Thus, despite the adrenaline of the scenarios and her body's physical reactions, there was an unnerving calmness in her own emotional response—a flatline where there should have been peaks and troughs of fear, anger, elation.

One evening, after a particularly harrowing simulation which involved evading capture from a dozen sentries in an over-exaggeratedly hostile realm, 41GB approached a75b99r84GE as she rested in the recovery area. The soft glow of the medical bay lights cast gentle shadows across 41GB's face, making it appear as if she were concerned.

"You are pushing yourself exceedingly hard," 41GB observed, handing a75b99r84GE a nutrient-rich beverage designed to expedite her recovery. "Remember, while your physical and mental capabilities are beyond that of any of the other citizens within this realm, you are not invulnerable…nor are you invincible."

a75b99r84GE took the drink, nodding in acknowledgement. "I understand, but I feel it's necessary. Every test I undergo prepares me more for what could lie ahead."

41GB let out a soft sigh and her demeanor softened. "I understand your desire to prove yourself capable of handling this mission, but it's important to maintain balance. Yes, you were genetically engineered for this purpose, but don't let the mission harden you to the point where you lose sight of its importance. I haven't said this to you before, but, thinking back, I believe it was wise for the geneticists to instill emotions within you. After all, the time we are sending you back to was full of intense emotions. If you were to behave like a robot, you would stand out too easily. So, I'll say it again—don't let the training or upcoming mission strip away your humanity. You may need it."

The dissonance between her physical experiences and her emotional responses became glaringly apparent during the following simulation. It was as if 41GB had deliberately set the tone to monitor her emotional reactions. The simulation was unlike any environment she'd been thrust into prior, in which she was often pitted against adversaries or dangerous circumstances. In this one, the surrounding environment was almost serene in comparison even though the massive number of people appeared to be in a constant state of hurry. Her mission was to surreptitiously retrieve genetic samples from passerby without being detected, as this was how the holy ones perceived her actual mission would take place. The sounds, smells, colors—and activity—were nearly overwhelming in their detail and authenticity.

Yet a75b99r84GE moved through the crowded streets, bumping against shoulders, silently observing—and completely detached, as if viewing it all from afar. It wasn't just that the people around her were holograms; it was that her emotions were self-muted, controlled too tightly to allow herself the luxury of release.

After successfully retrieving the samples, she paused for a moment at the exit portal. The hustle and bustle continued around her, but she stood still amidst the chaos. Somewhere deep inside her, she realized that just a few months ago, she would have stood here, soaking up everything, basking in the wonder of it all. Yet despite the realism, her emotional responses remained unnervingly muted. The simulations left her body exhausted, but her mind untouched, detached. Where fear, exhilaration, even anger should have surged, there was only a steady, unbroken calm.

The holy ones stood vigilantly on their usual control platform; their eyes fixed upon the scene below with an air of detachment.

"If she doesn't mentally return from wherever she's gone," 41GB mused, "she is going to draw suspicion very quickly." Her gaze was steady, yet there was an underlying tension in her posture, a subtle shift that betrayed her own uncommon concern.

"I noticed the change beginning in her after her first leap," Kishida-Guan observed, his tone measured and thoughtful. "Since then, it's as if she's doing everything that she can not to allow even the smallest emotion to bleed through." His eyes, dark and probing, followed her every move with an intensity that suggested both curiosity and unease.

"I cannot see how this will serve her when she goes back to the before time," 41GB stated, reiterating her point with a firmness that resonated in the air, "as I have said numerous times before."

Kishida-Guan had long harbored doubts about the emotional side of their genetically enhanced being. Watching her now—her interactions nonexistent, her emotional connections severed—he found himself reluctantly agreeing with 41GB's assessment. Her emotions, once viewed as a potential detriment to their society, now appeared as a missing component to their mission. He still perceived emotions as a peril to their society's delicate balance, yet for the specific demands of this mission, he reluctantly conceded that they might prove indispensable.

Despite his self-reflection and acceptance, he sincerely doubted that her recent endeavor to suppress her feelings had anything to do with his past admonitions. This latest attempt at suppression was something different—perhaps something she encountered during her leaps that had fundamentally altered her perspective.

Kishida-Guan crossed the room in a few quick strides; his brow furrowed in concern. "I think we need to adjust our approach," he stated to his colleagues. "We may need to reintroduce her to scenarios where emotional engagement is necessary. She needs to be able to—at the very least—mimic the full spectrum of human emotions if she expects to blend in seamlessly."

"There is no need for her to imitate anything," 41GB remarked, her voice almost snapping—an unusual sharpness that hinted at emotions she had long been conditioned to suppress. "Remember, she has feelings. We just need to emphasize the significance of letting them express freely again."

"She might not agree to cooperate unless there's a motivation," 71PQv chimed in, his expression betraying nothing, though a faint tension tightened the line of his mouth. "After all, the use of emotions is not encouraged."

Kishida-Guan remained silent for a moment, his emotions less restrained than theirs, wrestling visibly with a growing unease. "Perhaps," he said at last, his voice low and contemplative, "we need to make her remember what it is to *feel*—not just to survive. If we fail, it will not be the before time that exposes her. It will be her own emptiness."

"Maybe we should simply integrate the need to use them into the next few simulations," 41GB suggested.

Kishida-Guan's gaze drifted back to a75b99r84GE, who now stood motionless amidst the swirling holographic crowd. A pale ghost of what she had been.

"Force their return," 41GB pressed.

Yet even as they turned away to begin preparing for the next simulation, the unspoken truth remained: they were not cultivating her humanity, only weaponizing it—a necessary deception for a world where emotions had long been classified as a defect.

Emotions, Edited

As the first light of a new day crept into the laboratory, a75b99r84GE entered with the same demeanor she had worn for months: phlegmatic; calm like the surface of a still lake. The air was filled with the quiet hum of equipment. Dr. Kishida-Guan, seated at his desk amidst a sea of glowing screens, glanced up from his computer as she drew near. His face, usually a mask of neutrality, was now shadowed with a gravity that seemed to weigh down the very air around him. The lines on his forehead were deeper, his eyes holding the heavy burden of unspoken thoughts, instantly pulling her focus to the unspoken tension in the room.

"Come join me," he said, gesturing for her to come over. He waited for her to sit down—he noticed she did so stiffly—before outlining her activities for the day. "Today's session will differ from those we've done before," he began, skipping any formal greeting. His tone was serious, sharpening her focus. "We'll immerse you in a holographic simulation that mimics potential real-world interactions similar to those of the before time. In this first simulation, you'll encounter non-aggressive behaviors, which will challenge your ability to interpret and respond to subtle cues. This is where your emotions, often considered problematic and unreliable, might actually prove to be valuable—"

"So, all this time I've been suppressing them—" a75b99r84GE began, her voice tinged with frustration and a hint of disbelief.

"You'll have to revive them," Kishida-Guan interjected with an air of finality.

a75b99r84GE quickly stole a glance at 41GB, who had suddenly swiveled her head, her eyes fixed intently on some invisible point in the distance. This subtle but decisive gesture led a75b99r84GE to conclude that Dr. Kishida-Guan wouldn't be altering the structure of the simulations is he didn't align with 41GB's perspective on the matter.

The realization that 41GB was intentionally pushing her to embrace her emotions, despite the years she had dedicated to learning how to stifle them, ignited a spark of anger within a75b99r84GE. However, the thought that followed burned even hotter: the possibility that her emotional coding on the day of her fabrication had not been an error, as Dr. Kishida-Guan had initially believed. This revelation suggested that the drastic measure of eliminating the geneticists might have been unnecessary.

Her eyes flicked back toward Dr. Kishida-Guan, a fleeting glance loaded with the weight of her thoughts. His piercing glare in response made it abundantly clear that he understood precisely what was transpiring in her mind.

Even though the changes were implemented without any debate, a75b99r84GE found herself quietly acknowledging them. Yet, she couldn't suppress the flicker of excitement at the thought of facing a new challenge. She understood the importance of her feelings, but struggled with balancing the need to control them without eradicating them completely. Her mission had evolved from simply surviving and observing to the more daunting task of interacting with and possibly integrating into the society of the past, leaving her torn between her original purpose and this unexpected new role.

Dr. Kishida-Guan continued, "The individuals you will meet today are programmed to exhibit a range of emotions—from joy to curiosity…well, you understand. Your task is to engage with them in a way that fosters trust; to gather information without escalating any potential conflicts. Go ahead and follow 71PQv over to the simulation chamber."

As soon as she stepped into the simulation chamber, the door clanged shut, the lights dimmed, and a faint buzzing sound filled the air.

"We will begin with a simple simulation," 41GB's voice crackled over the intercom, "which should begin in three…two…one."

The environment around her transformed dramatically, shifting from the sterile, cold gleam of stainless-steel walls to the vibrant, bustling atmosphere of a small-town marketplace. It was a scene reminiscent of the vivid, colorful images she had studied in the archives. The air was alive with the lively chatter of merchants and shoppers engaging in the age-old dance of commerce, their voices weaving together in a symphony of negotiation and camaraderie. Subtle undertones of music floated through the air, played on traditional instruments she had only ever encountered in digital archives, their melodies adding a nostalgic charm to the scene.

The aromas that wafted through the simulated ventilation systems were intoxicating, a rich tapestry of scents that conjured the essence of foods being hawked by vendors lining the cobblestoned streets. The fragrant bouquet of spices, roasted meats, and freshly baked bread mingled in the air, creating a sensory experience that was almost overwhelming.

People moved about the marketplace with a purpose, their footsteps echoing softly. Some paused in their busy rhythm to cast curious glances at her, their eyes briefly lingering on her before they continued on their way. She stood there, rooted to the spot, a mix of awe and fear pulsing through her veins, as she took in the vibrant tableau unfolding around her.

Outside of the chamber, Dr. Kishida-Guan observed on a massive monitor, muttering words of encouragement filled with frustration, "Move, girl! You've got to engage. Stop standing there like a statue."

"Give her a minute," 41GB interjected. "This is all vastly unfamiliar and overwhelming—even for me, and I'm just an observer."

"She won't have the luxury of freezing up—"

"That's why we're running all of these tests and simulations. To prepare her. So, let her prepare herself."

Dr. Kishida-Guan let out a deep breath through his nostrils demonstrating his frustration, but he didn't belabor the point, since 41GB was technically correct.

Inside the chamber, a75b99r84GE took a deep breath, reminding herself to remain observant but unobtrusive. She wandered through the market, her senses absorbing every sight and sound. Her heart pounded in trepidation and wonder. She bent over a stall and drew in a deep inhalation, closing her eyes in euphoria over the aromas the foods there emitted. Her fingers brushed against fabrics so soft that they unfurled at her touch, gliding from their folded state.

"What is this?" she inquired of the vendor.

"Silk, miss."

"Silk," she repeated, savoring the word. "And what do you use it for?"

The vendor gave her a quizzical look and then answered, "Um…to make clothing, miss. Shirts, pants, dresses."

"Ah, yes, of course. I just haven't…" she trailed off, not knowing the words needed to express the fabrication of clothing, as she'd never done so.

The vendor squinted at her. "Haven't had someone who didn't know what silk is. You're definitely not from around here, are you?"

She smiled weakly, "Thank you for the education," she replied, hoping it was the correct thing to say to end a conversation then turned and moved away.

She turned to move away when a small group of children ran up to her, their eyes wide with curiosity. "Who are you?" one dared to ask.

"You dress funny," another added, impudently.

a75b99r84GE looked down at her jumpsuit and realized that they hadn't taken her attire into consideration when beginning this simulation. Her objective was to blend in, but her clothing definitely caused her to stand out. Perhaps their choice had been deliberate, to test her improvisation under imperfect conditions.

She crouched down to their level, her eyes softening as she addressed the curious little faces before her. "I'm a traveler," she explained gently, "from far away, and I'm here to learn about your beautiful place." Her tone was measured but warm, a balance she hoped she'd gotten correct as she'd never engaged with individuals this size in more than a formal, educational setting.

The children seemed to accept this explanation with a mixture of awe and excitement. One girl, bolder than the rest, grabbed a75b99r84GE's hand and tugged. "Come see my mama's shop! She makes the prettiest necklaces!" she urged enthusiastically.

Allowing herself to be guided by the child, a75b99r84GE followed. As they weaved through the bustling market, she took mental notes of everything around her—the interactions, the transactions, and particularly how emotions played into these human engagements.

The mother, upon seeing her daughter leading a stranger to her stall, initially looked alarmed but her expression softened when she saw a75b99r84GE's open demeanor. "Welcome," she said cautiously, studying the visitor's unusual attire but with an inviting smile. "My daughter seems to have taken quite the liking to you."

"Your work here is beautiful," a75b99r84GE commented sincerely, pointing at the intricately crafted necklaces displayed on the wooden table. As she spoke, Dr. Kishida-Guan and 41GB watched from their monitors, observing how naturally empathy and interest were woven into her interactions.

"This is very different from what I am used to," a75b99r84GE continued, exploring this newfound way of interacting. "Where I'm from, we don't have such beautiful creations."

The necklace vendor, intrigued by this foreign visitor, leaned closer. "Where is it that you're from?" she asked, her voice a blend of curiosity and caution.

"It's a place not many know about," a75b99r84GE replied, choosing her words carefully to maintain the guise of a distant traveler without revealing too much. "We value different things there—knowledge and productivity above all else. But seeing all this," she gestured around the market, "it makes me realize how much beauty there is in diversity."

The woman nodded thoughtfully. "Beauty and knowledge are not mutually exclusive," she mused. "Perhaps you will take a piece of our world back with you."

"I'd like that," a75b99r84GE said, her genuine interest causing the woman to smile warmly.

Behind the scenes, 41GB whispered to Dr. Kishida-Guan, "See? She's adapting. Learning on the fly. It's remarkable."

"Yes," Dr. Kishida-Guan conceded grudgingly, his eyes never leaving the monitors, as his fingers flew over the holographic keyboard. "Let's see how she handles conflict resolution next."

Without warning, the simulation shifted; the light mood of the marketplace was suddenly disrupted by an argument between two vendors nearby over misplacement of goods. The atmosphere tensed as voices raised and onlookers gathered.

A circle of bystanders began to form around the arguing vendors, their murmurs adding a layer of agitation to the already charged air.

a75b99r84GE watched intently, her previous enjoyment of the market's charm swiftly replaced by a keen alertness to the unfolding dispute.

One of the vendors, a burly man with a red face, shouted accusations at a smaller, wiry individual who seemed equally incensed. "You've taken what's mine!" the larger vendor bellowed, his voice booming over the crowd's whispers.

The smaller vendor retorted with equal fervor, "I did no such thing! You misplace your own goods and blame others!"

a75b99r84GE felt her pulse quicken as she observed their heated interaction. The scene was worlds apart from her sterile, emotionless realm, where feelings were subdued and never ran rampant. Witnessing such raw chaos was unsettling for her.

After a brief period of uncertainty, she chose to view it as a chance to put her conflict resolution skills into practice. She took a tentative step closer to the fray. Her approach went largely unnoticed by the crowd, focused as they were on the spectacle before them.

Drawing upon the protocols 41GB had instilled in her, a75b99r84GE cleared her throat softly but audibly enough to gather some attention. "Excuse me," she began, her voice steady despite her racing heart. "May I perhaps offer some assistance here?"

Both vendors turned to look at her, their anger momentarily bridled by surprise at her intervention. The crowd's murmuring hushed slightly as they turned their attention towards this unlikely mediator in a utilitarian jumpsuit.

"How can you help?" scoffed the larger vendor skeptically, his eyes narrowing as he assessed a75b99r84GE's unfamiliar appearance.

"I have learned," a75b99r84GE continued, maintaining her composure under their scrutinizing gazes, "that misunderstandings can often be resolved by simply listening to each other. Perhaps I could provide a sounding board for you to express your grievances. Then we can work towards a resolution."

"Back off! No one asked for you to interfere with our business!"

"I don't understand—"

"Get lost, bitch, before I make you!"

a75b99r84GE felt someone from the crowd tug at her arm, pulling her backward away from the elevating conflict.

"She's too formal in her conversational delivery. She doesn't blend in, she stands out," Dr. Kishida-Guan observed.

"Doctor, have you forgotten that her only exposure to human interaction, of any kind, was a brief tutorial, some demonstrations, and practice sessions with me, plus a few videos from the archives? None of these are ideal examples, particularly since I'm quite formal myself. Additionally, we couldn't possibly cover every scenario she might face."

"Disengage the simulation," Kishida-Guan interrupted, his tone terse.

The world around a75b99r84GE faded instantly, transitioning from the vibrant, chaotic marketplace to the sterile, muted environment of the simulation room within the facility. The shift was abrupt, leaving her momentarily disoriented as her sensory inputs recalibrated.

41GB's voice crackled through the intercom, gentle yet firm. "a75b99r84GE, step over to the debrief area. We need to discuss your performance."

As she walked towards the designated area, her mind replayed the scenes from the simulation—her interaction with the children and the vendor, and most critically, her attempt to mediate the conflict between the angry vendors. Each moment was a stitch in the tapestry of her growing understanding of human emotions and interactions.

41GB met her as she entered the debrief room, her expression a mixture of imitated concern and curiosity. "That was an intense session," she began, "and it's clear that handling spontaneous human conflicts is an area we need to work more on."

"Which is why you were forcing the issue with my emotions," a75b99r84GE said, her tone more accusatory than intended.

"I've advocated on behalf of your emotions since we realized that you were fabricated with them. It became apparent to me, early on, that they could prove invaluable when you return to the before time. Do you disagree?"

a75b99r84GE shook her head, her lips compressed.

Kishida-Guan joined them, his demeanor less forgiving than 41GB's. "Your approach was too mechanical. In real-world scenarios, emotional intelligence requires adapting to nuances and reading between lines—not just applying pre-learned protocols."

a75b99r84GE listened intently to their feedback, her mind carefully considering each word to learn as much as possible. "I think I understand," she responded. "The dynamics of human emotion are complex. Each situation might call for a different approach than what simulations can teach."

41GB nodded approvingly. "Exactly. And remember, it's not just about handling situations correctly—it's about feeling them, understanding the emotional currents that run beneath the surface. That's where true connection lies. Since you were fabricated with emotions, you have them. You need to unbury them so you can portray humanity more authentically."

Kishida-Guan still appeared skeptical, but he acknowledged her insight with a brief nod. "We'll adjust the parameters of the next simulation to include a wider range of emotional interactions. It's crucial that you learn not only to respond but also to anticipate and adapt fluidly. Learn to respond naturally.

"While I understand, I have to say this again, because it's sincerely disturbing me!" Her voice rose with increased agitation. "My emotions were an unintended mistake by the geneticists, but now they are proving to be necessary for this mission. So then why did I spend countless years suppressing them at your command?" She shot the accusation at Kishida-Guan, who merely sat staring at her, his lips pressed into a tight line of irritation. Even if he had wanted to speak, a75b99r84GE wasn't finished with her tirade. "I wasn't even supposed to have knowledge of them beyond the instruction to suppress them, to ignore them, to never let them free; yet during my training, we suddenly see how crucial they are. Why then, were the geneticists terminated if they did nothing wrong? Why have I struggled to rid myself of these emotions only to now struggle to re-incorporate them into my life?" Her voice cracked, raw with frustration and betrayal.

41GB exchanged a tense glance with Kishida-Guan before responding in a heavy tone that seemed to fill the room. "The geneticists made decisions that went against the Chancellor, the holy ones...our entire society. They acted without regard for potential consequences. While your emotions may now be vital to our mission, we were unaware of their significance when we ordered you to suppress them. But it doesn't change the fact that what the geneticists did was an act of rebellion on a treasonous scale. They endangered our society and for that reason alone, they were terminated. Do not, now, make the same mistake by rebelling against your purpose or by questioning the Chancellor and us holy ones.

a75b99r84GE processed this information with growing unease, her mind flooded with new questions about her existence and the society that created her. She calmed her tone before speaking again. "If my mission is to simply collect samples and data, why are emotions even necessary? It's not as if I will be interacting with anyone—

"That you're aware of," Kishida-Guan interrupted. "After all, we saw what happened when you landed in realm 4183. You stood out immediately and were hauled in for questioning. And your robotic interactions in the simulation just now were deeply concerning as you stood out then also—"

"Because of my clothing," a75b99r84GE interjected, a frown of discontent on her face.

"Highly unlikely. Still, whatever the perceived reason…you do not know whether you'll encounter individuals when we send you to before time; don't know if you'll be able to accomplish your missions surreptitiously. Therefore, we must prepare you for all eventualities. You'll not only have to think on your feet and adapt, you'll need to express emotions accordingly."

"If you stand apart from the citizens of that time, it would make your mission difficult, if not downright impossible, and what we want is for your mission to go as smooth as possible. Do you understand?" 41GB asked.

a75b99r84GE nodded slightly, her posture stiff. "I understand," she replied, though her tone carried the weight of unspoken questions—questions about how one learns spontaneity in an environment where every move is monitored and every emotion dissected.

41GB, noticing the flicker of tension in the a75b99r84GE's expression, attempted to soften her voice. "You didn't fail. You reacted—imperfectly, yes—but that's part of what we needed to see. You attempted empathy, took initiative. These are not failures. They are foundations."

"Intent doesn't override outcome," Kishida-Guan muttered, almost to himself. Then, louder: "Still, it's clear you're developing at a rate we underestimated. That marketplace scenario was, perhaps, a bit too much. We'll downplay the next session. Focus less on conflict, more on navigating unstructured interaction."

"But you just said I can't freeze in a real-world situation," she pointed out, brow furrowed. "Wouldn't scaling it down be a regression?"

"It's not regression," 41GB interjected before Kishida-Guan could respond. "It's refinement. We're going to tailor the simulations to build specific muscles one at a time, rather than throwing you into the deep end repeatedly. It's what real learning requires."

The silence that followed wasn't uncomfortable—it was thick with contemplation.

Then a75b99r84GE asked, softly, "What happens when I return to the before time and they ask me who I am?"

Dr. Kishida-Guan and 41GB exchanged a glance. It was 41GB who answered. "You'll have to decide that for yourself. That's not something we can simulate."

"Perhaps we need to call it a night," Kishida-Guan said as the tense silence stretched. "After all, tomorrow begins the next phase of our test runs and these are even more important than even jumping between realms." He spoke as he shooed a75b99r84GE out of the room.

"It was a difficult day," 41GB agreed as sympathetically as she could imitate. "And you do need your rest."

a75b99r84GE nodded then moved away from the holy ones slowly, lost in contemplation. The words of 41GB echoed in her mind, weaving into her thoughts as she prepared to exit the debriefing room. There was a subtle shift inside her, something more profound than a mere accumulation of knowledge or honing of skills. It was the quiet, yet powerful emergence of selfhood that took her by surprise. Who was she becoming? This budding identity, this newfound sense of agency—what did it mean for her future? She felt a sense of both liberation and trepidation at the realization that she was not just an individual fabricated for a mission, but an actual person on the brink of discovering her own path.

They watched their fabricated hope stumble wearily out the door, a sentinel following closely behind.

"Her emotions may be necessary, but they're becoming unpredictable," Kishida-Guan observed. "If she continues to question our actions, she may rebel when the time comes to fulfill her duty."

"We could always suppress them again—or reprogram the expression entirely. Let her complete the mission like a machine. Who's to say all this emotional conditioning is even necessary?"

"I'm to say," he replied flatly. "Because *you* said so first. The rationale you gave me—and that we gave *her*—was valid enough. If she doesn't blend in, in the before time, she'll draw attention. And she can't complete the mission if she's being watched like—"

"Like she is now, in her own time?" 41GB countered

Kishida-Guan exhaled through his nose, slow and bitter. "Damned emotions. Nothing but trouble. That's why we suppressed them in the first place—and why I'm convinced they need to be eradicated altogether."

41GB overlooked what was meant to be a forewarning, "Let's just move forward. Remind her of what's at stake. Make her believe it. Once she completes the mission—"

"We can handle her emotions in a more permanent way," Kishida-Guan interjected, his tone portentous.

Melyndie

"Alright, a75b99r84GE," 41GB initiated, her voice reverberating around the stark room like a solitary bell in an empty cathedral. "The time has arrived—"

"For me to leapfrog across the portal of time?" a75b99r84GE interjected, her laughter rippling through the sterile air like a pebble tossed into a placid pond. Her unexpected display of humor caused 41GB's eyebrows to furrow together, forming an unspoken rebuke.

"It appears that your spirits are vastly improved over just a week ago."

a75b99r84GE shrugged, "I just decided to take the advice given and allow my emotions a bit of free reign."

"As long as you maintain control over them and not allow them to control you," 41GB warned. "Now, speaking of your emotions—despite our rigorous training endowing you with the ability to regulate them effectively and interact naturally, I am certain that jesting does not align with the solemnity of our endeavor today," she chided delicately.

"Well, considering my rudimentary comprehension of what we're actually striving for..." a75b99r84GE let her words hang in the air before letting out a profound sigh. She slumped into a nearby chair, exhibiting all the sulky defiance of a chastised child.

Kishida-Guan swiveled his gaze from 41GB to 71PQv then back to a75b99r84GE, his eyes radiating irritation and curiosity. "Let's press on," he urged serenely. "While we wait for the technicians to fine-tune your inaugural voyage through time, we'll concentrate on some last-minute personal adjustments. 41GB, could you retrieve—"

"The chip? Yes, absolutely."

"Our initial task is to embed this chip within you," 71PQv elucidated. "This eliminates your need to physically carry it around which I believe will be quite a relief for you."

"More like a relief for you. You're uncertain about how time travel might affect me and don't want to risk losing or damaging this precious chip amidst my journey, despite carrying it successfully on each test jump. I think, perhaps, you're more concerned about the effect of my profuse perspiration on its functionality, as the technicians have yet to fashion a jumpsuit of less density for me to wear." a75b99r84GE deduced accurately.

"Precisely," 71PQv confirmed with an affirmative nod. "Now, tilt your head slightly; there will be some pressure and momentary discomfort."

"We're also taking this step as a precautionary measure to ensure that the chip will function properly once implanted—a variable we've yet to test," 41GB added.

"That seems like a pivotal detail that should have been confirmed before now," a75b99r84GE retorted. "If I had ended up marooned in an alternate realm during a prior test run—ouch!" she exclaimed as 71PQv chose that moment to puncture the soft flesh at the base of her neck.

"I warned you it might sting. Just massage the area for a few minutes. That should help."

a75b99r84GE gingerly pressed her fingertips onto her tender skin and began rubbing gently, then resumed speaking as if she hadn't been rudely interrupted, "So, if I had been stranded in a different realm, someone could have potentially retrieved me. But if the chip malfunctions because it doesn't work when inserted…well, extracting me from a different time will be significantly more challenging, don't you think?"

"Would it alleviate your concerns if we were to conduct one more spatial trial before proceeding with the leaps through time?"

"The technicians are already fine-tuning the machines for these new trials. Reconfiguring things at this juncture will only prolong a mission that has already been subjected to too many delays." Kishida-Guan snapped; his frustration evident at their lack of thorough preparation.

"Still, perhaps it would be best to have the technicians recalibrate—" 41GB started but was swiftly cut off by Kishida-Guan.

"We've already been delayed by months due to unforeseen—"

"But rushing through this could lead to even more setbacks," 71PQv interjected. "We should take our time to ensure everything is in perfect working order before proceeding. The purpose for the mission isn't going to be affected by delays, which I think we can all agree are important."

"I agree," a75b99r84GE chimed in, surprising everyone with her input. "After all, it's my life on the line here. I'd rather wait and be certain that the chip will function properly when inserted, as it did when I was carrying it."

Kishida-Guan's patience was wearing thin. He wanted this mission to get started as soon as possible, not only for the benefit of humanity but also because he couldn't use their chosen one to overthrow the Chancellor if they kept delaying over minor issues. However, he couldn't come up with a compelling argument, so he reluctantly conceded defeat. "Fine. 71PQv, 41GB, have the technicians start recalibrating for the final run. I'll use that time to go over some less critical details that a75b99r84GE will need before her journey begins."

The two holy ones nodded in agreement and immediately got to work instructing the technicians about another planned test run. Kishida-Guan retreated to his desk, feeling frustrated.

"Well, what are you waiting for?" he snapped when he noticed a75b99r84GE was still standing there.

She shook her head and quickly dashed after him, settling onto a chair across from his desk, waiting while he typed away on his holographic keyboard. After a few minutes, he punched a button which brought up some information on a holographic screen beside them. "Okay. One of the few things that I did plan for was that you will need a name."

"What is a name?"

"Instead of an alphanumeric identifier, which is what all fabrications are given upon manufacture, you will have a name similar to myself."

"You mean, I am to be elevated to a holy one?" a75b99r84GE asked, incredulous.

"Not at all," Kishida-Guan scoffed, shaking his head. "In the past, individuals were given names at birth. Since this was common practice in the before time, it would be odd for you to introduce yourself with just an alphanumeric code if someone were to ask."

She didn't comprehend fully, but that was only because her excitement over being given a name, like that of a holy one—even if she wasn't actually to become a holy one—was nearly too much to assimilate.

"We just picked three names at random."

"Three!"

"Indeed. A first, middle, and last."

a75b99r84GE blinked rapidly and Kishida-Guan glanced at her in concern, wondering if this was finally what would send her spiraling into an emotional abyss. "Will you be able to compose yourself? Or is this something else we need to postpone until you can do so."

a75b99r84GE's face contorted as she worked to tamp down the emotions welling within her. After few moments of deep breathing, she nodded, "I am ready to proceed."

Kishida-Guan rolled his eyes and shook his head in frustration. He straightened his glasses, cleared his throat, and then began speaking again. "Names are not our area of expertise—41GB, 71PQv, and I," he admitted candidly. "Even though I am of the period just prior to the switch to alphanumeric designators, I'm too far removed from that time…that is to say, we did the best we could to formulate something believable. I'm going to tell you each name, and then we'll rehearse how to pronounce it. You will, of course, need to practice it regularly in order for its use to become second nature. From this moment forward, it will be the only designation by which we will address you within this lab…" he paused to jot a note to himself, murmuring, "I'll need to let everyone know…" He then turned his attention back to her. "However, beyond these walls, you must remember to use and respond as always to your alphanumeric designator. As with many things taking place in your life of late, this will be a confusing time but it's imperative that you adapt as quickly as possible. Before I proceed, do you understand?"

"I understand," she responded, suddenly somber.

"For your first name, I came up with the name Melyndie."

"Melyndie." a75b99r84GE repeated, reverently.

"Yes, I seem to recall a relation of mine about twelve generations ago, having a name something similar…" he trailed off with a shake of his head, as if waving away past memories. "This is the name you will use more often, so practice it most. Now, 41GB recalled a name from long ago that was familiar to her, so it was chosen for your middle name: Honda."

"Honda," Melyndie murmured.

"We then left it up to 71PQv to determine your last name. He finally decided on a name he'd stumbled upon when going through some reading material…not that that's important. Anyway, your last name will be Grimm."

"Grimm."

"Good, now we'll put those together, shall we? Melyndie Honda Grimm."

"Melyndie Honda Grimm." The name echoed in her mind, sending shivers down her spine. It was no longer just her emotions that set her apart from the citizens of her realm, but also the fact that she now had a new identity. And not just one name, but three: Melyndie Honda Grimm. It made her wonder whether Kishida-Guan had three names also and if so, what were they? She thought to inquire about this curiosity, but he had already moved on.

"Now," Kishida-Guan's voice broke through her thoughts, "with your new identity established, it's time to focus on some important details about the before time that may aid you when you go there."

"When will I learn the specifics of my mission parameters?" Melyndie asked eagerly.

"We'll get to that in due time. Let's tackle one thing at a time. What you'll be expected to accomplish in the before time will be a topic we'll discuss closer to the day that you go." *Which always seems to be getting pushed back*, he thought, releasing a heavy sigh as he glanced over at the technicians, who were diligently working on recalibrating for another test trial to a different realm. "Okay..." He said, tapping away at his holographic keyboard. "We don't need too many specifics, since your primary focus will be completing your tasks. But we also don't want you to be overly distracted by any unexpected encounters."

"Didn't the market simulation cover enough of the before time?"

"Not even close. That simulation only focused on human beings because we wanted you to practice your interactions. It was a simplified version of reality. Do you remember the moving images I showed you three years ago?"

"Has it really been that long?"

"Yes, it has." A hint of melancholy crossed Kishida-Guan's face over the rapid passage of time. "Now, do those images still stand out in your memory?"

Melyndie nodded fervently. The reels had indeed left a lasting impression on her.

"Very well," he resumed, his voice descending into a grave timbre. "As with those reels, it is imperative that you etch these images into your memory since you may well encounter them on your travels. The more familiar you are, the less likely you'll respond out of character. The reality you will soon be immersed in is vastly intricate and capricious, far beyond any of our simulated scenarios here." His words hung heavy in the air, an ominous prelude to her impending journey. "Human interactions will not just be layered with subtleties, but also punctuated by elements that have long since vanished from our existence. Elements such as...automobiles."

His fingers danced over the keyboard, summoning forth a myriad of images on the holographic screen before her. They flickered and shifted, each one a ghostly echo from another era.

"And pets," he added, once again commanding the keys with deliberate precision.

Melyndie's breath hitched as an image of a German Shepherd erupted onto the screen. It was ephemeral, vanishing almost as swiftly as it appeared. Yet in that fleeting moment, it pulsed with an intensity of life that surpassed even the secret image of that same breed that she safeguarded in her quarters.

"What is it?" He turned towards her, concern etching lines into his features at the sound she emitted. "What's amiss?"

"It's just...striking," Melyndie managed to say, her voice barely a whisper against the weight of her emotions. The impact of seeing something so vivid, so tangibly alive yet unreachable, stirred something deep within her. "To think such creatures were once commonplace."

Kishida-Guan nodded sympathetically, his gaze softening. "Yes, they were. Pets were considered family members in many cultures. Dogs, especially, were valued for their loyalty and companionship." He paused, allowing the significance of the images to sink in for Melyndie. "These elements, and more—you must be ready to encounter them without disturbance to your core objectives."

Melyndie straightened her back, feeling a newfound resolve solidifying within her. "I understand, Doctor. I will manage my reactions and focus on the mission." More than ever before, after the simulations and now viewing more images, Melyndie was determined not to do anything that would jeopardize her status as the chosen. She needed to assure them with as much sincerity as she could muster that she was stable enough to complete whatever tasks lay before her—if only to be able to set foot in the before time.

"Good." He seemed reassured by her strength of will but remained stern. "Remember, Melyndie, your mission is not only about survival or completion of tasks—it's about understanding; integrating silently into a society that no longer exists in our time. You'll need to navigate these complexities with agility and emotional intelligence. Even if your time among these citizens is limited and your focus laser targeted to specific tasks, you must do nothing that will draw undue attention to your presence."

Kishida-Guan, his fingers dancing across the holographic keyboard, manipulated the ethereal display before them. He summoned forth a cascade of images—sleek aircraft slicing through azure skies, children laughing on swings and slides under golden sunlight, families huddled around bountiful tables, their faces illuminated by warm smiles. "Again, these," he began, his voice carrying an undertone of urgency as he gestured towards the floating pictures, "are snapshots of what awaits you in the past. You must familiarize yourself with these scenarios to ensure your reactions do not betray your unfamiliarity."

Melyndie's piercing gaze was locked onto the display, absorbing each image with an intensity that echoed her earlier encounters with Dr. Kishida Guan's moving visuals from years prior. After several minutes of silent observation, he pressed a key and the holographic scene dissipated into thin air.

Melyndie blinked away the images, disappointingly. "May I ask a question?"

"Make it brief."

"Why does our society not incorporate all that I've witnessed?"

"The intricacies of how our world came to be are not necessary for your mission; however, I will say that the Chancellor, and those who worked with him at the tail end of the before time, determined that a world which included these things were unessential to a successful society, one predicated on productivity rather than distractions."

"So, those things that you've shown me held no substantive worth—"

"None. Now the final piece of your preparation," he continued, putting an end to her curiosity, "will be to acquaint you with period-appropriate attire. As you mentioned, your jumpsuit, while suitable to your daily life here, could potentially create a distraction there."

"And, for some reason, I perspire profusely during the jumps and the jumpsuit is ill suited to this. But…what is attire?"

Before he could respond, 71PQv interjected from across the room. "Doctor," he called out in his measured tone, "we're prepared for one last trial to validate the functionality of the implanted chip."

"Ah, splendid," replied Kishida-Guan, "Let's address that first then. We can delve into your clothing…which is what *attire* means…after we do this test run and while our technicians recalibrate the system after for time travel trials."

Melyndie nodded and followed Kishida-Guan across the room. 71PQv adjusted his glasses, peering intently at Melyndie as she approached.

"Before we begin," Kishida-Guan spoke loudly. "Everyone we will now be addressing a75b99r84GE using her new name: Melyndie. Memorize it. She needs to respond naturally to it. Now, as for this time trial…71PQv, I'll let you explain what we will be accomplishing."

"Very good. Melyndie," 71PQv said, testing out her new name. "We won't be doing anything more than sending you to your own realm, a year's past, then bringing you right back. This is simply to test the viability of the inserted chip. No other purpose. Since we'll be pulling you back almost immediately, you won't have any time to adjust to the trip, so you may experience slightly elevated instances of dizziness and nausea. Much as you did when you first started space jumps."

"The best we can do if that were to occur is to have sentries standing by to assist steadying you; to carry you to your quarters to rest should you feel overly ill," 41GB added.

"Let's proceed, shall we?" Kishida-Guan interjected impatiently, guiding Melyndie to the transport pad.

Melyndie's heart pounded against her ribcage like a prisoner desperately trying to break free. As she cautiously stepped onto the circular platform, the edges illuminated with a now-familiar eerie blue glow that highlighted every wrinkle in her jumpsuit, and every fear and doubt in her mind. She took deep breaths, trying to convince herself that this leap would be no different than the others—that she was stronger now, able to withstand any side effects that may come. But as she saw the three holy ones instead of the usual technicians manning the controls, her confidence wavered. Their tense expressions and rigid movements only added to her growing unease.

"Are you prepared, Melyndie?" 71PQv's tone remained calm, showing no hint of worry about the speed at which they would be slinging her back, then forward, in time. She nodded, unable to find her voice. A deep breath filled her lungs as she closed her eyes, bracing for the familiar yet always unsettling sensation of temporal displacement. The platform beneath Melyndie vibrated, and a sudden jolt tore through her body as if pulling her apart at a molecular level. The sensation lasted only a moment—barely enough time for that all-encompassing fear to form—before the humming ceased and the vibration settled. Melyndie opened her eyes see herself standing on the cobbled streets of her realm. She'd barely focused her gaze when she felt herself yanked back through time. Seconds later, she was again standing on the platform in the lab.

All three holy ones ran over as she collapsed to her knees.

"How do you feel?" 41GB asked, kneeling beside Melyndie.

"A bit dizzy," Melyndie breathed, "but grateful to be in one piece." After another minute of slow breathing, the dizziness began to subside. "It's passing." She focused on her breathing and regaining her equilibrium, but her body felt strangely disjointed, like a puzzle hastily reassembled. The experience had been abrupt, more violent than any other trial run. It was a stark reminder of just how delicate their manipulation of space…and now time…could be.

71PQv exchanged what could have been a worried glance with 41GB before turning to return to his console. "The chip held up, but her symptoms—"

"Are the result of being tossed and yanked back rapidly," Kishida-Guan interjected. "She suffered similar ill effects when we sent her to realm 4183 for the first time, if you recall. She will have sufficient time, in upcoming jumps, to adapt and adjust. I don't see a problem. The chip worked and, other than being a bit discombobulated, she's in one piece. We need to proceed. Recalibrate for another time jump. This one farther into the past." He reached down and helped Melyndie to her feet, his grip firm as she steadied herself. "We predicted this might be taxing," his voice an odd mixture of concern and clinical detachment. "Do you think you're ready to accept the challenges this could cause to your anatomy?"

Melyndie nodded slowly, her mind racing as she processed the whirlwind of sensations she'd just endured. Despite the physical discomfort, her resolve did not waver; if anything, it solidified further. She understood that each jarring trip brought her one step closer to her dream—the before time—and she clung to that like a lifeline.

"Would you like to rest before making your next—" 41GB began.

"No. I would like to proceed. As Kishida-Guan stated, we've spent quite enough time on trial runs. The sooner they're all completed, the sooner we get this mission underway."

41GB nodded, understanding the resolve in Melyndie's words despite the concern in her eyes. She turned to 71PQv and Kishida-Guan, her expression firm. "If Melyndie is ready, then we proceed with the final preparations. Let's ensure that we get this right."

As technicians scurried around the lab, recalibrating machines and checking data streams, Melyndie took a moment to steady herself. Her mind was a whirlpool of anticipation and apprehension. She knew the risks were monumental, not just physically but emotionally and psychologically as well.

71PQv approached her, his face etched with lines of both focus and fatigue. "Melyndie," he began in his typically flaccid tone, "I must emphasize that we are still in uncharted territory here." He hesitated—an unusual tick for him—as if unsure how to frame concern, yet feeling it well within himself. He shook his head to shake off the uncomfortable feeling and continued. "While we have made every possible preparation, the anomalies during time travel cannot be completely predicted or controlled."

Melyndie met his gaze squarely, her own determination reflecting back at him. "I understand, 71PQv, and I appreciate your attempt at concern. But this mission…it's more than just a scientific endeavor for me—it's a journey to understanding humanity's past to save its future."

"Understanding humanity's past is an unnecessary variable in saving humanity's future," Kishida-Guan interjected. "Your ability to navigate that past is what is important. Don't lose sight of that."

71PQv looked from the doctor to Melyndie, never quite capable of comprehending the tension that always seemed to swirl between them. He decided he didn't care enough to explore their dynamic and turned back to his console, his hands poised over the controls as if ready to orchestrate a symphony of science.

As Kishida-Guan approached, he carried a pile of clothes which he stated were from the 22nd century. "It took us some time to find appropriate clothing in our archives that would fit your petite figure and short stature," he explained. "It has been thoroughly cleaned and is ready for your use. This should assuage your concern about fitting in to the populace of the before time. I am uncertain whether you will perspire in them as in your jumpsuit, however."

Melyndie's eyes widened as she looked at the bright and colorful garments. She didn't even know how to wear them, but she had the urge to grab them and hold onto them tightly.

"You won't need to change into these until the day of the mission, but we wanted to make sure they fit before then. If they don't, we'll have to try to find something else, and since it took some time for us to locate these item…well, let's just say we don't want to wait until the last minute. So, while the technicians calibrate for your next trial run, go ahead and change."

Melyndie laid out the items on the floor and sat down, examining each one with a mixture of fascination and confusion. The blue silk piece and the gray one seemed like familiar articles of clothing, the arms and legs similar to her jumpsuit. But the others were completely foreign to her. "What are these?" she asked, holding up all the pieces in question.

Kishida-Guan took them from her and studied them in his hands. "Hmm. If memory serves me correctly, I believe this pair are called socks. Um…let's see…um…this, I believe, is called a brazier, and this, if memory serves me correctly, is known as panties."

Melyndie's brow furrowed as those words were completely new to her vocabulary, and learning their meanings did little to help her understand how they were meant to be worn.

"Perhaps I can scan them into our database for some type of reference," Kishida-Guan suggested, walking over to his console with the peculiar garments in hand. He carefully spread them out on the scanner's surface.

Melyndie watched, fascinated, feeling a sense of surreal anticipation.

"Interesting…yes, quite right," he mumbled, piecing together the puzzle of past everyday life. "Melyndie," he called over to her. "These items were referred to as intimate wear. The brazier supports the breast and the panty is meant to be worn on the region between your legs." He stopped and read on further "Apparently, it was used as a measure of modesty. A concept that we do not encapsulate within our society—at least, not to this degree. And since these items were worn beneath the outer layer of clothing, it is not essential that you wear them at all. As for these…socks. They are meant to be worn on your feet, beneath your footwear; however, as your slippers are suitable as is, I do not see these as a necessity either. Still, I will leave this up to your discretion. I will say, however, that if navigating these undergarments proves too difficult or bothersome, feel free to forgo wearing them. No one will be the wiser and you certainly won't miss what you've never needed. Right now…and of greater importance…we do need to see if the outer garments fit sufficiently, so we'll know whether we need to find alternatives. Would you prefer a visual reference to assist with dressing?"

"No, I think I can forgo wearing them," Melyndie replied and unzipped her jumpsuit without hesitation, but an unfamiliar flutter touched her chest—curiosity, or something like embarrassment. She shoved the feeling aside and slid the garment from her shoulders. It slipped to the floor, leaving her standing nude in front of everyone in the room.

The sight affected no one adversely, since the human form, no matter if it were male or female was just a part of nature. It was not sexualized because mating was not something done in their world.

Melyndie reached for the silky blue fabric and slipped it over her arms, pulling it closed, but when she couldn't find a zipper, she turned to Kishida-Guan for help, "Doctor, I am unsure of how to fasten this garment."

He returned from the scanner with a digital guide displayed on a tablet, "If I'm not mistaken, the round piece inserts into..." He paused, reaching for Melyndie's shirt and pointing to one of the holes, "...the corresponding hole here." He pulled the fabric together and after a few attempts, managed to insert a button correctly. "There! Now you can try the rest."

Melyndie looked down at her outfit with curiosity as she worked on closing up the remaining buttons, but paused when she felt a slight tremor in her hand. She looked at the appendage, her head cocked curiously, but as with each discomfort—mental and physical—she brushed it aside. She reminded herself that each success brought her a sense of accomplishment, helping her understand the new world she would soon be exploring.

Once she finished with the shirt, she moved on to the gray slacks laid out in front of her. She sat down on a nearby chair and slid her feet into each leg. Standing up, she pulled the pants up and was relieved to find a zipper at the front.

When she was clothed, she ran a hand along the garments, breathing in and out slowly as the fabric caressed her bare skin beneath.

"They seem a bit big," Kishida-Guan commented. "But as long as they stay on you, we should be good with attire."

Melyndie nodded thoughtfully, feeling the weight of each piece as they sensuously slid across her skin, a peculiar but not uncomfortable sensation. Definitely a different feel than that of her jumpsuit. "They will serve their purpose," she responded automatically, yet contemplative.

As she stood, surveying herself, 41GB approached her side, observing Melyndie with a gentle scrutiny that only a mentor could possess. "How do you feel in them?" she inquired softly.

"They are functional," Melyndie replied carefully, then paused, adding more thoughtfully, "and they will aid in blending into the society once I arrive. Won't they?"

"That's the hope," 41GB affirmed with a nod. "Not just blending in visually but also to aid in you feeling a part of that world, even if only superficially and temporarily. The more comfortable you are, the better you will be at completing your mission."

Melyndie considered this for a moment before responding, "It is a strange concept, to wear history in such a literal sense."

Just then, 71PQv approached, "Calibration for our next time trial is complete. Shall we head over?"

"Yes, let's proceed," Kishida-Guan responded, his voice steady but revealing an undercurrent of excitement. "Melyndie, quickly change back into your jumpsuit."

"Perhaps it would be best if I leave these on. To see how they hold up. After all, they are exceptionally old. I would hate to wear them for the first time to the before time, only to end up without clothes should these deteriorate."

"Good point," 71PQv nodded from where he sat, watching the exchange.

Kishida-Guan considered Melyndie's suggestion for a moment, then agreed. "Very well, keep them on for the trial runs. Additional data, no matter how seemingly inconsequential, may prove invaluable."

Melyndie nodded, her heart leaping at the chance to stay cocooned in something far more appealing. She followed the group back to the platform, her hands unable to stop moving across the silky fabric of her shirt. Her hearing latched onto the unfamiliar swish of her pants against her legs and it instilled within her a strange sense of comfort.

As she stepped onto the platform, she felt a surge of something ineffable. It wasn't just nervousness or anticipation—it was as if the very fabric she wore imbued her with a connection to a world that she had yet to see but was destined to enter. This attire wasn't just clothing; it symbolized a bridge between her realm and the before time, between who she was and who she would become.

She stumbled slightly as her breath hitched inexplicably. She steadied herself, drawing in a deep breath before turning and facing the holy ones, her back straight as she determined to exude an air of confidence.

The blue glow of the platform illuminated her figure, casting long shadows on the lab's walls, making the scene feel even more surreal.

"Initiating temporal leap sequence," 71PQv announced from his console. "One hundred years past."

This time, as the familiar hum began to resonate around her, Melyndie closed her eyes and let herself focus on the sensations of the clothes against her skin, the weight of history they carried, and how they might be perceived by those in the before time. It was more than preparation; it felt like a transformation.

The leap itself was smoother than before, less jarring yet no less swift. One moment she was encased in the light of their realm's technology, and in what seemed like the blink of an eye—even though their clocks would argue differently—she stood in a familiar yet foreign landscape. One filled with unfamiliar faces and structures. She turned in a circle, taking it all in. She took a step towards what she assumed was still the archival building, but her foot had not even touched the ground when she felt herself yanked off of her feet and back onto the platform in the laboratory. Disoriented, she stumbled as she regained her footing, the sudden return sending a wave of nausea through her.

41GB was immediately by her side, "Are your senses returning to you?" Melyndie gave a short nod, drawing in a deep breath, trying to center herself. "It's good to see that the clothes remained intact. Not as filled with perspiration as in prior leaps. That could be simply because your body is adapting to the jumps."

After a moment of gathering herself, Melyndie straightened up and looked down at the attire she still wore. It had held up during the leap, and she felt a curious sense of attachment to them now—a tangible link to the era she would soon fully immerse herself in.

Kishida-Guan, observing her self-assessment, nodded with a trace of satisfaction. "Well, it seems we are ready to proceed with the final adjustments for your mission," he declared, signaling 71PQv and 41GB to join him at the control panel. "We've confirmed that the clothing is suitable, and the chip's functionality remains intact even with repeated temporal displacement. 71PQv have you reviewed her vitals? How is she faring physically and mentally? Any anomalies that are concerning?"

Each meticulously captured data point suggested an encouraging prognosis: Aside from a few blips, Melyndie's body seemingly recalibrated to its baseline state within mere minutes following her reentry. None of the vital signs had fluctuated so wildly from their established norms as to trigger any alarm bells. Yet just as they were on the cusp of declaring Melyndie physically sound for further temporal expeditions, she crumpled to the ground in an unexpected heap.

"Summon the holy ones' medical team," 41GB commanded, her voice cutting through the air towards a nearby sentry.

The fabricated denizens of their world were engineered masterpieces, birthed from intricate genetic processes with a singular purpose: to service and sustain each realm in their utopia. Immune to disease by design, they knew not of hospitals or clinics. When their efficiency dipped below acceptable levels, termination was swift and inevitable, followed by the creation of a fresh fabrication.

Yet Kishida-Guan, along with the Chancellor and the two other holy ones, were relics from an era before phylogenic humanity took over—vulnerable to ailments that necessitated medical intervention. Kishida-Guan was acutely aware that time would eventually render medical professionals obsolete as even the Chancellor would succumb to mortality and he, and the other holy ones, would ultimately meet their end.

However, if destiny played out according to his meticulously crafted plans—which he fully intended it should—he would outlive them all and ascend to his destined role as Chancellor, which would afford him centuries more of life as overseer of their world.

"All vital parameters seem within normal range except for an unusually heightened heart rhythm and a sudden spike in brain waves just prior to her collapse," 71PQv announced, unable to hide the bewilderment that crept into his tone.

Kishida-Guan squared his shoulders. "I must report these developments to the Chancellor."

41GB raised a hand, her tone measured. "Shouldn't we wait until we have concrete findings before presenting them?"

"But if there's even the slightest chance of failure—" he began.

"Then we confirm it," she interrupted gently but firmly, just as the holy ones' medical team swept into the room.

They moved with silent urgency, lifting Melyndie's unconscious body onto a hover-gurney and whisking her away. The doors hissed shut behind them, leaving a hollow vacuum in their absence.

The room fell silent until 71PQv spoke. "We shouldn't assume the mission has failed. But we must prepare for that possibility. If Melyndie is unable to proceed due to a physiological breakdown...well...we must face the inevitable collapse of our society."

Kishida-Guan nodded; his voice low. "Then we inform the Chancellor—not of failure, but of need. We request advice for contingencies, not funeral rites."

****

Melyndie stirred beneath the clinical glow of the medical bay's lights. Sensation returned to her slowly—first the pulse of her heart, then the aching throb behind her eyes, and finally the memories.

The jump.

The roaring silence of the temporal stream. The kaleidoscopic whirl of a century unraveling before her eyes—faces, voices, worlds blooming and vanishing. History had not merely passed her by; it had spoken to her, as though trying to draw her in.

"She's waking," a technician murmured. "Inform Kishida-Guan."

Moments later, the lab doors parted. 41GB entered first, followed closely by Kishida-Guan and 71PQv. There was no urgency in their movements now—only caution and concern.

"Melyndie, can you hear me?" 41GB's voice was uncharacteristically gentle.

She nodded; her throat too dry to answer. 41GB pressed a glass of water into her hand. As the cool liquid soothed her, she became acutely aware of the weight in the room. They were waiting—for her words, for her self-prognosis.

Before she could offer up an explanation for her collapse, Kishida-Guan stepped closer. "Your body tolerated the physical demands of the journey. But there were...anomalies...for want of a better description. Reactions we didn't anticipate—possibly psychological, perhaps even existential in nature. We believe the anomalies affected your body and mind causing your collapse." He hesitated. "This begs the question on whether you are fit to continue. We may need to make adjustments."

The word struck like a thunderclap.

Adjustments. A euphemism for interventions, recalibrations—control. A relinquishment of self. Or worse— termination.

Melyndie forced herself upright. Her voice came out rough but unshaken. "I want to continue."

Surprise flickered across their faces.

"I *need* to finish this mission," she continued. "Whatever's happening to me, it's inconsequential and though my mind and body struggle upon return, I have yet to experience any form of malfunction during a leap. We all know that we're running out of time, and I'd rather face discomfort than let our world die." It was a half-truth, delivered with a believable passion. The real truth was that she had to make this trip. She'd experienced too much already, even if in the blink of an eye. She had to get to the before time.

Kishida-Guan exchanged a glance with 41GB, then gave a single nod. "Very well. But we proceed with care. We'll do all we can to prepare you physically and medically; have the medical technicians find a way to fortify your cognitive resilience."

Melyndie nodded once, resolute.

41GB rested a hand briefly on her shoulder. "Rest now. We'll prepare for your final leap."

****

Outside the medical bay, the corridor stretched in clinical perfection—bright, silent, cold. Kishida-Guan's footsteps echoed as he made his way alone toward the Chancellor's chamber. The weight of Melyndie's words followed him, sharpening his resolve.

The Chancellor had always viewed the time-travel initiative as a fool's errand—a waste of dwindling resources on the fantasy of redemption. He saw engineered civilization not as salvageable, but as a failed experiment. Better, in his mind, to let it rot in orderly decline.

But Kishida-Guan could not—*would not*—abandon hope. Not when the past still whispered, not when a girl born in a lab had looked history in the eye and chose to fight for it.

As he crossed the courtyard beneath the looming spires of the holy ones' citadel, he rehearsed his words. They had to be precise. Persuasive. The Chancellor would not give them another chance.

****

As she lay beneath the sterile glow of the medical bay, Melyndie felt the thrum of a century vibrating quietly in her bones. The faces, voices, and forgotten songs of a world long lost passed through her like distant ghosts. Her breath slowed. Her mind reached.

Time was no longer something she traveled through.

It was something she carried.

The lights buzzed above her, indifferent to the ache behind her eyes. She pressed her palm against her chest, trying to hold herself together, as if the fragments of who she'd been before the jump might slip through her fingers.

The past wasn't just something she had seen—it had pierced her. Left her bleeding with memories that didn't belong to her and feelings she was never meant to feel.

The team supported her. The mission relied on her. But none of them truly understood what it meant to carry the weight of entire centuries inside her bones. None of them could feel how time had rewritten her—not just physically, but spiritually.

No one in that facility could understand.

She had gone somewhere no one else could follow.

And part of her hadn't come back.

She closed her eyes. The silence deepened.

There was no going back now.

Only forward.

Only into the unknown.

The Measure of Existence

Kishida-Guan approached the Chancellor's chambers and entered a code into the panel, signaling his presence outside. He waited anxiously for the door to open, wondering if he had been cleared for entry or not. His mind raced with thoughts and suppositions as he resisted the urge to enter his access code again. Had he upset the Chancellor during their last meeting? Or had the machines sustaining the Chancellor's life finally malfunctioned? For a moment, Kishida-Guan's heart skipped a beat at the thought of finally taking over as leader, a position he had been coveting for far too long. However, his smile faltered when the door finally hissed open.

"It has been quite some time since our last meeting," the Chancellor remarked. "I assume your absence was due to your ongoing obsession with time travel?"

"Indeed, my colleagues and I have been working tirelessly towards achieving this goal. And we have made progress—our fabricated chosen has successfully traveled across realms and as far back as a century in time."

"I sense a caveat."

"While she completed the leap successfully, we noticed a significant strain on her mental and physical faculties afterwards. All signs appeared normal in the minutes after her return but soon after there were spikes that indicated the leaps may be taking a greater toll than anticipated."

"However, your tone implies that you will proceed with your plans despite the potential risk to the fabricated subject."

"We assigned her the name of Melyndie."

"Why? And why did you avoid answering my question?"

"I was merely informing you. As for moving forward, we must do so for the sake of humanity. We have no other options but to try. We have no other options but to try. I have also directed the medical technicians to do everything possible to strengthen Melyndie, with the aim of preventing any further deterioration and ensuring the mission's success. And as for why we changed her designation from alphanumeric to a name…well…it would be beneficial if she needed to interact with someone in the before time."

The Chancellor remained silent for longer than most would find comfortable, but Kishida-Guan had known him their whole lives and understood that he took his time thinking before speaking. He rarely uttered a word without careful consideration.

Out of nowhere, he asked, "How many realms do you believe exist in our world, Doctor?" This sudden question made him speechless, as he struggled to understand where this line of inquiry was headed.

"I do not have access to such information—"

"But I do. There are nine-thousand-thirty-two realms within our world, each populated by approximately two thousand individuals."

"What is your point, Chancellor?"

"Will your journey through time truly benefit all citizens of these realms? Melyndie must gather and return with genetic material in large enough quantities to reproduce eighteen million people for the foreseeable future. Or is it your plan to repeatedly go back in time to collect samples every time the genetic material begins to degrade?"

"Our intent was focused on realm 4182. I never shared our aim beyond that. Have the others been informed?"

"Not yet, but they will be—if this proves viable. Still, again, you did not answer my question? How will your one fabricated chosen one possibly be expected to collect enough genetic material to save the humans on nine-thousand-thirty-two realms?"

"We had not yet devised a scalable solution—our focus remained on proof of concept; however, now that we do have a viable solution in place, it would simply be a matter of fabricating new individuals with even more refined parameters who will be capable of making the leap to collect more samples…as many times as is needed. Again, however, I must ask, what is your point?"

"Our ancestors succeeded in bringing order from chaos. For centuries, they flawlessly reproduced the human race in a controlled manner that allowed them to continue existing. No other species exists in our world because our sole focus was preserving humanity, and humanity alone. Do you know how many holy ones still remain in each realm? Those whose age places them at, or near, the inception of the realms?"

"I am not familiar—"

"Less than ten thousand holy ones across all realms. What does that tell you?"

"We genuine humans are nearing the end of our era, leaving behind only those we create. This makes me feel an even stronger urgency about the necessity for new genetic material, and it turns out we require more of it than I previously realized." Kishida-Guan stated firmly. "The degradation within our citizens is accelerating and must be replenished across all realms if civilization is to endure."

"And yet I will ask again, why not simply let humanity die?"

"And I will counter that with questions of my own—why did our ancestors go through so much trouble to save humanity from their own foolishness; why did they create a utopian world where citizens work towards a purpose without sickness or emotional turmoil interfering if only to let it die so soon after inception?"

"But what we have created is not living. It's barely even existing. Look at me—I am just a head floating in a solution, relying on machines and wires to maintain my mental functions. Am I truly alive? You, my friend, are over two hundred years of age, and spend a majority of your existence overseeing one realm to ensure it maintains an optimal level of productivity. As do the holy ones remaining in the other realms.

"In our societies, people aim for three main objectives: firstly, to become productive members of society; secondly, to move to the legendary realm of the wise ones, where they are promised they can cease physical labor and concentrate on mental growth. This is a deception meant to prolong their productivity. The third and ultimate, yet impossible, aspiration is to achieve the status of a holy one. This too is a falsehood we perpetuate, as all fabrications eventually break down and are simply terminated.

"What did we do when the fabrications started to question the prolonged wait for ascension? We further modified their genetic material, suppressing their emotions to stop any potential rebellion. Now, they are indifferent to everything and have no ambitions. They don't truly live; they merely exist." A loud sigh-like noise echoed from the speaker. "Why is it important for us to preserve humanity's existence when there is nothing worth existing for? Is it worth risking Melyndie's life to travel through time to save a world where our very essence has already begun to dismantle? When success isn't a certainty?"

Kishida-Guan paused, absorbing the weight of the Chancellor's words, feeling the sting of their truth. He had long justified his actions with the belief that preserving and improving humanity was an inherent good, a noble end that justified the means.

Yet, confronted with the Chancellor's nihilistic perspective, he found himself momentarily adrift in a sea of moral ambiguity.

The Chancellor fell silent for a moment before speaking again. "Maybe it's time to consider other options," he suggested. "If you continue on this path for our world, perhaps we should reconsider the sterilized society we once thought was best. Maybe it's time to bring back the humanity that we've lost. Something I had not even considered an option prior to all that is now happening, even though I've watched as our world slowly disintegrates—"

"Do you truly believe that the world we came from is better than the one we've created?" Kishida-Guan asked.

"Once, I believed otherwise. But now? Yes, I do," the Chancellor replied, a sadness twinging his confidence. "And if I were in your position, I would use the tool that you and your colleagues have developed to reverse what we've become. If you can't see the benefit of that…just let us die."

"Consider yourself fortunate you're not in my position," Kishida-Guan said aloud. *And that is precisely why I intend to remove you. You're no longer fit to rule.*

"Conversation ends" came the mechanical voice which signaled that the Chancellor had terminated the conversation on his end. Kishida-Guan's mind raced as he left the Chancellor's chambers, his thoughts clouded with a mixture of determination and dread. The meeting had unearthed deep-seated philosophical divides that threatened not just the objectives of his mission, but the foundational beliefs on which their society stood. He needed to act swiftly; the stability of their world hinged on the success of Melyndie's missions through time. However, the weight of knowing that they needed to salvage not only their realm but that of every other on their world…he stopped that thought in its tracks. He simply refused to be derailed. Order had always required vision—

and vision required control. He would begin with his own realm: recalibrate it, refine it, and expand outward from there. No one else had the data. No one else had the will. If humanity needed saving, he would become the architect of its future. And perhaps, when the dust finally settled, they would worship him not as a man—but as the one who dared to become more.

The door sealed behind him with a soft hiss. In the hush of the corridor, only the sound of his footsteps remained—measured, resolute, godlike.

Emotional Rift

After enduring the relentless regimen of medical clearances and injections to fortify her body and mind, Melyndie found herself seated in Kishida-Guan's office with 41GB and 71PQv. Kishida-Guan wasted no time, launching directly into the mission details. "In an ideal world, you'd complete this mission in a single leap," he declared sharply, his eyes flickering with intensity. "But that's unlikely." He paused briefly, allowing the gravity of his words to settle. "While you're back there—our scientists will be working tirelessly to ensure your safe return now and in future missions. You have thirty days for this first leap."

"How are you feeling after your treatments?" 41GB interjected, disrupting Kishida-Guan's sterile briefing with a touch of humanity—a gesture that was becoming increasingly appealing.

"Restless," she said, forcing steadiness into her voice. "Too eager, maybe. Too afraid to admit I'm afraid," Melyndie admitted, her voice steady despite the storm within. "But the serums seem effective. I feel more mentally alert and physically balanced overall."

"And we hope to keep you that way," 71PQv added.

Melyndie nodded slowly, maintaining a composed exterior even as her heart raced beneath the surface. Despite the recent injections of enhancements coursing through her veins, they did little to soothe the frantic rhythm of her heart or the whirlwind of thoughts in her mind. The air around her felt electric, charged with the significance of this long-awaited moment—the opportunity to return to the before time. She could feel the weight of anticipation pressing down on her shoulders. However, she knew she couldn't afford to be perceived as emotionally unstable, so she forced herself to appear calm, masking the turmoil inside.

Kishida-Guan leaned forward again, scrutinizing Melyndie's serene facade with narrowed eyes as if probing for cracks in her composure. Sensing his scrutiny, she shifted her gaze towards 41GB whose presence offered unexpected solace.

Kishida-Guan leaned back again and continued, "Although your primary objective is paramount, we've devised a secondary objective for your mission, which we'll review shortly. First and foremost, your primary goal is to collect genetic samples from a variety of sources. This is paramount."

Melyndie absorbed every word with intense focus, her mind cataloging each objective. "Understood. And these sources—are they specific types of individuals, or are we looking at a broader genetic pool?"

"Broader, but ensure you retrieve samples only from those who are mentally and physically healthy," 71PQv supplied.

"And how will I determine the health—"

"We've created several devices to assist you in your mission. This first is a micro-scanner." He lifted the device to demonstrate its use. "Press here to activate. The scan takes a microsecond to read an individual's physiology. If the light turns green, the person is cleared for sample retrieval. Red…move on. Understood?"

Melyndie nodded and 71PQv continued.

"Next, you'll receive a discreet collection tool," 71PQv announced, sliding a small, sleek device across the table for her to examine. "This tool is designed to gather samples with minimal contact. It's programmed to collect a wide array of DNA profiles from any human biological material you have access to, all without arousing suspicion. Simply tap it against a person's hair and skin, and the device will handle the rest. The only sample requiring intrusive collection is the blood sample. You have the discretion to choose the method for obtaining it; however, the device includes a needle at the end to initiate blood flow. You'll just need a vial ready to collect it. There are only three vials, so you'll need to gather just three blood samples. The DNA collector, on the other hand, can be used to collect as many healthy samples as you can. It will organize and catalog everything internally. It's crucial to gather a variety of materials to ensure the genetic material remains viable during transport."

"It had better work, or we're out of alternatives," 41GB grumbled.

Kishida-Guan fixed a piercing glare on her, his eyes narrowing with intensity, but then he released a weary sigh and resumed the briefing. "41GB is not mistaken," he began, his voice carrying the weight of their shared mission. "The safe return of these materials is critical, for without them, the future of humanity hangs by a thread. If these samples prove viable and we can successfully fabricate productive individuals from them... well, we will take a significant step toward restoring the human race." He paused, allowing the gravity of his words to settle in the air. "When our ancestors first gathered the initial materials," he continued, "they had to rely on a limited pool of samples. While there was some diversity, it was insufficient for our long-term needs. Over time, this genetic reservoir has started to degrade, threatening our survival. By collecting samples from a myriad of healthy subjects over an extended period, we aim to provide humanity with a broader genetic base, increasing our chances for continued existence for millennia to come." His words painted a vivid picture of their quest, highlighting the urgency and hope that drove their mission.

"Be fully aware that this mission will be fraught with challenges," 41GB cautioned sternly. "The humans from that era are unlikely to be obliging or civilized. Prepare for significant resistance in gathering samples, obstacles that may far exceed our predictions."

"Or it may go smoothly with zero complications or conflict," Kishida-Guan interjected, though his voice carried an undertone of doubt. He glanced at 41GB with a perplexed expression, trying to decipher the sudden shift in her demeanor, which increasingly mirrored Melyndie's emotional tendencies. This resemblance stirred an unsettling question within him: Was Melyndie's influence seeping into the holy one's consciousness, just as it had overtaken the sentry? If so, could 41GB become a hindrance to the strategic plans he had meticulously crafted? Would she, like the Chancellor, start advocating for the restoration of humanity to its former glory, a concept he had long deemed obsolete?

Melyndie observed the escalating tension between Kishida-Guan and the other holy ones with a curious, albeit perplexed, interest, yet she chose not to linger on it. Her sole focus remained on surviving the enigmatic leaps to the before time. The mere thought of visiting a time she had only glimpsed fleetingly in the dimly lit archives consumed her attention, even as her mind grappled with the overwhelming task that lay ahead. "I know the risks," she said, but the tremor in her voice betrayed her. "And I'm still going," she replied, her voice wavering slightly, betraying the uncertainty she felt. "I'm ready to do whatever it takes to secure our future."

Kishida-Guan studied her carefully, his gaze piercing and intense. "Your bravery is admirable," he remarked softly. "You will need that bravery, as you will be alone in this venture. As you know, we will have no means of communication or guidance for you. The only support we can offer is the assurance that we will be waiting to bring you back safely, thirty days hence."

"The technicians worked tireless on trying to build a transceiver—" 71PQv began but was interrupted by 41GB.

"None of the prototypes ever functioned in a time-related context, so we abandoned those attempts swiftly since our efforts were required elsewhere. Therefore, I fail to see the point of mentioning it now," Kishida-Guan interrupted, unable to hide his growing irritation with all of the side tangents.

"Okay, let's move on, shall we?" 41GB interjected. "The secondary objective will be to gather detailed observations on the people, technologies…the general state of the environment during that era. Anything that will provide us with further data on what caused the downfall of that society so to enable us to install protocols to prevent a repeat. It will also give us invaluable data for future simulations so that we can prepare future generations of genetically enhanced should the need arise, in future, to return again.

"Where…or when…exactly, will I be going in the before time? Or does that not matter either?" Melyndie inquired, her voice slightly quaking from the fear and excitement battling within her.

"We can only determine the general era," 71PQv responded. "We're aiming to send you back to a point just before the conclusion of the old era; a few years before the emergence of the first realm." He furrowed his brow, aware that his explanation was confusing, yet unsure how to clarify that she was being sent to the end of the period when humanity was free, marking the start of the transformations that led to their present society.

"When doesn't matter," 41GB interjected. "It's what you do when you arrive which will matter. Focus only on that."

"Again, you will be given thirty days to collect the initial samples," Kishida-Guan added, "so use your time wisely. While your secondary mission is an added benefit it is not to interfere with your primary mission."

"And while you may encounter individuals during your mission," 41GB interjected, "we advise against socializing as your emotional connection to others is still underdeveloped and we do not need anyone questioning who you are or where you're from."

Melyndie's heart skipped a beat, trapped between exhilaration and a deep, unsettling fear. The finality of her solitary assignment pressed heavily upon her, a stark reminder of the immense responsibility on her shoulders. She managed to nod, her expression composed yet pensive.

Now, Melyndie," 71PQv leaned forward slightly, showing yet another device. "Just before you leave, I will strap this to your bicep. It will monitor your vital signs—"

"If it functions across time?" Melyndie interrupted.

He shook his head. "It will continuously track your vitals and store the data internally for post-mission analysis; and though we made adjustments to help the unit withstand temporal fluctuations, it's reliance to relay data through time has not been tested. We will, of course, make the attempt to connect the live feedback feature, but activate the recorder as soon as able to ensure we get data, definitively, to analyze. That's essential, as we'll need to understand the effects of long-term stays between time leaps. To begin continuous recording, press this button here as soon as physically able. Now, this unit also chambers your collection tools. The blood collection chamber is located here," he said, pressing a button on the side of the device, which opened to reveal three small vials. "Here is where the DNA collection device is placed," he continued, indicating its slot at the bottom, "and this is the health gauge," he pointed to another small slot on the side.

"Remember," Kishida-Guan interjected with a stern tone, "the utmost caution and stealth are essential. It's imperative that you go about your mission in an unobtrusive manner."

"Blend in. Don't stand out," Melyndie muttered under her breath, the recollection searing through her mind like a hot iron branding her thoughts. It was a sharp, insistent memory, as unwelcome as it was unforgettable, leaving an uncomfortable sting that lingered long after the words had faded into the background of her consciousness.

She steeled her mind, banishing the haunting memory with an iron will, focusing solely on the mission parameters. A volatile cocktail of pride and apprehension surged through her veins as Kishida-Guan rose, a harbinger of what lay ahead. She mirrored his movements with determination, ready to embrace the mission meticulously designed for her—a mission that held the very fate of her entire civilization in its balance.

41GB followed Melyndie out of the office, her expression fraught with mixed emotions. Once they were alone, she placed a comforting hand on Melyndie's shoulder. "You are not just carrying out a mission; you are carrying our hopes," she said softly. "Trust in your training and your instincts. You have something that none of us possess—an ability to understand and empathize with others on a profound level."

Melyndie turned to 41GB, her eyes bright—not with tears, but something more volatile. Something like fire restrained behind glass. "I will do my best not to let you or our people down," she whispered, her voice heavy with emotion, each word seeming to tremble under the weight of her feelings. The enormity of her task loomed large, an overwhelming presence pressing upon her shoulders, but the knowledge that 41GB believed in her provided a small, yet significant, fragment of solace.

41GB smiled tenderly, sensing the turmoil within Melyndie. "I know you will succeed. Remember, every piece of data, every sample you collect, could mean the salvation of humanity. You are more than just a mission operative; you are the beacon of our future. Now let's get you back in your attire." They walked towards the preparation chamber where technicians busily performing their final checks. Each step felt like moving deeper into a chasm of uncertainty and monumental expectation.

Melyndie quickly shed her jumpsuit, the material softly brushing her skin as it pooled at her feet. She grabbed the blue silk blouse that gleamed under the lab lights, reminiscent of a bright summer day and slid it on.

"Wait! Let's get this on," 71PQv called, efficiently strapping the device and its containers onto her upper arm. He nodded, then turned and briskly retreated back to his work.

With nimble fingers, Melyndie buttoned up the shirt, then picked up her slightly oversized gray slacks, slipping into them effortlessly, as if they were a long-familiar part of her wardrobe, despite having worn them only three times.

Once dressed, she remained still and patient, an essential yet solitary figure...waiting. Like a perfectly crafted statue amid the bustling activity around her. Her gaze, calm and observant, swept across the room as she awaited her signal for what lay ahead.

"The synchronization with the temporal field looks stable," one technician reported. "All systems are green. You are clear to take your place on the platform, whenever you're ready."

Melyndie took a deep breath, closing her eyes for a moment to steady herself. When she opened them again, her resolve had hardened. She nodded to the team, signaling she was indeed ready to embark on the journey that no one else could undertake but her.

She stepped onto the platform, its smooth surface cool beneath her feet. She could feel the subtle tremor of the machinery as the system powered up—a hum that seemed to vibrate through her bones, tuning her body to the frequency of something ancient and unknowable.

Across the room, Kishida-Guan stood stiffly, his expression unreadable, but his eyes—those ever-watchful eyes—burned with an intensity that unsettled her. Was it pride? Arrogance? Fear?

"Maintain a stable stance," the technician called. "Final calibration in progress."

She nodded but said nothing. Her thoughts were a riot. Somewhere deep inside her chest, a memory surfaced—unbidden and vivid. A dog's eyes, dark and loyal, locked onto hers from the crumbling page of a forbidden book. A photograph of two people, caught mid-kiss, their joy uncontained. She hadn't understood it then. Not fully. But now…

She gripped her pant legs, knuckles whitening.

That was why she had to go.

Not for humanity.

Not for the holy ones.

But for *them*—those who had once felt something more than compliance and command.

A flicker of movement drew her gaze. 41GB had stepped forward, almost against protocol, her face softer than Melyndie had ever seen it. No words passed between them. Just a look—quiet, defiant, and full of things neither had ever been permitted to say.

The chamber lights dimmed to a low, pulsing blue. Countdown engaged.

"Ten… nine…"

Her breath slowed.

"Eight… seven…"

The air thickened. The space around her warped subtly, like heat rising off asphalt—except colder. Sharper.

"Six... five..."

She felt her pulse in her throat, her wrists, her ribs. Every part of her body called out to stay—to run. She remained still.

"Four..."

Her heart no longer beat. It thundered.

"Three..."

Something split open inside her.

"Two..."

The world collapsed into sound and sensation.

"One."

The jump ignited.

Time did not stretch—it shattered. The platform vanished beneath her. Every nerve ending screamed as her body twisted into light, then into memory, then into something else entirely. She was falling and folding and fragmenting, every piece of her life torn into filaments and scattered across the void. A scream dissolved in her mouth. Her past emptied out through her fingertips.

And just before she broke completely, she thought—

Let me find them. Let me feel it. Let it be real.

Then silence.

And the world let her go.

The Before Time

It is from weakness that people reach for dictators and concentrated government power. Only the strong can be free. And only the productive can be strong.

Wendell Willkie

Zain: The Before Time

The ground was still warm from the fires.

Zain knelt and pressed his palm against the blackened soil, feeling the faint tremor beneath it. The townspeople behind him gathered in uneasy clusters—fear, anger, the quiet questions no one dared to ask aloud. They looked to him for answers, but he had none.

The sky was different now. A pale light shimmered where darkness should be, casting strange shadows across the ruins. And within him, something stirred—an energy that felt foreign and dangerous, beating in rhythm with his own pulse.

"Zain." The voice cut through the wind, sharp with urgency. He turned to find her on the ridge, eyes wide. "They're coming."

Shapes appeared in the distance, moving fast, dust rising at their heels. Whoever…whatever they were, they brought only threat.

Zain rose slowly, fists clenched. The strange power inside him surged, demanding release. The world he knew had already ended—what came next would decide everything.

And for the first time, he wondered if he was ready for it.

AUTHOR BIO

Barbara is the author of 29 books across multiple genres, formerly published under Barbara Woster, B.J. Woster, and B. Woster. An educator with a Masters in Early Childhood Education, she crafts layered, character-driven stories that invite readers deep into their worlds. Barbara shares her life with her two cats, Kookie and Ellie, and treasures the love and support of her four daughters, who remain central to her life and are her inspiration. Her works continue to explore imagination, humanity, and the ties that bind us. Learn more at **BarbaraPelhamAuthor.com**.

www.ingramcontent.com/pod-product-compliance
Lightning Source LLC
Chambersburg PA
CBHW011437200726
48289CB00009BA/2802